W9-AFS-297

*Aunt Dimity and the Enchanted Cottage*

ALSO BY NANCY ATHERTON

*Aunt Dimity's Death*
*Aunt Dimity and the Duke*
*Aunt Dimity's Good Deed*
*Aunt Dimity Digs In*
*Aunt Dimity's Christmas*
*Aunt Dimity Beats the Devil*
*Aunt Dimity: Detective*
*Aunt Dimity Takes a Holiday*
*Aunt Dimity: Snowbound*
*Aunt Dimity and the Next of Kin*
*Aunt Dimity and the Deep Blue Sea*
*Aunt Dimity Goes West*
*Aunt Dimity: Vampire Hunter*
*Aunt Dimity Slays the Dragon*
*Aunt Dimity Down Under*
*Aunt Dimity and the Family Tree*
*Aunt Dimity and the Village Witch*
*Aunt Dimity and the Lost Prince*
*Aunt Dimity and the Wishing Well*
*Aunt Dimity and the Summer King*
*Aunt Dimity and the Buried Treasure*
*Aunt Dimity and the Widow's Curse*
*Aunt Dimity and the King's Ransom*
*Aunt Dimity and the Heart of Gold*

# *Aunt Dimity and the Enchanted Cottage*

NANCY ATHERTON

VIKING

VIKING
An imprint of Penguin Random House LLC
penguinrandomhouse.com



LIBRARY OF CONGRESS CATALOGING-IN-PUBLICATION DATA
Names: Atherton, Nancy, author.
Title: Aunt Dimity and the enchanted cottage / Nancy Atherton.
Description: [New York City] : Viking, [2022] | Series: Aunt Dimity ; 25 |
Identifiers: LCCN 2021029662 (print) | LCCN 2021029663 (ebook) |
ISBN 9780593295779 (hardcover) | ISBN 9780593295786 (ebook)
Subjects: GSAFD: Mystery fiction. | Ghost stories.
Classification: LCC PS3551.T426 A932 2022 (print) |
LCC PS3551.T426 (ebook) | DDC 813/.54—dc23
LC record available at https://lccn.loc.gov/2021029662
LC ebook record available at https://lccn.loc.gov/2021029663

Printed in the United States of America
1st Printing

Set in Perpetua MT Pro
Designed by Nerylsa Dijol

*For Michael Atherton and Cindy Walter,*
*the enchanted couple*

*Aunt Dimity and the*
*Enchanted Cottage*

# One

The Little Deeping River would never be mistaken for the mighty Mississippi or the Nile. A minor tributary of the Thames, its headwaters could be found in an unassuming meadow strewn with puddles fed by a bubbling spring. Swollen by snowmelt, rainfall, and a glittering web of narrow, nameless streams, the spring's trickle became a torrent by the time it reached the Cotswolds, a pastoral haven described in countless guidebooks as one of England's most picturesque regions.

Though no one had ever steered a paddle-wheeler down the Little Deeping, or constructed a pyramid beside it, the river had for centuries been a focal point for human activity. Romans had built villas near it, Saxons had littered its deep pools with votive offerings, and Vikings had explored it in their dragon-headed boats. In medieval times, a single-arch packhorse bridge had been built over a willow-draped stretch that flowed past the small Cotswolds village of Finch.

With its humpbacked bridge, its Norman church, and its golden-hued stone buildings, Finch was nothing if not picturesque. Its cottages and small business establishments faced one another across the village green, an elongated oval of tufted grass encircled by a cobbled lane. The pub, the greengrocer's shop, and the general store stood silhouetted against a rising landscape of dark woods and patchwork fields, while the tearoom, the vicarage, and the old village school, which had for many years served as the village hall, turned their backs on the water meadows that descended in a gentle slope to the river's edge.

Finch sat in a bend of the Little Deeping, as if cradled in the crook of a watery arm. Finch's residents agreed that the river could be tiresome after a wet winter, when it had the discourteous habit of overflowing its banks. No one relished the prospect of bailing out flooded cellars or clearing flotsam from waterlogged gardens, and local farmers heaved aggrieved sighs as they watched the swirling waters inundate their well-tended crops.

In the main, however, the Little Deeping was regarded as an asset to the community. A catch-and-release policy prevented Finch's anglers from dining on the trout they landed but did nothing to diminish their enthusiasm for the sport. Bird-watching was so popular that nearly every villager kept a pair of binoculars handy to observe the herons, egrets, coots, and mallards that nested near the Little Deeping as well as the feathered friends that were merely passing through. The river was too cold and its current too strong to entice casual swimmers, but a handful of hardy souls took the plunge on hot summer days.

As pleasant as it was to while away an idle hour near the river, the villagers never lost sight of the role the Little Deeping played in boosting the local economy. Though votive offerings had gone out of fashion and Roman villas had gone the way of Viking boats and packhorse trains, a boom in freshwater sports had brought a small but steady stream of kayakers, canoeists, and paddleboarders to the village. The influx of outdoor enthusiasts wasn't overwhelming, but it was large enough to keep Finch's tiny engine of commerce firing on both cylinders.

A significant number of damp and sunburned visitors popped into Peacock's pub for a refreshing pint after a long day spent on the river. Others feasted on the delectable pastries in Sally Cook's tearoom. With its mismatched tables, chairs, teapots, and crockery, the tearoom was as unfussy as it was charming.

Many visitors topped up their picnic lunches with fresh fruit from the greengrocer's shop, and many more prowled the aisles of Taxman's Emporium, Finch's grandly named general store, searching for sunblock, insect repellent, energy bars, bungee cords, and whatever else they'd forgotten to bring with them. As the villagers were fond of saying, the river kept Finch's businesses afloat.

The pub, the tearoom, and the Emporium also carried an extremely limited range of items produced by local entrepreneurs. Miranda Morrow, Finch's resident witch and a notable homeopathic healer, specialized in a line of ointments infused with elixirs she distilled from the medicinal plants she cultivated in her greenhouse. Felicity Hobson, a retired schoolteacher, sold hand-labeled jars filled with the honey she collected from the hives in her back garden. Elspeth Binney, Opal Taylor, Millicent Scroggins, and Selena Buxton, an industrious quartet of artistically inclined retirees, churned out miniature paintings of river scenes and notable village landmarks. The souvenirs didn't bring in a fortune, but they were a welcome source of pocket money for those living on limited incomes.

Businesses near Finch saw an uptick in custom as well, thanks to the river's allure. Leaflets advertising the local stables tempted diehard fresh-air fiends to follow a morning on the river with an afternoon in the saddle, exploring the bridle paths surrounding Anscombe Manor, where the stables were located. Emma Harris, who lived in the manor house with her husband, Derek, and their extended family, had grown accustomed to the sight of cars topped with dripping canoes, kayaks, or paddleboards cruising up the manor's curving drive.

St. George's Church wasn't a business, exactly, nor could it be called an entrepreneurial enterprise, but it, too, benefited from the river's popularity. A gratifying number of outdoor adventurers wandered into the church to admire its medieval wall paintings or simply to savor a moment of quiet reflection in the wake of an action-packed day. A few paused to give thanks for their safe deliverance after a day packed with a bit too much action. Hardly any of them left without dropping a pound or more in the donations box, either in payment for one of the guidebooks penned by Lilian Bunting, the vicar's scholarly wife, or as a kindly contribution to the church's upkeep.

While the vast majority of Finch's visitors behaved irreproachably, a few bad apples made fools of themselves after spending more time than was good for them in the pub. Finch was far too small a village to merit its own police constable, let alone a police station, but its residents had a pair of secret weapons upon whom they could rely to impose order on the unruly.

Their first line of defense was Peggy Taxman, a doughty woman known much less than half jokingly as the unofficial empress of Finch. Peggy Taxman reigned supreme over the Emporium, the greengrocer's shop, the post office, and every committee meeting that had ever been convened in the old schoolhouse. Having been on the receiving end of Peggy's tirades on numerous occasions, the villagers were confident that her imposing physique, imperious manner, and stentorian voice would frighten all but the most pugnacious pests into instant sobriety.

If Peggy's gimlet gaze and thunderous scolding failed to achieve the desired effect, the sight of Tommy Prescott bearing down on them would bring even the rowdiest offenders to heel. Tommy was a thirty-year-old army veteran who'd recently moved to Finch to live with his uncle, the highly respected handyman, Mr. Barlow. Tommy was so tall he had to bend at the waist to avoid hitting his head on nearly every lintel in Finch, and there wasn't an ounce of fat on his broad-shouldered, muscular frame. He'd lost the lower half of his left leg to a roadside bomb while serving in combat overseas, but an ingenious prosthetic allowed him to follow a fitness regimen that kept him in formidable shape.

Those who knew Tommy knew that he'd had his fill of violence. Those seeing him for the first time did their level best to avoid annoying him. When Tommy Prescott invited belligerent tipplers to share a pot of strong coffee with him in the tearoom, they suddenly became as pliant as lambs.

My family and I didn't have to rely on Peggy Taxman or on Tommy Prescott to rout drunks from our doorstep because our doorstep was a safe distance away from the pub. We lived two miles outside of Finch, up a narrow, twisting lane lined with tall hedgerows. We didn't have to worry about the Little Deeping invading our cellar, either, because several acres of farmland lay between the river and the honey-colored cottage we called home.

Although my husband, Bill, and I were Americans, as were our twin sons and our daughter, we'd lived in England for more than a decade. Bill ran the European branch of his family's venerable Boston law firm from a high-tech office overlooking the village green; eleven-year-old Will and Rob attended Morningside School in the nearby market town of Upper Deeping; and I juggled the challenging roles of wife, mother, friend, neighbor, gossipmonger par excellence, and community volunteer.

Our daughter, Bess, was navigating the hazardous shoals of the terrible twos. Bill and I were delighted when she learned how to throw a ball, but not quite as pleased when she used her newly acquired skill to fling fistfuls of food across the table at mealtimes. If we left her alone with a box of crayons, the living room walls became her coloring book. Her inability to defeat the childproof locks we'd installed throughout the cottage provoked titanic tantrums that sent our sleek black cat, Stanley, running for cover.

When Bess wasn't having a meltdown or wreaking havoc on her surroundings, she was a bundle of joy. Her smile could melt the heart of the grumpiest curmudgeon, her rapidly growing vocabulary filled us with pride, and her sense of wonder reawakened our own. Best of all—from a weary parent's point of view, at any rate—she was a champion sleeper. As long as we didn't disrupt her routine unduly, she was good for eleven hours of sleep at night and a two-hour nap during the day. In our estimation, this was a gift beyond price.

Though the Little Deeping wasn't on our doorstep, we still thought of it as "our" river. Bess quacked energetically whenever a duck family paddled into view during our riverside rambles, and she gave a friendly wave to any human who floated by. Bill and I never allowed ourselves to be distracted when our daughter was near the river. Left to her own devices, our fearless girl would have tried to shoot the rapids without a kayak.

Our sons enjoyed roving the riverbank with us on foot, but they preferred to ride beside it on their gray ponies, Thunder and Storm. Finch's visitors were so charmed by the sight of identical twins on matching ponies that Will and Rob had gotten used to being photographed. If the photographers were courteous, the boys would rein in their ponies near a particularly scenic stretch of river. If the photographers were intrusive, the boys would turn their backs—and their ponies' backsides—on them.

Will and Rob were well loved in Finch, but the villagers doted on Bess, an understandable preference given the scarcity of toddlers in a village populated primarily by retirees and middle-aged working folk. Bess would have weighed more than her brothers if we'd let her eat all the cookies the villagers baked for her, and she could scarcely take two steps across the village green without being swept off her feet by an admirer. Her most devoted fan, however, was Bill's father.

William Arthur Willis, Sr., was a courtly, old-fashioned gentleman who'd made our happiness complete when he'd retired from his position as the head of the family law firm and moved to England to fulfill his role as his grandchildren's only surviving grandparent. Willis, Sr.'s patrician good looks, impeccable manners, and hefty bank account had made him the most eligible widower in Finch until he'd made his own happiness complete by marrying the well-known botanical artist Amelia Thistle.

Willis, Sr., and Amelia lived down the lane from us in Fairworth House, a graceful Georgian mansion surrounded by a modest ten-acre estate. The wrought-iron gates that guarded the entrance to their tree-lined drive stood a short distance away from Finch's humpbacked bridge.

Amelia loved to walk beside the river, sketching the wildflowers that graced its banks. Willis, Sr., who loved to be wherever Amelia was, often served as her attendant, gallantly toting her camp chair, sketchbook, and paint box, as well as the picnic lunch they would share in the shade of their favorite willow.

The Little Deeping had always been a benevolent presence in my life and in the lives of everyone I knew. Even the sedentary could savor its beauty and find solace in its comforting murmur. An occasional flood seemed a small price to pay for the pleasure it gave to so many.

I had no idea that the river harbored a harrowing secret until a stranger in an enchanted cottage opened my eyes to a tragedy Finch had chosen to forget.

# *Two*

It was a glorious Saturday morning in late May. The sun shone serenely in a pristine blue sky, primroses bobbed in a balmy breeze, and busy birds flitted to and fro among the hedgerows, providing sustenance for their clamorous young. The Little Deeping had lost its lacy carapace of ice, and after a gloomy winter blighted by illness and miserable weather, the good people of Finch were once again hale and hearty and ready to embrace the splendors of spring.

The villagers were especially grateful for the fine weather because a momentous event was about to unfold before their highly observant eyes. A blustery thunderstorm would have dampened their spirits, though it wouldn't have kept them at home. No one who was anyone would dream of missing an occasion that would provide grist for the gossip mill for weeks, if not months, to come.

Bill and I called it the moving-van vigil and as far as we knew, it was unique to Finch. The rules of engagement were simple: Whenever someone moved to Finch, our neighbors would station themselves at carefully chosen vantage points in order to watch the parade of possessions that passed between the newcomer's moving van and the front door of his new home.

To avoid appearing overly inquisitive, the villagers would behave clandestinely, using innocent pursuits to disguise their true intentions. Some walked dogs, others touched up the paint on their own front doors, and still others tended the flowers in their window boxes, or examined the fruit in the greengrocer's bins, or threw themselves into their favorite outdoor hobbies. As soon as the moving van rumbled into view, however, every head would point in its direction.

My neighbors were, without doubt, among the nosiest people on the planet, but when they took part in the moving-van vigil, they weren't simply snooping for snooping's sake. Experience had taught them that, for better or for worse, a single individual could have an enormous impact on a small village. They reckoned quite reasonably that the more they knew in advance about a new neighbor, the better prepared they would be for the influence he would exert.

Would he be a good neighbor? Would he lend a helping hand with the bake sales, the flower shows, the sheep dog trials, the parish fetes, and the myriad other events that breathed life into the village? Or would he be a leech who'd use his cottage as a weekend retreat and contribute nothing to the community? The villagers were firmly convinced that a newcomer's possessions would give them a fair estimate of his character.

Their latest quarry was about to move into Pussywillows, the cottage that sat between the tearoom and the humpbacked bridge. His name was Crispin Windle and he was, unfortunately, a man of mystery.

Marigold Edwards, the delightfully indiscreet estate agent who handled all of the properties in Finch, hadn't had a lot to say about Mr. Windle. The villagers were past masters at gleaning useful information from Marigold, but after treating her to a pot of Earl Grey in the tearoom, a half-pint of cider in the pub, and two packets of crisps in the Emporium, even they had conceded defeat.

Despite, or perhaps because of, Marigold's imminent failure to disclose much of anything about Mr. Windle, his arrival had triggered an exceptionally high level of activity on and around the village green. Christine and Dick Peacock, who could usually be found serving drinks and hearty meals in their pub, were comfortably ensconced in the captain's chairs they'd placed on either side of the pub's entrance, their faces turned toward the sun, as if they were merely basking in its warmth.

Felicity Hobson sat on the bench near the war memorial, knitting industriously, while her husband, James, our local metal detectorist, swept his machine in wide arcs over the tufty grass. Jasper Taxman, Peggy's mild-mannered mate, slowly and methodically arranged a selection of colorfully packaged snacks in the Emporium's display window, and George Wetherhead, the most bashful man in Finch, perused the notice board on the old schoolhouse.

Like Jasper Taxman, Tilly Barlow had elected to stay indoors. Though Tilly appeared to be reading a book, she hadn't turned a page since she'd seated herself in the bow window of the house she shared with her husband and his nephew. Mr. Barlow, who detested snooping, was nowhere to be seen.

Elspeth Binney, Opal Taylor, Millicent Scroggins, and Selena Buxton, whom my husband had dubbed "Father's Handmaidens" because of their pre-Amelia devotion to Willis, Sr., stood before four easels, painting en plein air. Clad in capacious smocks and wide-brimmed hats, the Handmaidens peered intently at Pussywillows, as though they were competing to capture its manifold charms on canvas.

Homer, Elspeth Binney's scruffy little terrier, trotted back and forth across the green to visit his canine chums and to wag his stumpy tail at their owners. Homer wasn't much to look at—Bill thought he resembled a dust mop—but he was the most convivial pup I'd ever met.

Elspeth claimed that Homer had popped out of a hedgerow during one her walks, routed the mob of squawking magpies that had blocked her path, and escorted her safely to her front door. Homer's gallantry had won her heart and though she'd tried her level best to locate his owner, she'd been overjoyed when no one had come forth to claim him. She'd named him Homer because she felt that if he could talk, he would have great tales to tell.

While Elspeth kept a fond eye on Homer, the rest of the villagers busied themselves with familiar vigil-day chores—touching up the woodwork on their cottages, walking their dogs, or weeding their window boxes. As the morning wore on, they worked at an increasingly leisurely pace, pausing frequently to chat with one another and with anyone who happened to pass by. They also glanced with increasing frequency at their watches because Crispin Windle appeared to be running late.

I was content to remain where I was, seated at a table near the tearoom's large front window with my friends Charles Bellingham and Grant Tavistock. Charles sat on my right and Grant on my left, but the chair opposite mine was unoccupied. No villager in his right mind would choose to sit with his back to a window when there was so much to see on the green.

Grant and Charles ran a flourishing art appraisal and restoration business from their home in Crabtree Cottage, but they were never too busy to take part in a moving-van vigil. Tall, portly, and balding, Charles was the more demonstrative of the two. Grant, who was short, slim, and blessed with a healthy headful of salt-and-pepper hair, was more likely than Charles to think before he spoke.

I was more or less free to enjoy their company. Bill was in his office, the boys were at the stables, and Bess was playing "Catch me!" on the green with Tommy Prescott. The young giant had to rein in his long strides to avoid catching Bess too quickly, but he seemed to be having as much fun as she was.

Much to my delight, and to the delight of everyone else in Finch,

Tommy had recently become engaged to Bree Pym, the twenty-three-year-old New Zealander who lived down the lane from me in a house she'd inherited from her great-grandaunts, the late and sorely lamented Pym sisters. Bree's previous fiancé had dumped her a couple of weeks before Christmas, but the general consensus was that it had all worked out for the best. In our estimation—and in hers, too—she was a thousand times better off with Tommy.

Nevertheless, Bree had abandoned her beau to share the table beside ours with old Mrs. Craven and Miranda Morrow. Annabelle Craven was an elderly widow who spent most of her waking hours creating exquisite handmade quilts, but she'd set her work aside to participate in the vigil. She was dressed in her customary tweed blazer and skirt, and she'd wound her long white hair into a wispy bun at the nape of her neck. Miranda Morrow had bundled her strawberry-blond tresses into a demure French knot and slipped into a summery yellow sundress for the occasion. Nothing about her freckle-faced, wholesome appearance suggested that she was a practicing witch.

Bree Pym was a petite but sturdily built young woman with a heart-shaped face, lustrous brown eyes, and short, spiky hair. Though she'd been born a brunette, her hair color could vary from electric blue to cherry-red, depending on her mood.

Bree stood out in Finch, not only because of her youth, her Kiwi accent, and her ever-changing hair, but also because she had a nose ring in her left nostril and a large number of tattoos on her arms. She'd dressed for the day in a pair of rugged hiking sandals, khaki shorts, and a violently violet tank top that matched the tips of her spiky brown hair.

I, too, was wearing khaki shorts, but mine didn't have nearly as many pockets as Bree's, my sneakers were less rugged than her sandals, and my cotton blouse was less eye-catching than her tank top. Though a few gray strands had appeared in my curly brown hair, they'd come straight from Mother Nature rather than from a bottle.

The six of us sipped our respective cups of tea smugly, knowing that we'd nabbed the best seats in the house. Since the tearoom was directly next door to Pussywillows, its front window would afford us an unparalleled view of Crispin Windle's possessions. Unless Mr. Windle's handwriting was microscopic, we'd be able to read the labels on his boxes.

"Pussywillows looks a bit forlorn," Grant commented, "as though it's pining for Mr. Windle."

I nodded my agreement. Pussywillows wasn't derelict, but the small touches that made a house a home were missing. There were no curtains in the windows, no flowers in the window boxes, no curls of smoke rising from the chimney. The brass door knocker had lost its gleam, and spindly weeds had colonized the unswept, unused doorstep.

"It's like Sleeping Beauty, waiting for her prince," Charles put in.

"Sleeping Beauty wasn't waiting for her prince," Grant objected. "She was sleeping."

"If you're going to be literal-minded," Charles responded, "I shall not hesitate to point out that a cottage is incapable of pining. A cottage can look forlorn, certainly, but it can't pine."

"I may be literal-minded," Grant retorted, "but no one will ever accuse me of pedantry."

"Settle down, boys," I scolded. "If you don't play nicely, I'll send you home."

"Yes, Mummy," Charles muttered.

I ignored him and continued, "Pussywillows reminds me of something Mr. Barlow once said to me. He told me that houses like to be lived in. They go to rack and ruin, he said, if they're left on their own for too long."

"Pussywillows hasn't been empty long enough to go to rack and ruin," said Grant. "Tilly Trout lived there until a month ago, when she married Mr. Barlow and moved into his house. Still, it could do with a bit of sprucing up."

"Couldn't we all?" Charles said, gazing pointedly at the rumpled lapels on Grant's white linen jacket.

Grant smoothed his lapels as he addressed me. "What do you know about our new neighbor, Lori? Charles and I were in London when Marigold Edwards was making the rounds in Finch yesterday. We missed our chance to interrogate the world's chattiest estate agent, but you must have heard a thing or two about Mr. Windle."

"I've heard a few things," I acknowledged, "but not as many as you'd expect."

"Such as?" said Grant.

"Millicent Scroggins managed to coax Marigold into giving her Mr. Windle's name and his estimated time of arrival," I said.

"His badly estimated time of arrival," Charles interjected, tapping his wristwatch impatiently. "It's half past ten already. He was supposed to be here by nine, wasn't he?"

"You can't blame Marigold for Mr. Windle's tardiness," said Grant. "The poor man is probably caught in traffic."

"I hope he hasn't been involved in an accident," I said.

"As do I," said Charles. "Of course I do. I wouldn't wish an accident on anyone, but you must admit that a motorway pileup would supply him with an acceptable excuse for being late."

"I somehow doubt that he'll feel the need to explain himself to us," Grant said.

"He'll learn," Charles said airily.

"What else did you find out about Mr. Windle?" Grant asked me.

"Marigold told Sally Cook that Mr. Windle is a single gentleman," I said. "She told Opal Taylor that he's a retired university professor. And she told Elspeth Binney that he's from Derbyshire." I shrugged. "That's it."

"That's it?" Charles exclaimed. "Nothing about his age, his appearance, his income, his hobbies, or his field of expertise?"

"Nothing," I confirmed.

"Perhaps Marigold has learned the value of discretion," Grant suggested.

"Not a chance," I said. "As it turns out, Marigold has never actually met Crispin Windle. She's never even spoken to him on the telephone. She told Dick Peacock that she conducted the entire transaction through intermediaries. The reason she couldn't spill a whole lot of beans on her client is that she doesn't have a whole lot of beans to spill."

"You might have told us that to begin with," Charles said reproachfully.

"I was building up to it," I said.

"Mr. Windle sounds promising," said Grant. "A retired, unmarried professor from Derbyshire is unlikely to throw raucous parties or to leave beer bottles scattered across the green."

"True," said Charles. "He might even be willing to regale us with a series of lectures on his specialist subject. He should feel right at home in the old schoolhouse."

"I doubt that the old schoolhouse bears the least resemblance to his former workplace," said Grant.

"It'll make a nice change for him, then," Charles fired back.

"Wouldn't it be wonderful if he taught astronomy?" I interceded. "I've always wanted to learn more about the night sky."

"Or geology," Grant suggested. "I found the most beautiful stone on the riverbank the other day. I'd love to know what it is."

"Fool's gold," Charles said under his breath.

"I wouldn't mind literature," I said quickly, to head off yet another tiff. "Or architecture. Or engineering."

"Engineering?" Grant said in surprise.

"I like to know how things work," I said. "Don't you?"

"I suppose so," he said. "But I'd prefer literature, especially if Mr. Windle has a pleasant voice. I'm fond of hearing poetry read aloud, but only if the reader has a pleasant voice."

Sally Cook appeared at our table, bearing a serving dish piled high with the fruit scones we'd ordered. The tearoom's owner was short, round, and bursting with the kind of energy that propelled her out of bed at the crack of dawn to get the day's baking underway. She had bright blue eyes and she wore her white hair in a pixie cut that suited her pink face.

Sally had donned a traditional baker's apron to protect her floral blouse and her loose-fitting blue trousers from spatters, but I saw nothing more than a small streak of flour on it. When I thought of the state of my own apron after a day spent baking at home, I wanted to hang my head in shame.

"Who are you talking about, Grant?" she asked. "Who has a pleasant voice?"

"I'm rather hoping our new neighbor will have one," Grant replied.

"Why?" asked Sally.

"Because I'd enjoy hearing poetry read aloud by an ex-academic with a nice voice," said Grant.

"We were discussing Mr. Windle's possible area of expertise," I explained. "Literature seems as good a guess as any."

"You can guess if you like," said Sally, "but I can tell you one thing for certain."

"What's that?" Charles said eagerly.

"Crispin Windle will fall in love within the next six months," Sally declared.

My mouth fell open, Grant's eyebrows rose, and Charles sniggered.

"Why are you so certain that Mr. Windle will fall in love?" Grant inquired.

"Because," Sally answered portentously, "Pussywillows is enchanted."

# Three

"Pussywillows? Enchanted?" Charles gave a shout of laughter. "You must be joking!"

Sally's pink face turned a shade of red that, in her case, signaled mortal offense rather than embarrassment.

"Do forgive Charles," Grant said hurriedly, kicking his partner under the table. "What he meant to say was, how do you know that Pussywillows is enchanted?"

"It's as plain as the nose on your face." Sally turned her back on Charles, who was rubbing his shin. "Amelia Thistle moves into Pussywillows and the next thing you know, she's walking down the aisle with your father-in-law, Lori. Then Tilly Trout moves in, and hey, presto, she's married to Mr. Barlow. One cottage, two occupants, two marriages? Seems like magic to me."

"I have no trouble believing in romantic enchantments," Miranda Morrow said from the next table. She, Bree Pym, and old Mrs. Craven had interrupted their own conversation to listen in on ours, a common occurrence in the tearoom and just about everywhere else in Finch.

"Yes, but you're a witch, Miranda," said Charles, eyeing Grant resentfully. "One expects you to believe in, um, *unusual* things."

"It's not entirely out of the question, though, is it?" Mrs. Craven said thoughtfully. "You don't have to be a witch to believe that certain buildings are imbued with a special ambiance. I feel it every time I enter a cathedral. The Romans called it the genius loci—the spirit of a place. Perhaps a romantic spirit inhabits Pussywillows."

"I can see that I'll have to be the voice of reason this morning," Charles said with a long-suffering sigh.

Grant rolled his eyes.

Charles transferred an exceptionally fruity fruit scone from the serving dish to his plate before continuing, "Even if I did believe in magical cottages, which I can assure you I do not, your sample is too small to prove anything. Can you point to any other Pussywillows alumni who found true love in Finch, apart from Amelia and Tilly? Of course you can't, because there aren't any."

"Besides," I said, shifting my legs to one side to avoid an admonitory kick from Grant, "Tilly didn't find true love while she was living here. She was still living in Oxford when she fell in love with Mr. Barlow."

"Not true," Bree Pym piped up.

"Huh?" I said, caught off guard.

Bree glanced over her shoulder, as if to ensure that no one else in the tearoom was listening—a faint hope at best—then proceeded to explain authoritatively, "Tilly thought very highly of Mr. Barlow before she came to Finch, but she wasn't in love with him."

"She wasn't?" I said blankly.

"Of course she wasn't," Sally chimed in. "If she'd been in love with him, she wouldn't have bothered with Pussywillows, would she? She'd have married him and moved into his house straightaway."

"Sally has a point," said Grant.

"Possibly," Charles allowed, eyeing Bree speculatively, "but our young friend seems to know more than she's letting on. Out with it, my girl! Tell us everything!"

Bree lowered her voice to a confidential murmur. "I know for a fact that Mr. Barlow proposed to Tilly twice while she was still living in

Oxford and that she turned him down both times. It wasn't until *after* she moved to Finch that she said yes."

"Name your source," Charles demanded as he spread clotted cream on his scone.

"Tommy," Bree replied, referring to her intended. "Tilly confided in him and he confided in me."

"Plausible," said Grant as he, too, took a scone from the serving dish. "Since Tommy is Mr. Barlow's nephew, he's Tilly's nephew by marriage. I suppose aunts do sometimes confide in nephews."

"But do fiancés confide in fiancées?" asked Charles.

"Mine does," Bree said happily.

"It's the first I've heard of Mr. Barlow's multiple proposals," I said, feeling a little hurt that Bree hadn't shared the juicy piece of tittle-tattle with me as soon as she'd heard it.

"Sorry, Lori," said Bree. "Tilly asked Tommy to keep the story to himself because she didn't want to upset Mr. Barlow. You know how he feels about gossip."

"He disapproves of it," said Grant, "which makes him unique in Finch."

"It also explains why he's in St. George's, repairing the hinge on the vestry door," said Charles, "while the rest of us are waiting for Mr. Windle."

"Exactly," said Bree. "Tommy told me about the failed proposals because he knows he can trust me."

A reverberating silence enveloped the two tables. Charles allowed his gaze to travel slowly over the rest of the tearoom's occupants. Most sat frozen with their teacups halfway to their lips, their ears cocked in our direction, and a look of rapt concentration on their faces.

"My dear Bree," he said gently, "it goes without saying that *we* would never betray a confidence, but you've failed to take into account the tearoom's modest size and excellent acoustics." He turned to put a comforting hand on her shoulder. "I'm sorry to be the one to break it to you, but you've flung the cat so far out of the bag that you may as well have launched it from a cannon."

"Oh," said Bree, looking almost comically disconcerted. "I guess I have. I got so caught up in what Sally was saying about Pussywillows that I didn't stop to . . ." Her words trailed off as she peered through the window at her betrothed, who was chatting with the Peacocks while Bess played with Christine Peacock's shoelaces. "I don't think Tommy will mind *too* much. Do you?"

"If Tommy Prescott is going to make a home with you in Finch," I said, "he'll have to get used to the idea that everyone who lives here knows everything about everyone else who lives here."

"If I were you, I'd be more concerned about Mr. Barlow than Tommy," Charles advised unhelpfully. "Your adoring fiancé will forgive you anything, my dear, but Mr. Barlow might object to being known in the village as the man who was rejected twice by his future wife."

"I hope he won't be upset with Tilly," Bree said anxiously. "I'd hate to be responsible for their first marital spat."

Bree had more reason than most to value Mr. Barlow's good opinion. He'd taken her under his wing when she'd first arrived in Finch, taught her the tricks of the handyman's trade, and revealed a hitherto hidden talent for matchmaking when he'd invited his favorite nephew to live with him because, he'd told me confidently, Tommy Prescott was "the right lad" for Bree.

"Mr. Barlow will get over it," I said soothingly. "He may disapprove of gossip, but he knows what Finch is like and he doesn't expect miracles. He'll probably be astonished that the three of you were able to keep the story under your hats for as long as you did."

"I certainly am," said Charles.

"I hope you're right, Lori," said Bree.

"Mr. Barlow will get over it," I repeated firmly.

"I, for one, am grateful to you, Bree," said Grant. "Thanks to your insider knowledge, we can now confirm that both Amelia *and* Tilly fell in love while they were living in Pussywillows."

"You see?" Sally said triumphantly. "Pussywillows may not work its magic on everyone, but if Crispin Windle has an ounce of romance in him, the cottage will make sure that he finds true love in Finch." She held up two plump fingers. "Once is happenstance and twice is coincidence, but three times . . ." She raised a third finger and nodded knowingly. "Three times is a charm."

"If you say so," Charles said, sounding thoroughly unconvinced.

"I do say so," Sally retorted. "And if you had an ounce of romance in you, you'd say so, too, Charles." She gave him a withering look and returned to the kitchen.

"Superstitious nonsense," Charles said scornfully. "Enchanted cottages? Ha! What's next? Magical teapots?"

"You sound like Mr. Barlow," Miranda Morrow observed.

"High praise," said Charles. "Mr. Barlow is an intelligent and sensible man. He'd never be taken in by a fairy story about an enchanted cottage."

"Would you care to place a wager on the fairy story?" Grant extended his hand. "Ten pence says our new neighbor will find true love within the next six months."

"Done." Charles reached across the table to grip Grant's hand, then glanced at his watch. "Where is the wretched man? He should have been here ages ago."

Peering past him, Grant said, "Cometh the hour, cometh the van. Don't look now, my friends, but I believe the main event is about to kick off."

I craned my neck in time to witness a sea of heads swivel toward the far end of the green, where a maroon sedan was leading a boxy truck onto the cobbled lane.

At long last, Crispin Windle had arrived.

# *Four*

After a short pause during which nothing but the maroon sedan, the boxy truck, and a few wagging tails moved, the dog walkers continued to walk, the window box weeders took up their trowels, the Handmaidens bent over their canvases, and as if on cue, everyone else resumed the activities in which they'd been engaged before Crispin Windle's much-anticipated debut.

To maintain the fiction that I was in the tearoom for no other reason than to enjoy a pleasant morning's natter with my chums, I seized a scone, split it in two with my butter knife, and began to slather both halves with clotted cream. Like Charles and Grant, however, I kept a watchful eye on the pair of vehicles as they made their way up the cobbled lane to Pussywillows.

"Mr. Windle's Renault is twenty years old," Grant observed.

Since Grant wasn't known as an automobile enthusiast, I turned to him in surprise and asked, "How can you tell?"

"One of our London friends has the same make and model," he replied. "We're always teasing her about her antiquated Renault, but she refuses to replace it."

"She drives it for sentimental reasons," said Charles. "Why, I wonder, does Mr. Windle drive such an old vehicle?"

"I hope it's for sentimental reasons," I said, sucking the thumb I'd accidentally slathered with clotted cream. "I'd like to think that his car reminds him of long drives through the countryside with someone he loved."

"All this talk of enchanted cottages has gone to your head, Lori," Charles scoffed. "The most obvious reason for driving an old car is an inability to afford a new one."

"Not the sort of sentiment I was going for," I said resignedly, "but you could be right."

While Mr. Windle parked his aged Renault in the shed on the far side of Pussywillows, the moving van's driver executed a tricky maneuver that brought the vehicle's rear bumper to within a few yards of the cottage's front door. As soon as the engine fell silent, the driver and two brawny assistants climbed out of the cab and strode purposefully toward the cottage. A moment later, the front door opened and a hand motioned for the three men to enter. The hand withdrew, the men trooped across the threshold, and the door closed with a thump behind them.

"Mr. Windle must have slipped into Pussywillows through the kitchen door." I clucked my tongue disapprovingly. "Spoilsport. I still don't know what he looks like. I couldn't see his face clearly as he pulled into the shed—too much sun glare on the car's windows."

"I couldn't see his face, either," said Grant. "I could, however, see that he was alone. No one sitting beside him, no one in the backseat."

"You didn't expect to see a wife or kiddies, did you?" I said. "Marigold Edwards described him as a single gentleman." I pointed my butter knife at the four artists on the green. "That's why the Handmaidens are wearing their prettiest smocks. I don't know if you noticed, but those are the smocks they save for special occasions, like the art show."

"And the day a single gentleman comes to live in the village," Charles said, chuckling.

"I can't blame them for trying," Grant said tolerantly. "Mr. Windle is the first bachelor to move to Finch since George Wetherhead, and George is too introverted to even contemplate marriage."

"Especially to one of the Handmaidens," Charles murmured.

"Be nice," I said severely, though I smiled inwardly. The thought of bashful George proposing marriage to one of the four liveliest women in the village was as unlikely as the notion that one of them might accept him.

As the minutes ticked by with no sign of our new neighbor, Charles began to drum his fingers on the table.

"It's a bit inconsiderate of Mr. Windle to keep us waiting after he kept us waiting," he said querulously. "What's he doing? You'd think he'd want to get the job over and done with."

"He's probably showing the men where to place his furniture," I said. "It'll save time in the long run." I studied the moving van with a practiced eye. "It's not a very big van. It may be the smallest one I've ever seen in Finch."

"Dare we assume that Mr. Windle is a man with few possessions?" Charles asked in a melodramatic murmur. "If so, is he a minimalist? Or is he too poor to own much? Or is he fond of tiny furniture?"

"Hush," I said, laughing. "The curtain is rising."

The cottage's front door had opened and the three movers had emerged, followed closely by the man of the moment. I nearly lost my grip on my knife as I leaned forward to take a good look at him, unhampered by the sun's glare.

Crispin Windle was tall, pale, and painfully thin. He had gray eyes, a long, deeply lined face, and a receding shoreline of gray hair that suggested late middle age. His clothes were slightly shabby and remarkably ill fitting. His navy-blue crewneck sweater hung limply from his spare frame and his twill trousers appeared to be at least two sizes too large for him.

I felt a pang of pity for our new neighbor as I noted several small holes in his sweater, frayed cuffs on his trousers, and worn heels on his brown wingtip shoes, but I thought his air of genteel shabbiness might give the Handmaidens a reason to hope. It looked as though Crispin Windle needed someone to look after him.

While Mr. Windle exchanged a few words with the movers, Charles, Grant, and I exchanged quite a few words about him.

"He must have lost weight since he bought those trousers," I commented.

"I concur," said Charles. "Did he lose weight intentionally? Or has he been ill?"

"Either way," I said, "the Handmaidens will do what they can to fatten him up. They'll bombard him with so many welcome-to-Finch casseroles that he won't have a square inch of empty counter space left in his kitchen."

"He'll have to make room for everyone else's offerings," said Grant, "but at least the poor man will have three days of peace and quiet before the entire village converges on him."

"Yes, indeed," said Charles, nodding. "The three-day rule will keep all of us at bay until Wednesday."

The three-day rule was one of Finch's most hallowed traditions. My neighbors considered it common courtesy to allow a newcomer three days to settle in to his new abode before they inundated him with casseroles, cookies, and cakes as well as invitations to upcoming events and sign-up sheets for a veritable constellation of volunteer activities. If they met Mr. Windle anywhere other than Pussywillows while the three-day rule was in effect, they'd talk his ear off, but they wouldn't intrude on him in his home until the requisite time period had passed.

"He's not dressed to impress," Charles said, "but I wouldn't expect him to wear his Sunday best on moving day. How old do you think he is?"

"Hard to say," I replied. "Midseventies?"

"Too old for the Handmaidens?" Grant inquired.

"Not possible," Charles stated firmly. "As long as he has a pulse, they'll consider him fair game."

"He could do worse," said Grant. "A lot of men would give their eyeteeth to be pursued by four women at once."

"What's more," I said loyally, "the Handmaidens are interesting women—they paint, they cook, they attend all sorts of classes in Upper Deeping, and they play an active role in village life. They have a lot to offer."

"So if Mr. Windle ends up losing his heart to one of them," Charles said, glancing slyly at Miranda Morrow, "it will be because she has a lot to offer and not because his cottage is enchanted."

"It could be a bit of both," she responded, unfazed.

I peered at our new neighbor in silence, then said, "He doesn't seem to be very curious about his surroundings. He hasn't looked at anyone but the movers. If you were in his shoes, wouldn't you at least take a quick peek at James Hobson's metal detector? Wouldn't you react in some way to the sight of four easels pointed in your direction?"

"If I were in his shoes," Grant said, "I'd be too preoccupied to pay attention to the locals."

"If I were in his shoes," said Charles, "I'd have them resoled."

"I just hope he isn't antisocial," I said. "For his sake as well as ours."

Mr. Windle finished speaking with the driver, then retreated into the cottage. Under the driver's directions, the two burly men opened the van's rear doors, lowered a ramp, and began to unload a series of cardboard boxes.

"He hasn't labeled his boxes!" Charles exclaimed indignantly. "What kind of person moves house without marking his boxes?"

"An inexperienced one?" I suggested. "It could be that Mr. Windle hasn't moved house in a long time."

"If one owns very little," Grant theorized, "one may not feel the need to label one's boxes."

"But how are we supposed to tell what's in them?" Charles demanded. "By failing to mark his boxes, Mr. Windle has effectively prevented us from making educated guesses about him and his way of life."

"Try not to take it personally," Grant counseled dryly. "I doubt that Mr. Windle had our needs in mind when he packed his boxes."

"I hope he spends the next three days searching for his tin opener," Charles grumbled. He brightened suddenly and cried, "At last! A sofa!"

The furniture portion of the morning's entertainment had begun. Unfortunately, Mr. Windle's furniture wasn't entertaining. The plain beige sofa was followed by a succession of equally nondescript pieces that appeared to be older than his car but not old enough to qualify as antiques. Though they were serviceable, they were not in any way memorable, and there didn't seem to be enough of them to fill an entire cottage.

"I peg Mr. Windle as a practical man," I said charitably as the two burly movers carried a large but wholly unremarkable desk down the ramp. "His furniture may be boring, but it's easy to clean and there's not too much of it, so his rooms won't be overcrowded."

"Overcrowded?" Charles echoed incredulously. "Half the rooms will be *empty*. He hasn't even brought a bed for the spare bedroom. Has anyone seen a dining room table or chairs?"

"I haven't," I acknowledged. "I saw what could be a kitchen table, though. Maybe Mr. Windle likes to eat in the kitchen."

"A man without a dining room set doesn't expect to entertain guests," Charles said darkly. "It's a bad omen."

"Maybe he ordered a new dining room set for his new home," I proposed, "and arranged to have it delivered after he moved in."

Charles regarded me skeptically. "Does anything you've seen so far indicate that Mr. Windle is in the habit of buying new furniture?"

"Not really," I conceded.

The only items that piqued my interest were the last to emerge from the moving van, and they piqued my interest only because I couldn't figure out what they were. I could see that they were pieces of finished wood of varying lengths and widths, that some of them had holes drilled through them, and that they were tied in bundles, but their purpose eluded me.

My friends were equally perplexed.

"What do you suppose those bundles of wood could be?" Grant asked.

"Shelves?" I said tentatively.

"For what?" asked Charles. "Miniature books?"

"You have a guess, then," I retorted.

"Dining room table?" he said.

I laughed in spite of myself, then snapped my fingers as another explanation occurred to me.

"Annabelle," I said, turning to old Mrs. Craven, "could those lengths of wood be the parts of a dismantled quilting frame?"

"If they are," she replied, "Mr. Windle's quilting frame is unlike any I've ever seen, and I've seen quite a few."

"Any guesses as to what they might be?" I asked her.

"None," she said.

"Suggestions, anyone?" I looked from Bree to Miranda, but they offered nothing more constructive than a pair of mystified shrugs.

"Unmarked boxes and mysterious lengths of wood," said Mrs. Craven, smiling. "There's clearly more to Mr. Windle than meets the eye."

"I should hope so," said Charles. "There could hardly be less."

"The show's over," Grant announced.

The movers slid the ramp into the van and shut the rear doors before being admitted once again to Pussywillows. A short time later they reappeared, climbed into the cab, and retraced their route out of the village.

"Another moving-van vigil comes to a close," I intoned.

"By the looks of things, it came to a close some time ago," said Grant. With a sweeping gesture, he indicated a nearly deserted village green.

Apart from a pair of kayakers who were about to enter the Emporium, the only living souls in sight were Tommy Prescott and my daughter. Even the Handmaidens had packed up their paint pots and departed. It was the swiftest denouement to a moving-van vigil I'd ever witnessed.

"Mr. Windle was late," I reminded my friends. "If he'd been on time, I'm sure people would have stuck around to swap after-action reports. As it is, I imagine they've either gone to Upper Deeping for the Saturday sales or gone home to catch up on the chores they should have started two hours ago."

"I imagine they were too underwhelmed by the whole affair to have after-action reports to swap," said Charles. "I've never participated in a more tedious vigil. If Mr. Windle's furniture reflects his personality, I don't think we can count on him to enrich village life."

"I'll reserve judgment until I know what's in his boxes," said Grant. "His dreary furniture could be a neutral background for a fabulous collection of Ming porcelain or Venetian glass."

"Or he could be an ordinary man who owns ordinary things," I said. "What's wrong with ordinary? I'm nothing special and you still hang out with me."

"You're very special to us, dear," Charles assured me. He tucked a last bite of scone into his mouth and consulted his watch. "If we leave now, Grant, we can take in the needlework exhibition in Tewkesbury *and* treat ourselves to lunch at the Abbey Tea Rooms." He looked around expectantly. "Would anyone care to join us?"

"I would," said Mrs. Craven.

"Excellent," said Charles. "You can test us on our knowledge of whipstitches. Anyone else?"

"Sorry," I said, "but after romping with Tommy all morning, Bess will be in urgent need of a large lunch and a long nap."

"I'll have to beg off, too," said Miranda. "I have to plot a star chart for a client. No one from Finch," she added as our eyes lit up. "It's one of my online regulars—an *out-of-town* online regular."

Bree, who'd been unusually subdued throughout the vigil, got to her feet.

"Thanks for the invite, Charles," she said, "but there's something else I need to do."

"Going to St. George's?" I asked.

Bree nodded. "I have to speak to Mr. Barlow before anyone else does. I can't take back my idiotic blunder, but I can own up to it. At least he'll know who's to blame for turning his marriage proposals into gossip fodder."

"He'll appreciate your honesty," I said.

"I don't think he will," said Bree. She heaved a regretful sigh, then squared her tattooed shoulders and left the tearoom.

I felt a distinct sense of deflation as my friends and I paid our bills and went our separate ways. I wouldn't have had much to say about Mr. Windle if anyone had been around to listen, but I would have said something. The deserted green offered no scope whatsoever for analysis or speculation. A moving-van vigil without a flurry of follow-up conversations was, I decided, as disappointing as an Easter basket without chocolate bunnies.

My dejected mood evaporated when I spotted Tommy Prescott standing atop the humpbacked bridge with Bess the Fearless held securely in his massive arms. He was dressed in a flannel shirt with rolled-up sleeves, an old pair of cargo trousers, and a pair of sneakers, one of which covered the foot portion of his "everyday" prosthetic—he used a springy blade-style prosthetic when he worked out. Bess was speaking animatedly to him while pointing over the bridge's low stone parapet at the river. I wondered if she was teaching him how to quack.

As a Finch-trained snoop, I lacked the moral fortitude to walk past Pussywillows on my way to the bridge without glancing through Mr. Windle's curtainless windows. The living room held no surprises, but my eyebrows rose when I spied the mysterious bundles of wood lying on the dining room floor. Why were they in the dining room? I asked myself. Had Charles guessed correctly after all? Did Mr. Windle own a do-it-yourself dining set kit? It seemed improbable, but I could think of no other explanation.

The sound of Tommy's voice ended my musings.

"Lori!" he called. "Bess is teaching me how to quack!"

"Listen and learn!" I called back, laughing. "She's an expert!"

As soon as I reached the top of the bridge, I took Bess from Tommy and gave her a snuggly hug.

"Who's my clever girl?" I crooned.

"Look!" she replied, pointing at a group of paddling mallards. "Duck!"

"I see the ducks," I said. "Aren't they beautiful?"

Bess quacked her agreement, then continued to quack so enthusiastically that the mallards exploded into flight, adding their startled cries to the cacophony. Grinning, Tommy seated himself on the parapet, a move that spared me the trouble of tilting my head back to look up at him.

"Thanks for taking care of my little perpetual motion machine," I said, raising my voice to be heard above the ducky din.

"No thanks needed," he said. "Bess is a great kid, and I'm not one for keeping still. I had my fill of immobility when I was in hospital."

"I'll bet you did." Since potty training was still a work in progress, I gave my daughter an experimental sniff. "Did you change her training pants, too?"

"Bill did," he replied. "I paid attention, though. It's one of the many useful skills I'll need when Bree and I start a family."

"Is that likely to happen anytime soon?" I asked.

"If it were up to me, we'd get married tomorrow," said Tommy. "But it's not up to me. It's up to Bree. She doesn't want to make the same mistake she made with the Aussie bloke, so she's taking a good long look before leaping."

"Once bitten, twice shy?" I suggested.

"At least twice." Tommy looked past me, as if hoping to catch a glimpse of his fiancée. "Why did she run off to St. George's? My uncle didn't rope her into rehanging the vestry door, did he?"

"No," I said. "She went to St. George's because she needed to speak with your uncle."

"*Needed* to speak?" he repeated. "Must be serious."

"Bree thinks it is," I said. "Which is why I'll let her tell you about it."

"Fair enough," Tommy said amiably. He looked past me again and frowned. "What's he doing?"

"What's who doing?" I asked.

"Our new neighbor," Tommy replied. "He just came out of Pussywillows."

I swung around and saw Crispin Windle standing motionless before his opened door.

"What's he up to?" Tommy asked.

"I don't know," I said. "Maybe he's . . ." My voice faded into silence as Mr. Windle turned to face us.

His gaze drifted slowly from the bridge's arch to the river's rippling surface and back again. His pale features were expressionless, as blank and empty as a block of stone until, abruptly, and for no more than an instant, his breath seemed to catch in his throat and his gray eyes filled with tears. He looked in that brief moment like a man bereft of hope, a man so broken he could scarcely bear the weight of his own thoughts. I could almost see a cloud of anguish close around him as, silently, and once again blank-faced, he reentered his new home and shut the door.

# *Five*

I turned to stare at Tommy, who'd risen from his perch on the parapet, as if propelled to his feet by the sheer force of Mr. Windle's pain.

Shaken, I whispered, "Did you see—?"

"I saw," he broke in tersely.

"What did you see?" I pressed, unwilling to trust my own eyes.

"I saw a man in trouble," Tommy said grimly. "I saw a man in trouble looking at the bridge."

I felt a shiver of apprehension. "You don't suppose he's—"

"Thinking of chucking himself into the river?" Tommy ran a hand through his short, dark hair. "Odd thing to do after he's gone to all the trouble of moving here. He's from Derbyshire, isn't he? There are plenty of rivers up there. Why didn't he chuck himself into one of them?"

"I don't know," I said. "Maybe he thinks there'll be less of a fuss if he does away with himself in a place where nobody knows him."

"If he thinks that," said Tommy, "he has a lot to learn about Finch."

I turned again to peer at Mr. Windle's door. I didn't know what was going on behind it, but the terrible image of a noose dangling from a rafter flashed through my mind. Without a second thought, I passed Bess to Tommy.

"Hold on to Bess for me, will you?" I asked as I began to clamber down the bridge.

"Why?" he asked. "Where are you going?"

"To Pussywillows," I replied. "If I have to break a window to get in, I'll need to have both hands free."

Tommy came up beside me, shortened his stride to match mine, and stated emphatically, "If anyone breaks a window, it'll be me."

"Bye-bye, ducks," said Bess, gazing over his shoulder at the river.

Curtains began to twitch in a handful of cottages as a few sharp-eyed villagers interrupted their Saturday chores to watch Tommy and me race toward Pussywillows.

"We'll be slammed for breaking the three-day rule," I warned.

Tommy eyed me quizzically. "Want to wait until Wednesday to find out if Mr. Windle needs help?"

"Are you crazy?" I replied. "He could be at the bottom of the Little Deeping by then!" I glanced at my neighbors' twitching curtains, then clenched my fists determinedly. "There are times when fine old village traditions have to be set aside for the sake of basic human decency."

"And this," said Tommy, "is one of them."

I felt a sickening sense of foreboding when we reached Pussywillows.

"If he doesn't answer the door," I murmured, "we'll break a window."

"We should probably try the back door before we smash anything," Tommy suggested. "If he's in the kitchen, he might not hear a knock on the front door."

"Okay," I said tensely. "But if Mr. Windle doesn't answer the front door *or* the back door—"

"*I'll* break a window," he interrupted. "But I'll give Bess to you first."

Bess quacked.

"Good idea," I said. "Wait until I step well away, though. Broken glass flies everywhere. Do you have a handkerchief?"

"Always," he said, pulling a blue bandanna from the back pocket of his trousers.

"Wrap it around your hand so you don't cut yourself," I advised.

"I'm not going to use my hand to break a window," said Tommy, shoving the handkerchief back into his pocket. "I'll use my elbow."

"Have you done it before?" I asked interestedly.

"Would you like to hear about my career as a window breaker?" Tommy asked with a hint of exasperation. "Or would you like to check on Mr. Windle?"

"Sorry," I said, chastened. "Here we go."

I lifted the dull brass door knocker and rapped it smartly against the door. When nothing happened, Tommy thumped his fist on the door, but his thumps appeared to have no more effect that my raps. I was on the verge of sprinting to the back door when the front door swung inward.

Mr. Windle's face was again expressionless, but he appeared to be unharmed. He held a crumpled sheet of newspaper in his left hand, as if we'd interrupted him in the midst of unpacking. He didn't complain about the intrusion, however, or apologize for taking so long to answer the door. He didn't even greet us. He simply peered at us vaguely and let the silence spiral.

"Hi," I said. I hadn't given a moment's thought to what I would say next, but I plunged ahead regardless. "I'm Lori Shepherd and I was on the bridge just now. When you looked my way a few minutes ago, I couldn't help but notice that you seemed to be . . . distressed."

"Did I?" said Mr. Windle.

I'd expected his voice to be thin and reedy, but it was clear, supple, and altogether pleasant. I wondered fleetingly if he ever read poetry aloud.

"You did," I replied. "You looked very distressed. Are you okay?"

"Yes, thank you," he said. "I'm quite well."

Though I'd hoped he'd have a Derbyshire accent, I detected nothing in his speech to indicate that he was from the North.

"Are you sure?" I asked. "Because you didn't seem okay when you looked at the river. To be honest, you scared us a little. We were afraid you might be contemplating a watery, er . . ."

"Grave," Tommy put in helpfully.

"And we'd rather you didn't," I said earnestly. "Contemplate a watery grave, that is. Or any sort of grave, really. Even a dry one."

Mr. Windle blinked at me in silence for a moment, then said quietly, "I'm grateful to you for your concern, Mrs. Shepherd, but I can assure you that I do not intend to kill myself."

"Wonderful," I said, wishing fervently that I'd prepared an exit strategy. "I'm glad you're okay. And, um, welcome to Finch. Also, I'm not Mrs. Shepherd. My husband's name is Bill Willis, but I didn't change mine when I married him, so I'm still Lori Shepherd, but please, call me Lori. Everyone does."

"I shall bear it in mind." Mr. Windle's gaze shifted to Tommy. "How old is your daughter, Mr. Willis?"

"I'm not Mr. Willis," said Tommy, startled. "I'm Tommy Prescott."

"And Bess isn't his daughter," I clarified swiftly.

Bess quacked again and Mr. Windle's long, thin face seemed to brighten slightly.

"Bess is my daughter," I continued. "Well, mine and my husband's. My husband works a few doors down from here, in Wysteria Lodge." I pointed at the car parked in front of the vine-covered building that housed Bill's high-tech office. "The canary-yellow Range Rover is mine. My husband chose the color to make it easier for other drivers to see me," I jabbered. "He's an estate attorney."

"Daddy work," Bess explained.

"That's right," Tommy said to her. "Bill's your daddy, not me." Turning to Mr. Windle, he went on. "I'm engaged to Bree Pym. Bree's in the church right now, chatting with my uncle."

"Is your uncle a clergyman?" Mr. Windle inquired courteously, though he shifted his meager weight from foot to foot, as if the sheer effort of standing on his doorstep with two voluble strangers tired him.

"No," Tommy replied. "Theodore Bunting is the vicar at St. George's. My uncle is the village handyman and mechanic. If you have engine trouble or a loose floorboard, my uncle is the man to ring."

"Good to know," said Mr. Windle. The ghost of a smile flickered across his thin lips as he looked at Bess. "How old is your daughter, Lori?"

"She turned two in February," I told him.

"I two," Bess confirmed, holding out two fingers.

"I thought you might be. It's very nice to meet you, Bess." Mr. Windle's faint smile lingered as he addressed Tommy and me. "It was very nice to meet you, too, but I'm afraid you'll have to excuse me." He held up the crumpled sheet of newspaper. "Lots to do."

"Of course," I said. "Sorry to bother you."

"Not at all," he said, and closed the door.

I stared at the door in mortified silence, then grabbed Tommy's arm and dragged him away from Pussywillows, no small feat for someone who was a foot shorter and considerably less muscular than he was. I could feel Sally Cook eyeing me beadily as we passed the tearoom, but I fixed my gaze on the ground until we reached the Range Rover.

"That went well," Tommy said dryly.

"Dear Lord," I groaned, burying my face in my hands. "'Are you going to kill yourself and welcome to Finch'? I must have sounded like the village idiot."

"I must have sounded like a door-to-door salesman," said Tommy. "Car trouble? Ring Billy Barlow!"

"I have no idea why I told him where I park the Rover," I said with a helpless shrug.

"He must think Uncle Bill runs his business out of St. George's," said Tommy.

"You should have seen your face when he mistook you for my husband," I said, with a giggle.

"You should have seen yours!" he shot back.

My giggle turned into a chuckle, which prompted a sheepish laugh from Tommy.

"Bess down!" Bess commanded.

Tommy obeyed, setting her gently on the cobbles. As soon as her feet hit the ground, she made a beeline for her father's office. I kept half an eye on her while she fiddled with the door latch, ready to chase after her if she changed her mind and headed for the green.

"We may not have made the best first impression on Mr. Windle," I said to Tommy, "but we didn't go to Pussywillows to charm him. We went there to save his life."

"Our intentions were pure," Tommy agreed. "It was our execution that was a bit wonky."

"More than a bit," I said ruefully. "Even so, we were right to be worried about him. I'm still worried about him. He may not be contemplating suicide, but I could tell just by looking at him that he's sad, deep-down sad, the kind of sad you can feel from twenty yards away."

"The way his face changed when he looked toward the bridge,"

Tommy said reflectively. "I've seen faces change like that before, Lori. It's never a good sign."

"What do you mean?" I asked.

"I mean—" Tommy began, but he broke off when a familiar voice roared, *"Thomas Prescott!"*

I wheeled around and saw Mr. Barlow and Bree Pym walking toward us from the direction of St. George's. The stocky handyman had a face like thunder and Bree's head was bowed.

"Thomas?" Tommy murmured, his eyebrows rising. "The last time Uncle Bill called me Thomas was after I spilled a quart of motor oil on his workbench. I was twelve."

"I think you're about to find out why Bree needed to speak with him," I said.

"If he's upset her," Tommy growled, "I'll—"

"You've got it backwards," I interjected. "She's upset him. You have, too. So has Tilly. There's no point in going all knight-in shining-armor, Tommy. I suggest that you take your medicine like a big boy and apologize. Humbly."

Tommy looked down at me, bewildered. "Apologize for what?"

"You'll find out," I answered.

Mr. Barlow and Bree came to a halt a few feet away from us. Bree kept her head down, but Mr. Barlow glared at Tommy.

"Morning, Mr. Barlow," I said lightly, as if I hadn't noticed the angry sparks flying from his eyes.

"Morning, Lori," he replied in a much less breezy tone. "Sorry to intrude, but my nephew is wanted at home." He nodded to me, motioned for Bree to follow him, and strode across the green toward his house, shouting over his shoulder, *"Now,* Thomas!"

"If I were you," I said, "I wouldn't keep him waiting."

"Right," said Tommy, and he took off at a loping run to catch up with his furious uncle and his woebegone fiancée.

I didn't envy him. Mr. Barlow didn't lose his temper often, but when he did, he lost it good and proper. I'd thought he'd let Bree off with a mild reprimand for her unfortunate disclosure, but I'd clearly misjudged the situation. Charles Bellingham had come closer to the mark when he'd observed that Mr. Barlow might object to being known throughout the village as the man whose future wife had rejected him twice. Mr. Barlow, it seemed, did object. *Strenuously.*

The morning had been filled with far too much drama, even by Finch's high standards. Rattled, I turned to assist my daughter in her efforts to invade her father's office.

# *Six*

Since Bill was in the midst of a three-way conference call with a client in Milan and a colleague in Cologne, the invasion was short-lived. I blew a kiss to my husband, seized Bess's hand, and led her back to the Rover before she could cause an international incident. While I buckled her into her car seat, I assured her that she could tell Daddy about the ducks when he came home from work.

As I drove slowly up the cobbled lane toward the humpbacked bridge, I wondered again what Tommy had meant when he'd said he'd seen other faces change in the same unsettling way as Mr. Windle's. I'd never seen anything like it, but Tommy had witnessed a range of human suffering I could scarcely imagine, both in combat and in the hospital where he'd spent months recuperating from his injuries. It would never have occurred to me to compare our new neighbor to a wounded veteran, but it might have occurred to Tommy.

I glanced uneasily at Pussywillows. The profound sadness I'd sensed in Mr. Windle reminded me that some wounds were invisible. Though he'd stated unequivocally that he had no desire to do away with himself, the rushing waters of the Little Deeping were much too close to his new home for my liking.

I'd hoped that Bill would say something sensible to restore my peace of mind, but my conversation with him, like Bess's, would have to wait. Thankfully, I knew where to find a friend who was never too busy to say sensible things to me.

I could always share my worries with Aunt Dimity.

---

Aunt Dimity wasn't, technically speaking, my aunt. Nor was she, in the strictest sense of the word, alive. The former was a lot easier to explain than the latter.

Dimity Westwood, an Englishwoman, had been my late mother's closest friend. The pair had met in London while serving their respective countries during the Second World War, and the bond of affection they forged during those dark and dangerous years was never broken.

After the Allied forces declared victory in Europe and my mother sailed back to the States, she and Dimity strengthened their friendship by sending hundreds of letters back and forth across the Atlantic. When my father died shortly after my birth, those letters became my mother's refuge, a tranquil retreat from the everyday pressures of teaching full time while raising a rambunctious daughter on her own.

My mother was extremely protective of her refuge. She told no one about it, not even me. As a child, I knew Dimity Westwood only as Aunt Dimity, the redoubtable heroine of a series of bedtime stories invented by my mother. I was unaware of her true identity until both she and my mother were dead.

It was then that the fictional heroine of my favorite stories became very real to me. At the lowest point in my life, when I was broke, alone, and still grieving for my mother, Dimity Westwood bequeathed to me a considerable fortune, the honey-colored cottage in which she'd grown up, the precious correspondence she'd exchanged with my mother, and an apparently unused journal bound in blue leather.

It was through the blue journal that I finally came to know my benefactress. Whenever I gazed at its blank pages, Aunt Dimity's handwriting would appear, an old-fashioned copperplate taught in the village school at a time when the whisper of scythes heralded the harvest. I nearly fell off my chair the first time it happened, but I soon came to realize that Aunt Dimity was a wise and kindly soul who had nothing but my best interests at heart.

I couldn't explain how Aunt Dimity managed to bridge the gap between the living and the not-quite-living, and she wasn't too clear about it herself, but the *how* didn't matter to me. The one thing I knew for certain, the only thing I needed to know, was that Dimity Westwood was as good a friend to me as she'd been to my mother.

If anyone could restore my peace of mind, it was Aunt Dimity.

Bess alternated between quacking and singing as we drove home, though she also bellowed "Grandpa!" when we passed the entrance to Willis, Sr.'s tree-lined drive; "Bree!" when we passed Bree Pym's mellow redbrick house; and "Toby! Toby! Toby!" when we passed the curving drive that led to the Anscombe Manor stables. Since Toby was Bess's favorite pony, he received a longer and much louder salutation than either her grandfather or Bree.

By the time we reached our honey-colored cottage, I was yearning for earplugs and we were both ready for lunch. I parked the Rover in the graveled driveway, liberated Bess from her car seat, and walked with her up the flagstone path, through the front door, and into the front hall. After saying hello to Stanley, who was curled into a sleek and somnolent black ball on the living room's cushioned window seat, we toddled up the hallway to the kitchen, where I threw together a quick meal of cheese sandwiches, steamed vegetables, and sliced bananas.

Bess was so tuckered out from chasing and being chased by Tommy Prescott that she allowed me to carry her up to the nursery after lunch. Once I'd settled my sleepy girl in her cot, I grabbed the baby monitor and hurried downstairs to sequester myself in the study.

The study was still and silent and, I suspected, decidedly more tranquil than Mr. Barlow's house would be for the next little while. Sunlight streamed through the strands of ivy that crisscrossed the diamond-paned windows above the old oak desk, making the supple leaves glow like stained glass. I lit a fire in the hearth for comfort rather than warmth, then paused to speak with my oldest friend in the world.

"Hi, Reginald," I said. "I hope you've had a less exciting morning than I have. There's a lot to be said for monotony."

Reginald was a small rabbit made of powder-pink flannel. He had black button eyes, hand-sewn whiskers, and a faded purple stain on his handsome snout, a souvenir of the day I'd shared my grape juice with him. Reginald had entered my life shortly after I'd entered it, and he'd been my companion in adventure ever since. He'd absorbed more tears than any pillow I'd ever owned and he'd kept every secret I'd ever shared with him. A sophisticated woman would have put him away when she put away childish things, but I wasn't a sophisticated woman. I kept Reginald close at hand because I never knew when I'd shed more tears or have more secrets to share.

"I called on our new neighbor this morning," I said. "I'll probably catch all sorts of flak from the villagers for breaking the three-day rule, but I was afraid Mr. Windle would do something drastic if I didn't step in."

Reginald's black button eyes gleamed supportively as he gazed at me from his special niche in the floor-to-ceiling bookshelves. I twiddled his pink ears fondly, took the blue journal down from its shelf, and sat with it in one of the pair of tall leather armchairs that faced the fire.

"Dimity?" I said, opening the journal. "I have so much to tell you that I may not get through it all before Bess wakes up from her nap."

I breathed a sigh of relief as the familiar lines of royal-blue ink began to loop and curl across the page.

*Good afternoon, Lori. Has our unmarried, retired professor from Derbyshire taken possession of Pussywillows?*

"Crispin Windle has arrived," I confirmed.

*Then I'm not surprised that you have a lot to tell me. You always do, after a moving-van vigil.*

"It wasn't an ordinary vigil, Dimity," I said. "I mean, I shared a table with Grant and Charles in the tearoom, as usual, and the green was swarming with villagers, as usual, but the vigil itself was less informative than usual, and the morning as a whole was . . . complicated."

*In that case, I suggest that you begin at the beginning and proceed from there until you reach the end. Telling the story back to front will only complicate matters further.*

"The beginning?" I said, scratching my head. It felt as if half a lifetime had passed since I'd spread clotted cream on my fruit scone. "Well, I guess things took a turn for the strange when Sally Cook announced that Pussywillows is enchanted."

*I beg your pardon?*

"You heard me correctly," I said. "Sally's convinced that the cottage has become a magical launchpad for lovebirds."

*A magical what?*

"A magical launchpad for lovebirds," I repeated. "My words, not Sally's."

*I'm dazzled by your verbal dexterity. What do your words mean?*

"According to Sally," I said, "anyone who lives in Pussywillows is destined to find true love."

*Nonsense. I could list dozens of people who lived in Pussywillows without finding true love.*

"Amelia and Tilly did," I pointed out. "That's two launched lovebirds in a row. Since three's a charm, the enchantment is bound to work for Mr. Windle—according to Sally."

*I was under the impression that Tilly fell in love with Mr. Barlow before she moved into Pussywillows.*

"So was I," I said, "but Tilly told Tommy, who told Bree, who told us, that she didn't fall in love with Mr. Barlow until after she came to live in Finch. Mr. Barlow proposed to Tilly twice at her home in Oxford, but it wasn't until he proposed to her in Pussywillows that she accepted him."

*I've always wondered why Tilly moved into Pussywillows before she married Mr. Barlow. It seemed like a waste of time and energy, but if she wasn't in love with him until then, her decision makes sense. Why on earth did Bree wait until this morning to reveal such a scintillating bit of gossip to you?*

"She wasn't supposed to reveal it to anyone," I explained. "It was a family secret told to her in the strictest confidence, but when Sally started talking about the enchanted cottage, Bree felt compelled to set the record straight about Tilly, which meant that she had to tell us about Mr. Barlow's romantic setbacks."

*Bree discussed a closely held family secret in the tearoom? Good grief. She might as well have shouted it from a rooftop.*

"She didn't realize what she'd done until after she'd done it," I said, "but by then it was too late. Everyone in the tearoom had heard her."

*They could hardly avoid hearing her, and though it would be theoretically possible for them to keep the news to themselves, they won't.*

"Mr. Barlow's private life will be the talk of the village by teatime," I agreed. "When the vigil ended, Bree did the honorable thing. She ran off to tell Mr. Barlow about her blunder before he could hear about it from someone else."

*She may be impulsive, but she doesn't lack courage. I suspect that Mr. Barlow did not receive the news with unalloyed gladness.*

"I saw the two of them together before I left the village," I said. "Bree looked like a condemned prisoner and Mr. Barlow was breathing fire. Unless I'm very much mistaken, which I'm not, he is at this moment giving her *and* Tommy *and* Tilly a stern lecture about keeping certain family stories within the family." I leaned back in my chair and propped my feet on the plump ottoman. "Honestly, Dimity, I don't know why he's kicked up such a fuss. If I were him, I wouldn't care if the woman I loved rejected me a dozen times, as long as she married me in the end."

*Tilly's refusals must have bruised Mr. Barlow's pride as well as his heart, poor lamb. He wouldn't want such a sensitive subject bandied about by his neighbors.*

"No one would," I said, "but he's lived in the village for decades, Dimity. You'd think he'd know by now that the only way to keep a secret in Finch is not to have one."

*True, but hope springs eternal. Once Mr. Barlow calms down, I'm sure it will occur to him that his situation, as embarrassing as it is, could be worse.*

"How?" I asked.

*His romantic setbacks could be the ONLY subject of gossip in Finch. As it is, the villagers have Crispin Windle to distract them. Indeed, if the Handmaidens believe that Pussywillows is a . . . a magical launchpad for lovebirds, to use your mellifluous phrase, they won't waste any time on Mr. Barlow. Their sole concern will be to shower our new, unmarried neighbor with attention.*

"I'm counting on them to do just that," I said. "Mr. Windle is in dire need of some tender loving care."

*Are you jumping to a conclusion about Mr. Windle, my dear? If you're not, the vigil must have been as revelatory as Bree's comments about Mr. Barlow's love life.*

"The vigil nearly put us to sleep," I said. "Mr. Windle didn't label his boxes, so we couldn't tell what was in them, and he has barely enough furniture to fill one room, let alone a whole cottage. He doesn't even own a dining room table, Dimity, and the few pieces he does own are as plain as porridge. We were captivated for a few minutes by some bundles of finished wood, but no one could figure out what they were, so we lost interest in them as well."

*How old is Mr. Windle?*

"Seventy-five, maybe?" I said. "Tall, pale, gaunt. Long face, gray eyes, thinning gray hair. Ratty old clothes that made him look like a scarecrow. He drives an old car, too, but it's not a flashy collectible. It's just old."

*And his manner?*

"Distant," I replied. "He didn't look at or speak to anyone except the movers. He acted as though the rest of us were invisible, but everything about him was so dreary that the villagers cleared out before the moving van was empty."

*No one lingered to discuss the distant Mr. Windle? Most unusual. Did you and your friends in the tearoom leave early, too?*

"We stayed put until the bitter end," I replied, "but since we'd already said all we had to say about Mr. Windle, our party broke up when the moving van left. I intended to come straight back here afterwards, but Tommy had taken Bess to the bridge to quack at the ducks, so I chatted with him for a little while." I sighed. "I almost wish I hadn't."

*You didn't tell Tommy about Bree's indiscreet remarks, did you?*

"Of course not," I said indignantly. "I may not think things through as often as I should, Dimity, but even I know better than to tell a young man that his fiancée is a blabbermouth."

*I'm relieved to hear it. However familiar he is with his fiancée's foibles, he would not wish to hear about them from you. But I digress. You and Bess and Tommy were on the bridge, chatting and quacking, and then . . . ?*

"Then the strangest thing happened," I said. "Mr. Windle stepped out of Pussywillows. At first, his face was perfectly blank, as if it had been wiped clean of all emotion. Then he looked toward the river and it was as if"—I struggled to find the right words—"as if some sort of bone-deep pain bubbled up to the surface, as if his suffering soul were on display for all the world to see, except that Tommy and I were the only ones there to see it. His expression changed for maybe two heartbeats before his face went blank again. Then he went back into the cottage and closed the door." I frowned in frustration. "I wish I could describe the moment better, Dimity, but—" I broke off as the graceful handwriting sped across the page.

*You've described it very well, Lori, very well indeed. You and Tommy caught a glimpse of Mr. Windle's inner turmoil, which was quickly suppressed. It must have been very disturbing to witness such a sudden, public eruption of private pain.*

"It scared the bejesus out of Tommy and me," I said, "especially since the eruption happened when Mr. Windle looked at the river. We thought he was going to drown himself, Dimity, so we"—I braced myself for a reprimand—"we marched right up to Pussywillows and knocked on his door."

*I would expect nothing less of you, my dear.*

"Really?" I said, at once gratified and taken aback. "You're not going to scold me for breaking the three-day rule?"

*Don't be ridiculous, Lori. You could hardly wait until Wednesday to help a man who appeared to be in imminent danger of harming himself. Did you speak with him?*

"Yes," I said. "When he answered the door, I told him what we'd seen. He didn't seem to remember the eruption, and when I asked him if he was planning to kill himself, he said he wasn't."

*I see. So you know better than to tell a young man that his fiancée is a blabbermouth, but you don't know better than to ask a perfect stranger if he's suicidal. I understand what you mean about not thinking things through as often as you should.*

"I didn't have time to tiptoe around the question," I protested. "I was afraid Mr. Windle would top himself as soon as our backs were turned."

*Of course you were. Forgive my ungenerous jibe. Sometimes a direct approach is the best approach. Did Mr. Windle's answer reassure you?*

"No," I said. "It didn't reassure Tommy, either. Tommy told me he'd seen faces change like that before, and that it was never a good sign, but before he could elaborate, Mr. Barlow came along and brought our conversation to a screeching halt."

*You and Tommy will have a chance to continue it after church tomorrow.*

"Will we?" I said. "Something tells me that the villagers will be less forbearing than you are about our breach of the three-day rule. A few of them—or a few more than a few—will probably take us aside after church to explain how things are done in Finch. As if we didn't know . . ." I sank more deeply into the chair and gazed grumpily into the fire before asking, "Did Tommy and I overreact, Dimity? Did we read too much into a fleeting expression? Mr. Windle came close to smiling when he looked at Bess, and he listened politely to Tommy and me even when we were behaving like a pair of babbling buffoons. Could it be that, when he looked at the river, he was simply feeling the effects of a tiring day?"

*A tiring day might generate a powerful desire for a long soak in a hot bath, but I doubt that it would provoke a brief flash of intense suffering. It seems to me that Mr. Windle isn't at all well. Instead of wondering if you overreacted, you should be asking yourself what you can do to rescue our new neighbor from his inner demons.*

"What can I do?" I asked. "Offer him free therapy sessions? He already thinks I'm a nutter. Imagine what he'll think if I show up again, demanding that he tell me his deepest, darkest secrets." I tossed my head. "He'll lock his door and hide behind his sofa."

*As would I. A direct approach isn't always the best approach, Lori. I suggest that you try something a little more subtle.*

I eyed the journal doubtfully. "Are you telling me to spy on him?"

*Certainly not. I'm suggesting that you do what you always do when someone new comes to the village. Be a good neighbor. Become a good friend. If you take an active, honest, openhearted interest in Crispin Windle, he'll soon realize that he doesn't have to fight his demons on his own because he isn't alone anymore—he's a valued member of our small community.*

I stared at the journal in disbelief. "Is that what I do when someone new comes to Finch?"

*Need I remind you of the pivotal role you played in welcoming Amelia, Tilly, and Bree to the village? If you hadn't offered them your hand in friendship, who knows how long it would have taken them to recover from the blows that befell them before they came to Finch?*

"Amelia, Tilly, and Bree were little rays of sunshine compared to Mr. Windle," I said. "I don't think I'm equipped to deal with a man who's as damaged as he appears to be."

*I've never known you to back down from a challenge, Lori.*

"I back away from Bess ten times a day," I muttered.

*Mr. Windle is not a toddler having a tantrum, Lori. He's a grown man in dire need of some tender loving care. The Handmaidens are well intentioned, as are the rest of the villagers, but they didn't see what you saw, did they?*

"No," I admitted reluctantly. "They were long gone by the time Mr. Windle's emotions erupted. Everyone was."

*Not quite everyone. Tommy was on the bridge, too. He was as disturbed by the eruption as you were.*

"Tommy knows a lot more about damaged men than I do," I said. Bolstered by the thought, I slid my feet from the ottoman and sat upright. "Okay, Dimity. I'll give it my best shot. I'll team up with Tommy to do whatever needs to be done to keep Mr. Windle's head above water."

The baby monitor emitted a faint quacking noise.

*It sounds as though Bess is awake.*

"Either that or she smuggled one of her ducky chums into the nursery," I said.

*I wouldn't put it past her. She's very much like her mother.*

"I'll take that as a compliment," I said, smiling. "Thanks, Dimity. I'll let you know what happens next."

*I'm counting on it! Give Bess an extra hug from me.*

"I always do," I said.

When the curving lines of royal-blue ink had faded from the page,

I closed the blue journal and returned it to its shelf. I stood staring into the fire for a moment, then touched a fingertip to Reginald's snout.

"I hope to heaven that Pussywillows *is* enchanted," I said to my pink bunny. "If Tommy and I are going to wrestle demons, we'll need all the help we can get."

# *Seven*

Hours later, after the children were in bed and the fire in the living room was burning low, I drew Bill down beside me on the overstuffed chintz sofa and told him about my encounter with Crispin Windle. When I finished, he wrapped his arms around me, pulled me close, and advised me very gently to tread carefully.

"Mr. Windle may not be like you and me, Lori," he said. "He may prefer solitude to neighborly solicitude. Try to befriend him, by all means, but don't blame yourself if he rejects your overtures. The best thing you can do for him right now may be to respect his right to deal with his problems, however dire they may be, in his own way."

"Even if his own way isn't working?" I asked.

"Even then." Bill smiled down at me. "I don't believe for one moment that you'll take my advice, but I had to offer it."

"You're a good husband," I said, nestling closer to him. "It's been a long day. Shall we go up?"

"The sooner the better." He tilted my head back and kissed me softly on the lips. "I'm always willing to accept your overtures."

The sky on Sunday morning was as blue as Saturday's had been, and the breezes were just as balmy. Bill and I rousted the children out of bed early, but thanks to a sticky situation involving Bess and a pitcher of maple syrup, we left for church late.

With Bill behind the wheel, I could savor the scenery without endangering myself or my family. I smiled as a pair of lambs bounced playfully in a pasture and watched enraptured as a goshawk soared high above the treetops, but when we crossed the humpbacked bridge, my head turned automatically toward Pussywillows.

"He's hung curtains in his windows," I said.

"Wise man," said Bill.

"Beige curtains," I added.

"No surprise there," said Bill. "Beige seems to be his favorite color."

"I don't see any other signs of life," I said, frowning.

"He's probably beaten us to St. George's," said Bill, "along with everyone else."

We bumped along the cobbled lane to the far end of the green and parked the Rover on the verge beside the churchyard's low stone wall. To avoid further delays, Bill carried Bess while Will and Rob led the way through the lytch-gate, past the lichen-splashed tombs and the mossy headstones that flanked the graveled path, through the south porch's heavy oak door, and up the south aisle to our customary places in the back pew. Our neighbors were so used to our tardiness that no one but Peggy Taxman glared at us, and she would have glared at the Archbishop of Canterbury if he'd shown up late.

While Charles Bellingham, Grant Tavistock, old Mrs. Craven, and a few other friends nodded affably to me, the rest of the villagers seemed determined to ignore me.

"The cold shoulder," I murmured to Bill as we took our seats. "My punishment for calling on Mr. Windle."

"Could be worse," he murmured back. "Could be dirty looks and disapproving sniffs."

"They're saving those for after church," I whispered in his ear.

Bill disguised a snort of laughter with a cough.

Will and Rob were old enough to behave themselves in church, but I provided Bess with a tactile picture book about a kindly orangutan and his cheerful relatives that would, with a bit of luck, keep her from chattering nonstop during the service. Once her busy mind was engaged, I surveyed the rows of bobbing heads in front of me.

The Sunday-morning service was always well attended, but it drew an even bigger crowd after a moving-van vigil. Those hoping to learn if their new neighbor was a churchgoer were, however, doomed to disappointment. Crispin Windle was not among the faithful. Whether he attended another church or none at all—or whether he was enjoying a well-deserved lie-in after his exertions—remained to be seen, but his absence would, I knew, frustrate many of the villagers, not least those who'd wished for nothing more than to get a good look at him.

Bree Pym didn't appear to be in St. George's, either, but in her case appearances could be deceiving. It was not uncommon for Bree to spend an entire church service in the stumpy bell tower. She'd once told me that she liked to look out over God's green earth while singing His praises, but since she was currently in Mr. Barlow's black books, it seemed probable that she'd climbed up among the pigeons to avoid running into him.

Mr. Barlow stood at the rear of the church, his head bent and his hands clasped before him. I couldn't tell if he was praying or attempting to keep his temper in check, because he didn't even glance at us as we shuffled past him.

Tommy Prescott sat beside Tilly Barlow in the front pew, as was their privilege, since Mr. Barlow served St. George's as both usher and sexton. Tommy and Tilly shared the pew with Lilian Bunting, the vicar's wife. Lilian seemed to be studying her prayer book, but I was willing to bet that her ears were attuned to every whisper that passed between the villagers. While the vicar was too unworldly to attend to gossip, his wife had her fingers firmly on Finch's pulse.

Tommy must have felt my eyes on the back of his head, because he turned to look at me mere seconds after my gaze came to rest on him. Since he towered over the rest of the congregation, and since my family and I were habitués of the back row, he had no trouble picking me out. He regarded me soberly, then gave me a brief nod, as if to say, "I haven't forgotten," before facing forward again.

Willis, Sr., and Amelia, who were never late for church, sat in the front pew across the center aisle from Tommy, Tilly, and Lilian. If Bess had spotted her grandparents, Bill and I would have spent the next hour or so chasing her up and down the aisle while Peggy Taxman tutted, but my daughter was too entranced by the orangutan's adventures to be aware of her surroundings.

Elspeth Binney struck the opening chords of the processional on the fine old organ, and the service began. Peggy Taxman's booming alto caught Bess's attention during each hymn, but after pointing at Peggy and laughing uproariously, she settled down again with her book. My daughter was one of the few people Peggy Taxman failed to intimidate.

To everyone's relief, the vicar gave the sermon he always gave after a newcomer moved to Finch. Tall, slender, and gray-haired, with a mournful face and a deep affection for obscure biblical texts, Theodore Bunting was not famous for his gripping sermons. Most of his flock struggled to stay awake until the final blessing, and on one memorable occasion, his learned dissertation had been accompanied by a chorus of Dick Peacock's rumbling snores.

On the first Sunday following a vigil, however, his chosen text was refreshingly brief and comprehensible. After exhorting us to "be not forgetful to entertain strangers: for thereby some have entertained angels unawares," he delivered an uncomplicated homily on the role of hospitality in a Christian community.

"Ready for the scrum?" Bill asked as the recessional began.

"As ready as I'll ever be," I replied.

The churchyard scrum was Bill's pithy name for the group of villagers who gathered in the churchyard to catch up on local news after a service. Since the Cooks, the Taxmans, and the Peacocks had businesses to run, they rarely took part in the scrum, but I had no doubt that the Handmaidens would be on hand to opine loudly about transgressors who trampled on traditions.

"Do you want me to run defense for you?" Bill asked as the congregation straggled slowly out of the church.

"Thanks, but no," I said. "I'm kind of hoping to divert the gossip stream away from Mr. Barlow."

"A noble sacrifice," said Bill.

Braced for the onslaught, I followed my family through the south porch and into the light of day. Will and Rob, who had not the slightest interest in listening to adults prattle, ran down to the river to skip stones, while Bess led Willis, Sr., to her favorite grave, a tomb featuring two marble lambs watched over by a marble shepherd Bess had for her own inscrutable reasons named Dennis.

Bill stood manfully by my side as we were joined by Amelia, Charles, Grant, old Mrs. Craven, Lilian, and the vicar. The Handmaidens were nowhere to be seen.

"Where are Elspeth, Opal, Millicent, and Selena?" I asked.

"They scarpered off home," said Charles. "No idea why. I expected them to linger long enough to lambaste you for visiting Crispin Windle."

"You're not going to lambaste me, are you?" I asked.

"Wouldn't dream of it," he replied. "I admire your rebellious spirit."

"Why did you rebel?" Lilian asked.

Before I could answer, Tilly and Tommy emerged from the church, unaccompanied by Mr. Barlow. Tilly Barlow was a plump, middle-aged woman with tightly curled iron-gray hair. She was dressed plainly but neatly in a short-sleeved pink blouse, a brown skirt, and brown pumps. She and Tommy made a slightly odd-looking couple, as she was even shorter than I was.

"Morning, all," said Tommy as he and Tilly joined our circle.

He was greeted by a round of "Good mornings," but all eyes were on Tilly.

"I presume you've heard about my husband's proposals," she said.

As if to demonstrate the efficacy of the village grapevine, those who hadn't heard the story firsthand nodded as readily as those who had.

"Is Mr. Barlow terribly upset?" Lilian asked sympathetically.

"The silly old bear growled at us," said Tilly, "but I told him not to be so precious."

"I told him not to be so pompous," said Tommy.

"And Bree?" I asked.

"Bree went full penitential," Tommy replied. "After Uncle Bill took us down a peg or two, she announced that she wasn't fit to marry into his family."

"Whereupon she returned Tommy's lovely ring," said Tilly, "and ran from the house in a flood of tears."

The combined gusts of our shocked gasps could have rung the bells in the church tower, if the bells hadn't been replaced by an automated recording device in 1973.

"Bree called off the engagement?" I said, astonished.

"I'm afraid so," Tilly said. "I could have boxed Mr. Barlow's ears."

I couldn't imagine calling Bill "Mr. Willis," but as soon as Tilly had realized that Mr. Barlow shared a first name with my husband, my son, and my father-in-law, she'd revived the old-fashioned custom of referring to her husband by his surname when in company, to avoid confusion. The quaintness of her solution suited her.

"Did you go after Bree?" Charles asked, gazing avidly at Tommy.

"I did," said Tommy. "But she hopped into her car and hightailed it out of the village before I could stop her. She hasn't answered her door or her mobile since."

"Forgive me if I'm crossing a line, Tommy," Grant said, eyeing the young giant judiciously, "but you don't appear to be as heartbroken as I would expect a jilted lover to be."

"Bree hasn't broken my heart," Tommy explained. "She hasn't really broken our engagement, either. She made a dramatic gesture to prove to Uncle Bill that she's truly sorry for disappointing him, but that's all it is—a gesture. My ring will be back on her finger before the day is out."

"You sound awfully sure of yourself, young man," Mrs. Craven said warningly.

"I'm awfully sure that Uncle Bill will apologize to Bree as soon as he simmers down." Tommy's smile held just a touch of self-satisfaction as he continued, "Also, I've written her a love letter."

"By hand?" Mrs. Craven inquired.

"By hand," Tommy replied proudly. "I slipped it under her door first thing this morning."

Several breasts, including mine, heaved rapturously.

"Bree won't be able to resist a handwritten love letter," said Charles.

"No one could." He clapped Tommy on the shoulder. "Well done, sir. Mr. Barlow's apology will mean a lot to Bree, but she'll treasure your letter for as long as she lives."

"I hope Mr. Barlow does apologize," said Lilian.

"He will," Tilly said complacently. "He thinks the world of Bree. Once he climbs down from his high horse, he'll be thoroughly ashamed of himself for making the poor girl cry."

Grant laughed suddenly.

"What's so funny?" I asked.

"The Handmaidens," he replied. "They'll tear their hair out when they realize what they've missed."

While the rest of us chuckled and exchanged knowing nods, Charles peered owlishly at Tommy and me.

"The Handmaidens may have thrown away a chance to give you several pieces of their collective mind," he said, "but I haven't forgotten about your little rebellion."

"Nor have I," said Lilian. "Why did you visit our new neighbor yesterday? You must have realized that there would be repercussions."

"We did," said Tommy, "but we had no choice. Go ahead, Lori. Tell them what happened."

I took a deep breath and repeated almost word for word everything I'd told Aunt Dimity about our brief, disturbing glimpse of Mr. Windle's inner demons. When I finally fell silent, the vicar was the first to react.

"Dear Lord," he said, pressing a hand to his breast. "It sounds as if the poor man is in torment."

"I'm glad you called on him," said Lilian. "I would have done the same thing."

"Any decent person would," said Grant. "What did you say to Mr. Windle?"

"I told him what we'd seen," I replied, "and I asked him if he planned to kill himself."

"You didn't," said Charles, sounding awestruck.

"I did," I admitted.

"I salute your Yankee penchant for plain speaking," said Grant. "A Brit would have been incapable of approaching such a delicate subject head-on."

"I was worried," I said, blushing.

"I'd have done exactly as you did," Lilian said soothingly. "How did Mr. Windle respond?"

"He said he was grateful to us for our concern," I told her, "and he assured us that he did not intend to kill himself."

"Thank God," said the vicar.

"I'd be thankful, too," said Tommy, "if I could be sure that Mr. Windle had told us the truth."

"Do you think he was prevaricating?" the vicar asked.

"I don't know what to think," said Tommy, "but I've seen men crack like that before. I've seen it happen to soldiers who've been pushed beyond their limit. They shut down, clock out, refuse to feel anything until one day they feel everything, all at once." The neat scar above his left eye puckered as his brow furrowed. "It's too much for some of them. If they don't get the help they need, they clock out permanently."

Amelia, who'd lost a brother to suicide, groaned softly. Bill put an arm around her and shot an urgent look at Willis, Sr., who began to herd Bess away from Dennis the marble shepherd and toward our chattering circle.

"Do you still believe that Mr. Windle might harm himself?" Amelia asked anxiously.

"I'm not a mental health professional," said Tommy, "but I think he would have been more defensive if Lori's question had hit too close to home."

"He wasn't defensive," I said quickly. "If I'd been in his situation, I'd have told the nosy stranger on my doorstep to take a hike, but he replied as pleasantly as if I'd asked him for the time of day. He wasn't exactly outgoing, but he was perfectly polite."

"Polite or not," said Tommy, "he's a troubled man."

"He's the stranger at our table," said the vicar. "We must do something to help him."

"I agree," said Charles, "but what can we do?"

"We can be good neighbors," I piped up, recalling Aunt Dimity's sage advice. "We can take an interest in him. We can make him feel as if he belongs. We can give him a whole raft of reasons to go on living."

"We certainly can," Lilian said stoutly. "And we won't wait until Wednesday to begin. Teddy and I will call on Mr. Windle this afternoon."

"Indeed, we will," said the vicar.

"I'll fill a tin with lemon bars as a housewarming gift," said Lilian. "I baked a fresh batch last night."

"Your lemon bars always cheer me up," Charles interjected. "I don't suppose—"

Lilian shook her head. "Mr. Windle needs them more than you do, Charles. You can wait until I bake another batch."

"I'll drop in on Mr. Windle tomorrow morning," Amelia said. "I finished a pretty little study of a flag iris the other day. It'll add a touch of local color to his new home."

"Grant and I will visit him tomorrow afternoon," said Charles. "We'll offer to help him arrange his furniture."

"And we won't comment on how dull we think it is, will we, Charles?" Grant said pointedly.

"We might drop a few gentle hints," said Charles, but when Grant bridled, he added haughtily, "I'm joking, *obviously*. I shall, in fact, be as good as gold."

"Tuesday morning for me," said Mrs. Craven. "I'll give Mr. Windle a lap quilt. If I'm lucky, he'll allow me to drape it over the back of his sofa." Her blue eyes twinkled mischievously. "I want to know what he's done with those bundles of wood!"

"If the vicar and I find out," said Lilian, "we'll let you know."

"As will I," said Amelia.

"You can depend on Grant and me," said Charles.

"I'll take the Tuesday-afternoon slot," said Tilly. "If Mr. Windle is a book lover, we'll have lots to talk about."

"He must love books," said Grant. "He has four bookcases, each of them taller than Charles."

"What if he uses his bookshelves to display his fabulous collections of Venetian glass and Ming porcelain?" Charles asked.

"Then we'll talk about glass and porcelain," Tilly replied.

No one doubted Tilly's ability to converse intelligently about glass and porcelain. She'd read a great many books on a great many subjects.

"It looks as though I'll have to wait until Wednesday morning to renew my acquaintance with Mr. Windle," I said.

"He'll be thrilled to see you again, Lori," said Charles. "What will you do this time? Ask to read his diary?"

"Hilarious," I said in a voice devoid of hilarity. "What happens after I visit Mr. Windle?"

"We start the rota over again," said Lilian, "and we continue until we're certain that Mr. Windle is out of danger."

"Between visits," Tommy interjected, "I think we should keep an eye on him."

He couldn't have proposed a more welcome course of action. If there was one thing my neighbors and I were good at, it was keeping an eye on one another.

"We see Dennis," Bess announced as she and Willis, Sr., inserted themselves between Amelia and me.

"I'm sure Dennis was happy to see you," said Lilian. "He loves company."

"Are you quite well, my dear?" Willis, Sr., asked Amelia.

"I'm better now," she replied, kissing him on the cheek. "I'll tell you all about it on the way home."

Will and Rob bounded through the churchyard like a pair of playful lambs, rosy-cheeked and wet to the knees after their stone-skipping competition.

"Twelve!" Rob proclaimed triumphantly.

"He found the perfect stone," muttered Will.

"And the perfect technique," said Rob, elbowing his brother.

"Aren't you ready for brunch yet?" Will asked plaintively, looking from his parents to his grandparents. "I'm *starving*."

The twins always looked forward to Sunday brunch at Fairworth House, in part because it was a family tradition, but mainly because Willis, Sr.'s cook spoiled them rotten by preparing copious quantities of any dish they requested.

"We're on our way," said Amelia, smoothing Will's ruffled curls.

"Amelia and I shall walk Bess to your vehicle," Willis, Sr., informed Bill. "Unless we are distracted by another tomb, or a butterfly, or a colorful pebble, or an interesting stick, we should arrive in approximately five minutes."

I envied my friends for living in the village. Since Sunday brunch would last until early evening, and since I lived two miles outside of Finch, I wouldn't be able to keep an eye on Crispin Windle until Monday morning, after I dropped Will and Rob off at school. As my family and I departed the churchyard, however, I felt as if I were leaving our troubled neighbor in good hands.

# *Eight*

I telephoned Bree Pym repeatedly from Fairworth House, to no avail. She seemed to be as determined to shut me out as she was to keep Tommy at bay. I was relieved to catch a glimpse of her through her living room window as we drove past her house after a light supper in Willis, Sr.'s orchid filled conservatory, but when I asked Bill to stop, he shook his head.

"Bess is getting cranky," he said. "She should be in bed, the boys have to get ready for school tomorrow, and you need to give Bree some space." He reached over to squeeze my hand. "You're her best friend, Lori. She won't leave you out in the cold for long."

"I just hope she doesn't do anything stupid," I said unhappily. "And I speak as someone who's done more stupid things than I care to recall."

"Stupid," said Bess. "Stupid, stupid, stupid."

The boys guffawed, but I could only manage a weak smile.

"Our girl is always listening," I murmured. "How stupid of me to forget."

"Two-year-olds bring out the stupid in all of us, love," Bill murmured back. He gave my hand another comforting squeeze and we drove on.

I sank into one of the tall leather armchairs in the study, propped my stockinged feet on the ottoman, and opened the blue journal. Will,

Rob, and Bess were asleep and Bill was getting ready for bed, but I'd nipped downstairs for a quick word with Aunt Dimity.

"Dimity?" I said. "Prepare yourself for a shock."

*Good evening, Lori. Consider me prepared.*

"Here goes," I said. "Bree's broken her engagement to Tommy Prescott."

I expected the announcement to hit Aunt Dimity like a bombshell, but her graceful copperplate unfurled across the page without a trace of perturbation.

*Did Bree take Mr. Barlow's scolding to heart and decide that she's unworthy of his nephew?*

"Uh, yes," I said, wondering, not for the first time, if Aunt Dimity could read my mind. "How did you guess?"

*You've often described Mr. Barlow as the father Bree wished she'd had.*

"Her real father was an alcoholic and a gambler," I said, nodding. "Since her mother wasn't in the picture, Bree spent most of her childhood coping with him on her own. She was only eighteen when the drink finally killed him. By the time I caught up with her, she was a bit of a mess."

*I remember. So does Bree. She was in desperate need of a steady, stable, and above all sober father figure when you brought her to Finch, and she was lucky enough to find one in Mr. Barlow. That's why his approval means so much to her. Having lost it, she must have felt as though she'd also lost the right to marry Tommy.*

"She ran out of Mr. Barlow's house in tears," I said.

*Do you know where she went?*

"Home," I said. "I saw her there tonight when we drove past. Bill thinks I should give her some space, but I'm worried about her."

*You'll never stop worrying about her, my dear, but Bill is right. Bree isn't the broken teenager you rescued in New Zealand, Lori. She's a strong and capable young woman. Once she recovers her equilibrium, I'm sure she'll realize that Mr. Barlow didn't mean half of what he said. Tommy hasn't given up on her, has he?*

"Quite the opposite," I said. "He's more determined than ever to marry her. After she returned his ring, he wrote a love letter to her and slipped it under her door."

*He appears to have the situation well in hand. I'm afraid you'll have to stand aside while Tommy and Bree work things out on their own. Since they love each other dearly, I'm confident that they will.*

"I'm not very good at standing aside," I reminded her. "I'm more of a jump-in-with-both-feet sort of friend."

*I seem to recall writing quite recently that a direct approach isn't always the best approach. It's doubly true when it comes to affairs of the heart. If Bree wants you to jump in, my dear, she'll invite you to jump in. Until then . . .*

"I should back off," I said reluctantly.

*It's not as though you have no one else to worry about! Any news to report about Crispin Windle?*

"I'm not quite as anxious about him as I was." I explained what had taken place in the churchyard after I'd told my friends about the moment on the bridge, then continued, "When I repeated the advice you gave me, it was full steam ahead on the good-neighbor project. Tommy and I won't have to watch over Mr. Windle unaided, Dimity. Everyone who was in the churchyard is going to make a special effort to look after him."

*Of course they will. Even those who believe he's under the protection of an enchanted cottage will be eager to do their part, if only to keep up with their neighbors. Now go to bed, Lori. If you're to do your part tomorrow, you'll need to get some sleep tonight!*

"I will," I said. "Good night, Dimity."

*Good night, my dear.*

I waited until Aunt Dimity's elegant script had faded from the page, then returned the blue journal to its shelf. As I held out a hand to twiddle Reginald's powder-pink ears, I couldn't help wondering if either Bree or Mr. Windle was enjoying a good night's rest.

"I hope so," I said, "but I doubt it. I don't think I'll sleep well, either. Asking me to stand aside while someone I love is hurting is like asking the vicar to preach a rousing sermon. I'll try, but I'm not at all certain that I'll succeed."

I tried very hard to give Bree space on Monday morning, but, predictably, I didn't quite succeed. Having taken Will and Rob to school in Upper Deeping, I felt that it was my duty to slow the Range Rover to a creeping crawl as I approached Bree's redbrick house on my way to Finch.

"Do you see what I see, Bess?" I asked, coming to a full stop.

"Bess see tree," Bess replied from the backseat.

"I see the tree, too, sweetie," I said, "but I'm talking about the white patch on Bree's front door. It looks like a piece of paper. Shall Mummy take a closer look?"

"Mummy look," parroted Bess.

Encouraged by my daughter's ringing endorsement, I parked the Rover in Bree's graveled driveway, opened her creaking gate, and dashed through her front garden to examine the folded sheet of notepaper taped to her door. When I saw my name written across it in capital letters, I smiled ruefully. Bree clearly knew me well enough to know that I wouldn't drive past her house without investigating anything that appeared to be out of the ordinary.

I took the note from the door, unfolded it, and saw that Bree's message to me was disappointingly brief.

> Lori,
>
> Don't fret. I'm okay. I just need to be alone right now.
>
> Bree

"So be it," I said.

I refolded the note calmly and tucked it into the back pocket of my jeans. I did not succumb to an almost irresistible urge to pound on Bree's door until she opened it, but I did take a short detour on my way back to the Rover. After getting down on my hands and knees, I lowered my head to the ground and peered through the gap beneath her garage door. Satisfied, I pushed myself to my feet, brushed gravel from my hands, knees, and cheek, and climbed into the Rover.

"Bree's car is still in the garage," I informed Bess. "At least she hasn't taken off for parts unknown."

"Take off," said Bess.

Her suggestion helped me to stick to my nonintervention pact as I backed out of the driveway, negotiated the sharp curve in front of Bree's house, and cruised down the narrow, twisting lane, past Willis, Sr.'s wrought-iron gates, over the humpbacked bridge, and into the village.

After the hustle and bustle of the moving-van vigil, Finch had resumed the appearance of a somnolent backwater. No one I knew was out and about, though a pair of wet-suited paddleboarders were surveying the Little Deeping from the bridge. As it was another sunny spring day with barely a breath of wind, I was fairly certain that they would enjoy a non-life-threatening adventure.

Apart from a ribbon of smoke rising from its chimney, Pussywillows looked much as it had on Sunday. If it hadn't been for the beige curtains, there would have been no other sign of Crispin Windle's presence in the cottage. I could scarcely miss Amelia and Lilian, however, as they waved to me from one of the tables near the tearoom's front window.

I parked the Rover in front of Bill's office, set Bess free, and chivied her into the tearoom, where I was greeted by Henry Cook, Sally's chubby, mustachioed husband. Bess accepted a grandmotherly hug from Amelia, but when she refused point-blank to sit in the high chair Henry provided, he offered to let her tag along with him as he took orders, cleared tables, added baked goods to the glass-fronted display case, and worked the register.

"Henry, you are an angel," I declared as he escorted me to the third chair at Amelia and Lilian's table.

"So my wife tells me," he said, smoothing his handsome mustache, "but she may be biased."

I had to sit with my back to Pussywillows, but after asking my friends to keep an eye on Mr. Windle, I could hardly complain about them having better views of the cottage than I had. I ordered a pot of Lapsang souchong and a Chelsea bun, then planted my elbows on the table and asked Lilian the question I'd been dying to ask her ever since I'd left the churchyard.

"Well?" I said. "Did you and the vicar visit the enchanted cottage yesterday? Did you meet Mr. Windle?" It suddenly dawned on me that neither of my companions had been in the tearoom when Sally Cook had disclosed her remarkable theory. "By 'the enchanted cottage' I mean—"

"Pussywillows," Lilian interjected. "We know. Sally was kind enough to describe its magical properties to us." She lowered her voice. "Has she been reading romance novels again?"

"Her marriage is more romantic than any novel," I said. "Maybe she just wants everyone to be as happy as she and Henry are."

"I think it's a delightful conceit," said Amelia. "I find it quite easy to believe that Pussywillows played a role in bringing my William to me. I could feel its benevolence when I lived there."

"I hope our new neighbor feels it, too," I said. "To judge by what I saw from the bridge, life hasn't been very benevolent to him lately." Turning to Lilian, I repeated, "Well? Did you meet Mr. Windle?"

"In a manner of speaking," she replied. "He opened his door to us and he accepted my tin of lemon bars. He said he was very pleased to meet us"—she shrugged—"and that was that."

"He didn't invite you in?" I said.

"He did not," said Lilian.

"What about you?" I asked, facing Amelia, who sat across the table from me.

"Rinse and repeat," she said. "I called on him about thirty minutes ago. He admired my study of the flag iris, thanked me for it, said what a pleasure it was to meet me, and left me standing on the doorstep."

"When you told us he wasn't outgoing, you may have understated the case," said Lilian. "Teddy and I were rebuffed in the nicest possible manner, but we were rebuffed all the same."

"Perhaps Mr. Windle is a recluse," Amelia suggested.

"Would a recluse move to the heart of a small English village?" Lilian asked. "Surely he would find it less challenging to lead a life of solitude in a remote cavern or on a deserted island."

"He must have a lot to do," Amelia said reasonably.

"I don't know why he would," I said. "It's not as if he owns a ton of stuff. It would take me about an hour to unpack his boxes."

"He may be more fussy about the arrangement of his possessions than you are," said Amelia.

"He could hardly be less fussy," I acknowledged equably as Bess toddled by, clutching two fistfuls of clean spoons. "It's hard to be fussy with three children tearing around the house."

Henry delivered my tea and my Chelsea bun, then scurried after Bess, who was carefully dropping the spoons in the wastepaper basket behind the display case.

"I haven't seen hide nor hair of Mr. Windle since Amelia called on him," Lilian informed me. "And I've been seated at this table since half past eight."

"To be on the safe side," I said, "we should post someone behind Pussywillows. If Mr. Windle slips out by the back door, we wouldn't see him from here, and you know how close the back door is to the river."

"The possibility occurred to us as well," said Amelia. "But there's no need to worry. Sally's watching from the kitchen. If Mr. Windle leaves Pussywillows through the back door, she'll ring us."

"Excellent," I said.

"What's this?" Lilian said alertly, leaning forward to peer through the window. "What's Opal up to?"

Opal Taylor had emerged from her cottage at the far end of the village green, bearing a covered casserole dish. She straightened the belt on her shirtdress, glanced left and right at the neighboring cottages, then made her way across the green.

"Judging by her trajectory," I said, "she's heading for Pussywillows." I slapped the table and laughed. "Now I know why she didn't stick around after church to read the riot act to Tommy and me. She must have run home to cook something special for the new boy in town."

"No one had to ask Opal to keep an eye on Mr. Windle," said Amelia. "Once she learned that he was a bachelor, she was bound to watch him like a hawk."

"The more eyes on him, the better," I said.

"You and Tommy set a precedent," Lilian said, as if a marvelous truth had just revealed itself to her. "You gave Opal permission to break the three-day rule."

"So did we," Amelia pointed out.

"Guilty as charged," Lilian conceded.

"She hasn't let the grass grow under her feet," I said, grinning.

"You know what they say about the early bird," said Lilian.

"New dress?" said Amelia. "I don't recall seeing it before."

"She must have rushed off after the vigil to look for a dress at the Saturday sales," I said.

"I applaud her for making an effort," said Amelia.

"First out of the blocks," I said. "I'll bet half my Chelsea bun that the rest of the Handmaidens will be hot on her heels."

"Will they, too, be wearing new dresses?" Lilian queried.

"Can't guarantee it," I said, "but I'll bet the other half of my bun that Opal wasn't the only one who made a mad dash to Upper Deeping to look for a new frock."

"I hope Opal prepared her chicken-and-dumpling casserole for Mr.

Windle," said Amelia. "It must have a thousand calories in every bite, but the poor man could do with some filling meals. He's so frail that a light breeze might carry him away."

"Perhaps he's been ill," Lilian said thoughtfully. "It's a well-known fact that physical illness can lead to depression."

"It would explain why he didn't invite us in," said Amelia. "If he's recovering from an illness, he may not yet be strong enough to entertain guests."

"Let's see if he entertains Opal," I said, swinging around in my chair to look at Pussywillows.

We watched attentively as Opal Taylor presented her dish to Mr. Windle. He took it from her, uttered a few words, and closed the door. Opal blinked in surprise, then glanced furtively at the tearoom. When she saw the three of us looking back at her, she blushed fiery red and scuttled back to her cottage.

"I wonder which Handmaiden will be next?" I said.

"No need to wonder," said Amelia. "Here comes Millicent!"

# *Nine*

Opal Taylor was still closing her door when Millicent Scroggins opened hers. Like Opal, she carried a casserole dish, wore a dress none of us recognized, and strode diagonally across the village green toward Pussywillows.

"New dress," said Lilian. "Check."

"Casserole," said Amelia. "Check."

"The air of a huntress stalking her prey," I said. "Check."

My friends sniggered discreetly and I took a large bite of my Chelsea bun, secure in the knowledge that I wouldn't have to give away any of it.

"I hope Mr. Windle likes sausage casserole," said Lilian. "Millicent would be mad to make anything else for him. It's her best dish."

"It's delicious," said Amelia. "And it reheats beautifully."

Best dish or not, Millicent's culinary offering received precisely the same treatment as Opal's. Mr. Windle took it from her, spoke to her briefly, and withdrew. Millicent's nonplussed expression mirrored Opal's, as did the color that flooded her cheeks when she realized we'd witnessed her discomfiture, and the speed with which she fled the scene to hide her blushing face in her own cottage.

"I'm beginning to see a pattern," Lilian said dryly, resting her chin in her hand.

"Indeed," said Amelia. "It appears that Mr. Windle is an equal-opportunity rebuffer."

"I wonder what it will take to storm the castle?" I mused aloud.

"Flaming arrows?" said Lilian. "A trebuchet?"

"Selena's relying on a more traditional approach," said Amelia as Selena Buxton left her cottage, casserole dish in hand, and walked toward Pussywillows.

"Definitely not a new dress," Lilian observed, sitting upright. "I've seen it in church at least a half dozen times."

"I'd wear it more than once if it belonged to me," said Amelia. "It's lovely."

"Selena was a wedding planner," I reminded her. "Her wardrobes are filled with lovely dresses."

"What do we think?" said Lilian. "Vegetarian casserole?"

"Yes," Amelia and I chorused.

"She's brought it to every potluck supper since the beginning of time," I said.

"It's not as hearty as the other casseroles," said Amelia, "but it's tasty."

While I fed my foraging daughter a piece of Chelsea bun, Selena Buxton failed to storm the castle. The only difference between her experience and her friends' was her reaction to it. When she saw us, she raised her hands, palms upward, as if to say good-humoredly, "What can one do?" before beating a hasty but dignified retreat to her cottage.

"Wedding training," I said admiringly. "You have to be on your best behavior, no matter what happens."

"Elspeth should be coming along soon," said Lilian.

We gazed expectantly at Elspeth Binney's front door for at least five minutes, but it didn't open.

"A change in tactics?" said Amelia.

"Seems like it," said Lilian. "Elspeth must have seen you and the others beat a path to Mr. Windle's door. She's probably decided to give the poor man a chance to catch his breath."

"We'll stay here until she calls on him, won't we?" asked Amelia.

"I'm not going anywhere until the fourth Handmaiden tries her luck," said Lilian. "It would be a pity to leave before we've collected the set."

"I'm staying, too," I said. "I will, however, follow Elspeth's example and give Henry a break."

I took my daughter for a romping toddle on the green, changed her training pants in Bill's office without disrupting his videoconference with a client in Strasbourg, and returned with her to the tearoom. When she consented to sit in the high chair, I ordered a biscotti for her to gnaw and gave her a sippy cup Sally filled with fresh milk in the kitchen. Henry, who was busier than ever, hid his relief behind a doting smile.

Thirty minutes passed. Bess finished her milk and played with the damp biscotti crumbs on her tray as if she were in a sandbox. I pulled six brightly colored plastic dinosaurs from my capacious shoulder bag and added them one by one to the tray whenever she seemed to be losing interest.

"Elspeth is taking her time," Lilian commented as the recorded church bells chimed half past eleven.

"Perhaps she's playing hard to get," said Amelia.

"I doubt it," I said. "It's more likely that her casserole went wrong and she had to make another one."

"Her boeuf bourguignon is superb," said Lilian, "but it can be tricky to cook the beef to exactly the right degree of tenderness."

"She'd want it to be properly tender for Mr. Windle," said Amelia.

"Bess will have to eat lunch soon," I said, "or she'll get properly grouchy."

"Lunch sounds like a good idea to me, too," said Lilian. "Why don't we—"

"Not yet," I interrupted. "Elspeth is on her way."

I dropped the fourth dinosaur on Bess's tray absentmindedly as Elspeth Binney closed the door of her cottage and headed for Pussywillows with a large book cradled in her arms and Homer trotting faithfully at her heels.

"A blouse and trousers instead of a dress," Amelia said in a hushed voice.

"A book instead of a casserole dish," I marveled.

"And a terrier," said Lilian.

"In short," said Amelia, "a breathtakingly comprehensive change in tactics."

"She's starting as she means to go on," I said. "If Mr. Windle doesn't like Homer, that's it. Elspeth won't give him a second look."

"Love me, love my dog," said Lilian. "Or my cat, obviously. I suppose the same rule would apply to parakeets, ferrets, and tortoises."

"I'll give you parakeets and ferrets," I said, "but no one could dislike a tortoise. They're noble creatures."

"I wish she'd loosen her hold on the book," said Amelia. "She's blocking the title."

"It's a rather large volume," said Lilian. "It looks like a coffee-table book to me."

"Elspeth's niece is a photographer," I said. "Could it be a coffee-table book of her niece's photographs?"

"It could be," said Amelia. "Why would Elspeth bring a book of her niece's photographs to a man she's never met?"

"To find out if they have anything in common?" I hazarded. "Hush, now. It's showtime."

I fully expected to witness yet another brief encounter, but the sequence of events that occurred after Elspeth and Homer arrived at Pussywillows was unprecedented.

Homer sat obediently at Elspeth's feet and tilted his scruffy head back to gaze up at Mr. Windle's door while she made use of the tarnished brass knocker. When nothing happened, Elspeth shifted the book to one arm and followed her initial light taps with a series of forceful knocks. Again she received no response.

Elspeth frowned, then cocked her ear toward the door, as if she were listening. She straightened and sidled stealthily to her right, with Homer trailing after her, until she reached the curtained dining room window. She stood stock-still for a moment, hugging the book to her chest, then shook her head and retraced her steps, looking utterly perplexed.

"What on earth . . . ?" said Lilian.

"No idea," I said. "Here she comes."

"We can't let her get away," said Amelia, and she rapped the tearoom's window with her knuckles. When Elspeth looked in our direction, we all beckoned to her to join us.

Elspeth was only too eager to comply. Homer followed her into the tearoom, wagging his stubby tail, and responded to Bess's rapturous cries with a happy tap dance. I swung Bess to the floor so that she could give him some flat-handed pats on the back, then returned her to the high chair. As Stanley would testify, she couldn't be trusted near tails.

Elspeth was so discombobulated by her nonencounter with Mr. Windle that she willingly sat with her back to the window, still clutching the book to her chest. Homer lapped up the crumbs that had fallen from Bess's tray, then trotted to Elspeth's side and stretched out on the floor with his chin on his paws, the very model of a gallant and well-mannered little pup.

"Shall we order lunch?" Lilian asked.

"Don't be silly," said Amelia, and, turning to Elspeth, she asked, "What happened at Pussywillows?"

"I don't know what Mr. Windle is doing in there," Elspeth replied, "but whatever it is, it's noisy!"

# Ten

Lilian, Amelia, and I exchanged mystified glances.

"Noisy?" I said. "What kind of noise?"

"A thumping noise," Elspeth replied. "It came from the dining room. I expect it's why Mr. Windle didn't answer his door. He couldn't hear my knocks over the thumping."

While I grappled with the notion of Crispin Windle making thumping noises in his dining room, Elspeth set her book aside. Since our table was too cluttered to accommodate the oversized tome, she lowered it to the floor and leaned it upright against a table leg. Homer's expressive eyebrows rose and fell independently as he followed her every move. I suspected that treats from the table were not unknown to him.

"Perhaps Mr. Windle is shifting furniture," Lilian proposed.

"Or hanging pictures," said Amelia, thinking, no doubt, of her flag iris. "A hammer would make a thumping noise."

"I don't believe he was shifting furniture or hanging pictures," said Elspeth. "It was a continuous, rhythmic noise."

"Maybe he's doing jumping jacks," I offered.

"In the dining room?" Elspeth said, eyeing me skeptically.

"Why not?" I said. "He doesn't own a dining room set. Maybe he's transformed his dining room into a home gym."

"Mr. Windle doesn't strike me as the sort of man who would use a home gym," said Amelia. "He's too frail."

"He doesn't look like a gym rat," I conceded. "His leg bones would probably snap if he did a continuous series of jumping jacks."

"Charming," Lilian said with a moue of distaste. "But I won't deny that a similarly gruesome thought occurred to me."

"If he's recovering from a serious illness," said Amelia, "he wouldn't exercise without medical supervision, would he?"

"Depends on the illness," I said.

"And the exercise," Lilian added.

"Is he recovering from an illness?" Elspeth asked, leaning forward attentively.

"We don't know," Lilian told her, "but a prolonged bout of ill health would explain his apparent fragility."

"He's terribly thin," Elspeth agreed.

"He won't be after he gets stuck into the casseroles Opal, Millicent, and Selena delivered to him this morning," said Amelia. "I must say that it came as something of a surprise to see you with a book, Elspeth. I expected you to introduce Mr. Windle to your excellent boeuf bourguignon."

Elspeth's cheeks colored slightly, as if to confirm my theory that her signature dish had gone wrong.

"My niece sent the book to me for my birthday," she explained. "You remember Jemima, the photographer?"

"We do," I said, silently congratulating myself for having been the first to mention Elspeth's niece and the book in the same sentence.

"It would never do to give away a birthday present," Elspeth continued virtuously, "but I thought I might loan it to Mr. Windle. It's a compilation of photographs taken in the Peak District. Since our new neighbor is from Derbyshire, I thought he might enjoy leafing through it. The Peak District is a national park in the North of England," she continued, presumably for my benefit. "It sprawls across six different counties, but most of it lies in Derbyshire."

"I hope the photographs don't make Mr. Windle homesick," said Lilian. "I wouldn't want him to have second thoughts about moving to Finch."

A look of consternation crossed Elspeth's face. She glanced down at the book, then lifted her gaze and smiled impishly at us. "Perhaps it's just as well he didn't answer his door!"

"I'd bring the boeuf bourguignon next time," Amelia advised. "One taste and he'll never want to live anywhere else."

"You're too kind," said Elspeth.

I foresaw another casserole wending its way to Pussywillows in the not-too-distant future.

Henry Cook arrived with a bowl of water for Homer, who received it gratefully. After washing down the biscotti crumbs, he resumed his recumbent position with his chin on his paws. Inspired, perhaps, by the sight of his satisfied expression, Lilian reiterated her lunch query. No one accused her of being silly the second time around. It was a quarter past noon and we were hungry.

I ordered a shepherd's pie, which I could easily share with Bess, while the others requested various salads—tuna for Lilian, egg for Amelia, and chicken for Elspeth, each served on a bed of mixed greens. Having made an inevitable joke about serving the chicken salad before the egg salad, Henry delivered our orders to the kitchen, then cleared the table. While we waited for our food to arrive, three of us continued to survey the village, though I had to dive for a plummeting dinosaur from time to time.

"I never thought I'd see the three-day rule flouted so brazenly by so many, including myself," Lilian mused aloud. "All in a good cause, mind you, but still . . ."

"It's the best possible cause," Elspeth said earnestly. "Everyone knows that Mr. Windle requires special treatment. He's the exception that proves the rule."

I smiled inwardly as Elspeth used Finch's favorite phrase: "Everyone knows." Whenever I heard it, I knew that the village grapevine had done its job. Though none of the Handmaidens had been in the churchyard when Tommy and I had expressed our concerns about Mr. Windle's mental health, I was fairly certain that each and every one of them could repeat our words verbatim.

"I didn't see what Tommy and you saw, Lori," Elspeth went on, proving my point, "but I could tell that Mr. Windle wasn't entirely well when he moved in. If I'd included him in my painting, I would have portrayed him as a little lost waif—undernourished, ill dressed, with no one to give him the . . . support . . . he needs."

"We're trying to give him our support," said Lilian, "but he hasn't been very receptive so far."

"We must simply keep trying," Elspeth said firmly.

"We shall," said Lilian.

"Who's next on the Windle Watch rota?" Amelia asked.

"Grant and Charles," I replied promptly. "They're taking the afternoon shift."

"Perhaps they'll discover the source of the thumping noise," said Lilian.

"They'll have to get through the door first," said Elspeth.

Bess began to amuse herself by hurling dinosaurs at random targets, but our food arrived before she hit any of them. While Henry

Cook gave Homer a saucer filled with daintily diced pieces of poached chicken—Sally Cook was very fond of Homer—I plopped a heaping spoonful of shepherd's pie on a plate, blew on it to bring it to room temperature, and passed it to my ravenous daughter. She proceeded to squeeze the mashed potatoes between her fingers before stuffing them into her mouth.

"If Bess is ruining anyone's appetite," I said, "I can take her to the kitchen."

"It's not the first time we've seen her eat," Lilian reminded me. "We know what to expect."

"My granddaughter is incapable of ruining anything," Amelia declared, beaming soppily at Bess. "You're my precious messy Bessy, aren't you, darling?"

"Mmmph," Bess replied through the mashed potatoes.

Elspeth said nothing, but the speed with which she averted her gaze from the gooey spectacle spoke volumes.

I was about to dig into my portion of pie when Mr. Barlow's paneled van appeared on the humpbacked bridge. Tommy Prescott was behind the wheel and the passenger seat was empty. When Tommy parked the van in front of the workshop adjacent to his uncle's house, I lowered my fork. I hadn't shown my friends the note I'd found taped to Bree's door because I'd decided that her former fiancé should see it first. Opportunity, I thought, seemed to be knocking.

Elspeth craned her neck to follow my gaze, then asked sotto voce, "Is it true that Bree has broken off their engagement?"

"It's true," said Lilian, not bothering to lower her voice, "but Tommy's not convinced that her decision is final."

"Why not?" Elspeth asked.

"He's a young man in love," Lilian answered.

"Would you excuse me?" I said, getting to my feet. "I need to have a word with Tommy. If Bess asks for another spoonful of pie, give it to her, but be sure to cool it off first."

Lilian and Amelia rolled their eyes, as if to say, "We know how to feed a toddler, Lori!" but I was gone before they could express themselves aloud.

I dashed across the village green and arrived at the workshop in time to accost Tommy, who was sliding a gray toolbox into the back of the van. A powerful barnyard scent wafted from his filthy cargo trousers, his oil-streaked chambray shirt, and his muddy work boots.

"Where's your uncle?" I asked in a bid to gauge the mood in the Barlow household.

"Jim Teller's farm," Tommy replied, closing the van's doors. "Jim's manure spreader is on the blink again." He raised a boot to display the fragrant stains. "Uncle Bill and I started working on it this morning, but it looks as though it'll be a two-day job."

"So you and Mr. Barlow are still working together," I said cautiously.

"We are." Tommy leaned back against the van and folded his arms. "But I'm in no hurry to bring him the spanners he needs."

"Right," I said. Though the sun was shining, I detected a distinct chill in the air.

"I see that the front table's taken," Tommy said, nodding at the tearoom.

"I'd be sitting there if I weren't talking to you," I said. "Windle Watch is well underway."

"Windle Watch?" Tommy smiled wanly. "I like it. Anything to report?"

"Thumping noises," I said. "Elspeth Binney heard them through the dining room window, but she doesn't know what was causing them. And even though Mr. Windle has had a constant stream of visitors, he hasn't let anyone into Pussywillows, not even Lilian and the vicar."

"A man who values his privacy," said Tommy, with the merest hint of bitterness in his voice. "Good luck to him, I say. There are times when I long for a place of my own."

"You'll share it with Bree, won't you?" I asked anxiously.

"If she'll let me," he said. He drew a white envelope from a leg pocket in his trousers and held it out for me to see. "It's the love letter I wrote to Bree. Please observe that the envelope is unopened. I found it taped to her door when I stopped by her place after breakfast." He turned the envelope over to show me the message Bree had written on the back.

*I'm sorry, Tommy. It's no good.*
*You deserve better.*

*Bree*

"Oh my," I said as he stashed the letter in his pocket. "She really has gone full penitential."

"She'll probably ask Sally to knit her a hair shirt," he said. Sounding far less cocky than he had in the churchyard, he continued, "She's not answering my phone calls, Lori."

"Nor mine," I said.

"She won't reply to my texts, either," he told me.

"Early days yet," I said bracingly. "She taped a note to her front door for me, too." I pulled the folded sheet of paper from my back pocket and handed it to him. "It's not nearly as dramatic as yours."

Tommy read the note, then passed it back to me.

"How can she say she's okay when she's clearly anything but?" he demanded.

"She doesn't want me to worry," I said.

"Is it working?" he asked.

"No," I replied. "I can't help worrying about Bree, which is why I checked the garage to see if her car was still there. As of a couple of hours ago, it was, and I haven't seen her drive through the village. I think it's safe to assume that she hasn't made a mad dash for the border."

"What border?" Tommy asked.

"Any border," I replied. "She hasn't done a runner, Tommy. She's staying put. It's a hopeful sign, isn't it?"

Tommy's cell phone pinged. He took it out of his back pocket, glanced at it, tapped the screen, and put it away again.

"Uncle Bill," he explained, "asking why I'm taking so long." He began to lean against the van again, then jerked upright. "Don't look now, Lori, but Mr. Windle is on the move."

I looked, naturally, and sure enough, the reclusive Mr. Windle had emerged from Pussywillows. I was pleased to see that his short-sleeved yellow shirt and his khaki trousers were less shabby than the ensemble he'd worn during the moving-van vigil, though they, too, looked as if they belonged to a much larger man.

"He's crossing the green," I said in a muted tone. "He's walking toward the Emporium."

"You sound like a golf commentator," Tommy remarked.

"He's entering the Emporium." I tore my gaze away from the general store's front door and looked at Tommy. "Would you mind if I . . . ?"

"Not at all," he said, folding his arms and leaning against the van. "I'm getting used to women running out on me."

# *Eleven*

Since Mr. Windle had a tin of Lilian Bunting's peerless lemon bars as well as three hearty casseroles in his larder, I doubted that he'd gone to the Emporium to stock up on food. Perhaps, I thought, he needed fresh milk for his tea. Or aspirin for a thumping-induced headache.

The sleigh bells dangling from the Emporium's door jingled merrily as I stepped inside. I slipped quietly behind a display of sunblock, sunglasses, and adjustable sunglass straps and almost instantly recoiled from a thunderous roar that seemed to shake the shelves. Though I was accustomed to Peggy Taxman's powerful voice, it always took me a moment to recover from the initial blast.

Peggy stood behind the long wooden counter at the front of the shop, facing wispy Mr. Windle, who stood across the counter from her, seemingly unfazed by her majestic physique or her deafening pronouncements. The pair were evidently continuing a conversation that had begun before my arrival, though I suspected that their dialogue had so far been a bit one-sided.

"No need to drive to Upper Deeping," Peggy bellowed. "There's nothing there you won't find here, and at a better price." Since the streets of Upper Deeping were lined with shops, Peggy was indulging in a slight exaggeration, but I couldn't fault her for speaking well of her own business. "What are you looking for?"

"I would like to purchase a pair of scissors," Mr. Windle replied.

He spoke so softly that I had to strain my ears to hear him, but Peggy had no such difficulty.

"What kind of scissors?" she boomed. "Kitchen? Pinking? Left-handed? All-purpose?"

"Snips, if you please," said Mr. Windle.

"Right you are." Peggy stood back to scan the shelves below the counter, plucked a small item from one of them, and handed it to Mr. Windle. "Snips."

"Thank you," he said, slipping the purchase into his trouser pocket.

Peggy rang up the sale on her old-fashioned cash register, handed him a receipt, thanked him for his custom, and watched him depart before turning her attention to me.

"Not the chattiest of chaps," she observed at the tops of her lungs. "I asked him if he'd unpacked his boxes and all he said was 'Yes.'" She pursed her lips speculatively. "Polite, though. I wouldn't put him in charge of a stall at the village fete, but he might be useful behind the till."

Like everyone else in Finch, I was woefully familiar with Peggy's habit of "volunteering" the unwary for various roles at village-wide events. If Mr. Windle was too weak to resist her blandishments, he'd find himself behind the till at the flower show and the bake sale as well as the village fete.

"Well?" Peggy roared through unpursed lips. "Are you going to buy something, Lori, or should I put you to work tidying shelves?"

I snatched a tube of sunblock from the display, paid for it, and fled, wondering what snips were. Though I could have asked Peggy, I hadn't wanted to risk further damage to my eardrums.

Since Mr. Barlow's van was no longer parked in front of his workshop, I presumed that Tommy had taken pity on his uncle and headed for Jim Teller's farm with the spanners. I doubted, however, that he would break any speed records on his way there. Sighing, I returned to the tearoom to find a pristine daughter in a pristine high chair, playing with a pile of pristine teaspoons.

"Did you turn a hose on her?" I asked my tablemates, astonished.

"After my granddaughter had eaten her fill of *properly cooled* shepherd's pie," Amelia said pointedly, "I took her to the ladies' room for a wash and brushup."

"Henry wiped down the high chair and provided the spoons," said Lilian. "I retrieved the dinosaurs and put them in your purse."

"I'm surrounded by angels," I marveled. I planted a kiss on Bess's head, dropped the sunblock into my shoulder bag, and resumed my place at the table. What was left of my shepherd's pie was lukewarm, but I dug into it anyway. It had been a long time since breakfast.

"Don't be coy, Lori," said Amelia. "We saw you follow Mr. Windle into the Emporium. Did he buy anything?"

"If so, what?" Lilian added.

I swallowed mightily before replying, "Mr. Windle bought a pair of snips. What are snips?"

"Small scissors used for snipping threads," said Amelia. "Mrs. Craven has several pairs. You used them during the quilting bee, Lori. We all did."

"The sharp little scissors with the weird handles?" I said. "Mrs. Craven called them nippers."

"Nippers, clippers, snips," said Amelia. "Different names for the same type of scissors."

We contemplated Mr. Windle's purchase wordlessly, though I continued to eat.

"Could Mr. Windle be a quilter?" Lilian asked. "Or a tailor?"

"I've never heard of a quilter or a tailor who makes thumping noises," said Elspeth.

"The snips may have nothing to do with the thumping noises," Lilian pointed out.

"If he's engaged in sewing in some capacity," said Amelia, "why would he buy a pair of snips in Finch? Wouldn't he already own a pair?"

"Perhaps he's taken up a new hobby," Elspeth ventured. "New life, new hobby?"

"If he planned to take up a new hobby," said Lilian, "wouldn't he acquire the necessary tools before he moved?"

"He could have left his snips behind by accident," Amelia suggested, "or he could have misplaced them during the move."

"I'll bet he couldn't find them," I said. "Serves him right for not labeling his boxes." My gaze strayed to the window. "Oh, look! Here come Grant and Charles!"

Amelia and Lilian turned their heads and Elspeth turned her entire body to watch Grant Tavistock and Charles Bellingham approach Pussywillows.

"They're early, aren't they?" Amelia asked.

"It's past noon," I said, "and they're the afternoon shift. Technically, they're on time."

"I like Charles's cornflower-blue suit," said Amelia, "and Grant's straw fedora is very debonair."

"Do we think they dressed up for the occasion?" I asked.

"Hard to tell," said Lilian. "They're always well dressed."

"Grant's carrying a bottle of wine," Amelia observed.

"It makes a change from casseroles," said Lilian.

"But will it help them to storm the castle?" I asked.

"Not unless they use it as a battering ram," said Elspeth.

I jumped as a pile of pristine teaspoons cascaded to the floor.

"Bess needs to stretch her legs," I announced.

I collected the scattered spoons and left them on the table before lifting Bess from the high chair and carrying her to the green. While she toddled energetically from dandelion to dandelion, I divided my attention between her and Pussywillows.

It quickly became apparent that a bottle of wine was not the key to Mr. Windle's kingdom. He accepted the gift, thanked Grant and Charles for it, and closed the door in their faces. Instead of returning posthaste to their cottage, the two men sauntered across the green to join me as I followed Bess.

"Welcome to Windle World," I said to them. "You're not the first friendly natives he's left standing on the doorstep."

"We know," said Grant.

"We've been glued to our bay window all morning," said Charles.

"*You've* been glued to the bay window," Grant countered. "*I've* been working."

"Poor lamb," Charles said with mock sympathy, "slaving away without respite, except for the breaks you've taken every five minutes to ask if anything's going on at Pussywillows."

"I'll admit to a certain amount of curiosity about the enchanted cottage," Grant acknowledged gracefully.

"Enchanted cottage," Charles scoffed.

"You saw him rebuff the Handmaidens, then," I interjected before Grant could retort.

"I did," Charles replied. "I saw him rebuff Lilian, the vicar, and Amelia as well."

"Charles would have slept in our bay window if I'd let him," said Grant.

"What do you think of Mr. Windle's voice, Grant?" I asked swiftly. "Can you imagine him reading poetry to us in the schoolhouse?"

"His voice is pleasant enough," Grant allowed, "but he'd need an amplifier to perform in public."

"Perhaps he packed an amplifier in one of his unmarked boxes," Charles said, "along with his Ming porcelain."

Grant allowed the jibe to pass unremarked, observing thoughtfully, "I'd say that Mr. Windle is either a shy man or a fastidious one."

"Fastidious?" I queried.

"He may wish to have everything in place in his new home before he admits visitors," Grant explained. "First impressions count."

"He hasn't made a good impression on Opal, Millicent, or Selena," said Charles. "They looked as if he'd fed them sour apples. Has Elspeth erased him from her dance card? I might have, if he'd refused to open his door to us."

"She doesn't seem to be upset with Mr. Windle," I said. "She reckons he couldn't hear her knocks because of the thumping noises. And before you ask, I don't know anything about the thumping noises Elspeth heard, except that they were coming from the dining room."

"Thumping noises in the dining room," Grant murmured, stroking his chin. "Intriguing."

"Did Mr. Windle buy anything in the Emporium?" Charles asked. "A new pair of drumsticks, perhaps? A drummer would make thumping noises."

"He bought a pair of snips," I said.

"The sewing scissors Annabelle Craven uses?" Grant inquired.

"The very same," I replied.

"An odd purchase to make on his second full day in Finch," said

Charles. "I'd expect him to buy milk or eggs or some other perishables. Why snips?"

"Perhaps he's decided to alter his shirts and trousers," said Grant.

"If he has, he must be a talented tailor," said Charles. "His clothes would fit me better than they fit him, and I must be twice his size."

"Only twice?" Grant said under his breath.

"Beg pardon?" said Charles, eyeing his partner suspiciously.

"I said it would be nice," Grant lied. "It would be nice to have a talented tailor in the village, don't you think?"

"Indeed I do," Charles agreed, brightening.

Bess's energy was beginning to flag. I picked her up and returned to the tearoom, flanked by Grant and Charles. They called greetings to all and sundry and scratched Homer between the ears before informing Lilian, Amelia, and Elspeth that the afternoon shift was ready and able to relieve the morning shift.

"I take it you want our table," Amelia said dryly.

"Naturally," Charles replied. "It's one of the perks of the job."

"I was leaving anyway," I said as Bess's head drooped onto my shoulder. "My baby girl needs a nap."

"I must be going, too," said Lilian. "Meals on Wheels won't run itself."

"I was just about to leave," Amelia chimed in. "William misses me if I'm gone too long."

"Your marriage is a perpetual honeymoon," Charles observed.

"So it is," Amelia agreed, smiling.

"I'm staying put until the tearoom closes," Elspeth declared.

"Surely Homer will need a walk before then," said Grant.

"Yes, he will," said Elspeth, "but you can save my place for me while

I'm walking him. And my place will be in Lilian's chair. I'm sick of sitting with my back to the window."

"If there's breaking news, you'll ring us, won't you?" Amelia asked, getting to her feet.

"There's breaking news right now," said Grant, peering through the window. "Opal, Millicent, and Selena are moving en masse in our direction."

"They've got their prune faces on," said Charles. "I'll wager they're coming to the tearoom to air their grievances about Mr. Windle."

"Glad I'm leaving," I said, slinging my shoulder bag over my unoccupied shoulder.

Amelia, Lilian, and I fled the tearoom mere moments before the three disgruntled Handmaidens entered it. I offered Amelia a lift to Fairworth House, but she declined, saying that she preferred to walk.

"When shall we four meet again?" I asked, amending Shakespeare's text to include Bess.

"First thing in the morning, I should think," said Amelia. "Mrs. Craven is next in line for Windle Watch, and she's an early riser. We don't want to miss her attempt to storm the castle with a lap quilt, do we?"

"We do not," said Lilian.

"If Mr. Windle invites her in, the Handmaidens will go ballistic," I said, grinning.

"I'll secure our table as soon as Henry opens the tearoom," said Lilian.

"I won't be far behind you," said Amelia, gently stroking my baby girl's silken curls.

"Bess and I will join you after we take the boys to school," I said.

"We'll save a seat for you and a high chair for Bess," said Amelia. "Until then!"

We parted ways. I carried my dozing daughter to the Rover, strapped her in her car seat, climbed into the driver's seat, and drove slowly around the green, over the bridge, and up the narrow, twisting lane. I dutifully resisted the temptation to stop at Bree's house on the way home, but a glance at her front door confirmed that no messages were taped to it.

"At least Tommy hasn't knocked the door down," I said. "Yet."

Bess, who was fast asleep, didn't comment.

# *Twelve*

I was about to turn in to my graveled driveway when I noticed a head bobbing above the rippling rows of spring wheat in the field across the lane from my cottage. The figure was so far away that I wouldn't have known who it was if I hadn't caught a glimpse of spiky hair. Bree Pym was striding toward the river on a dirt track that would put a good two miles of breathing space between her and the village. It was, I thought, a simple way to clear her mind while avoiding human contact.

I was slightly surprised that she hadn't climbed the hill behind her house, her usual retreat in times of trouble, but I understood the river's appeal. The Little Deeping's soothing murmur had calmed my jangled nerves on more than one occasion. I hoped it would have the same effect on Bree.

I watched her until I could no longer see her, then pulled into the drive, parked the Rover, and began the delicate task of extricating Bess from her car seat without waking her. After settling her in the nursery, I tucked the baby monitor into my pocket and went downstairs to freshen Stanley's water bowl, wash and dry the plastic dinosaurs, and remove the tube of sunblock from my shoulder bag. Since I already had two tubes of sunblock in my overburdened bag, the tube I'd bought to appease Peggy Taxman was excess to requirements.

Only then did I repair to the study, where I paused briefly to speak with Reginald, whose black button eyes gleamed softly in the ivy-filtered sunlight.

"Sorry, Reg," I said. "I don't have enough time to give you *and* Aunt Dimity a review of the day's events, so you'll have to listen in."

He made no objection, so I patted his pink flannel head, took the blue journal from its shelf, and seated myself in one of the tall leather armchairs facing the hearth.

"Dimity?" I said as I opened the journal. "I'm pleased to report that Crispin Windle is still alive and kicking."

I leaned back in my chair as Aunt Dimity's elegant copperplate began to unfurl across the page.

*I'm very glad to hear it. Did the good-neighbor project get off the ground as planned? Have the villagers cast a protective shield of neighborliness around Mr. Windle?*

"We're calling the project Windle Watch now," I said, "and yes, Windle Watch is well underway. I spent half the morning and a little less than half the afternoon with Lilian and Amelia at the tearoom's most coveted table, watching Mr. Windle's front door, while Sally Cook kept an eye on the back of the cottage. If he'd headed for the river, one of us would have sprung into action and tackled him before he could throw himself in."

*Heroic interventions can be effective, but I hope you won't have to tackle Mr. Windle.*

"So do I," I said. "I'd scrape my knees and he'd break in two."

*Has anyone pursued a less drastic course of action, such as having a friendly chat with him?*

"Many have tried and all have failed," I said. "Lilian and the vicar paid a visit to Mr. Windle after church yesterday and a whole horde of villagers called on him today—Amelia, Opal, Millicent, Selena, Charles,

Grant—but he didn't invite any of them into Pussywillows. He accepted their housewarming gifts, thanked them, and left them standing on the doorstep."

*Where was Elspeth Binney? Don't tell me that she sat at home, twiddling her thumbs, while her friends laid siege to Pussywillows.*

"Elspeth went there, too," I said, "but Mr. Windle didn't even open his door to her."

*Mr. Windle may be self-conscious about the disheveled state of his new home.*

"He may be," I said, "but I wish he'd let someone in anyway. If he had, we might have identified the source of the thumping noises."

*I beg your pardon?*

"Elspeth Binney heard thumping noises coming through his dining room window," I explained. "She's convinced that he didn't respond to her knocks because they were drowned out by the thumping." I gazed ruminatively into the hearth's shadowy recesses, then looked down at the journal. "I think it may have something to do with tailoring. Or quilt making."

*You've lost me, Lori.*

"Sorry," I said. "I forgot to mention that I followed Mr. Windle into the Emporium, where he bought a pair of snips. Since old Mrs. Craven uses snips to clean up the loose threads on her quilts, it seems reasonable to assume that Mr. Windle might be a quilter. Or a tailor."

*Quilting and tailoring are quiet occupations. They do not produce thumping noises. Although . . .* The handwriting's steady flow came to a halt.

"Although?" I prompted after a few seconds had elapsed. "Have you been struck by a scathingly brilliant idea, Dimity?"

*I don't know if my idea is scathingly brilliant or not, but it would tie the thumping noises to the snips.* The handwriting paused again, as if Aunt

Dimity were mulling over her idea. *I'd describe the sound as clattery rather than thumpy, but I suppose the bar thingy does make a thump when one pulls it towards oneself, and one might not hear a knock above the clattering.*

"The bar thingy?" I said uncomprehendingly.

*Forgive me, my dear. I'm unfamiliar with the proper nomenclature. An old friend used one, but whenever she attempted to explain the parts to me, I'm afraid my eyes glazed over. It was so very complex.*

"What was complex?" I asked.

*Her loom. Didn't I say?*

I blinked down at the journal in undiluted amazement. I felt as if a multitude of scales had suddenly fallen from my eyes.

"No, you didn't say," I replied, "but it doesn't matter. Dimity, you are a scathingly brilliant genius. You haven't merely tied the thumping noises to Mr. Windle's snips. You've also tied his mysterious bundles of finished wood to his missing dining room set."

*Have I?*

"You have!" I exclaimed joyously. "Don't you see? Mr. Windle must have disassembled his loom and bundled the parts together before he left Derbyshire. When he finished moving his stuff into Pussywillows, he reassembled his loom in his new dining room."

*And since he couldn't squeeze a table, some chairs, and a loom into his dining room, he decided to dispense with a dining room set?*

"Yes!" I crowed.

*He must be a devoted weaver. Assuming I'm right about the loom.*

"You must be right," I insisted. "A loom explains everything!"

*You're giddy, my dear. If you weren't, you'd realize that a loom doesn't explain very much at all. It certainly doesn't explain the disturbing emotions Mr. Windle displayed when he looked at the river.*

"No," I agreed, momentarily subdued, "it doesn't explain the eruption Tommy and I witnessed, but it solves four niggling little mysteries that have so far baffled the finest minds in Finch." I couldn't suppress a gurgle of laughter. "I can't wait to tell Amelia and Lilian about the loom. They'll be absolutely blinded by your stroke of genius, which I will, in self-defense, claim as my own."

*I should hope so.*

"Amelia and Lilian are broad-minded women," I said, "but they'd probably urge me to see a psychiatrist if I told them about you."

*Indeed. Best to keep our conversations private. Has Bree emerged from her cocoon?*

"Sort of," I said. "I saw her just now, but I don't think she wanted to be seen. She was walking toward the river on the old farm track Bill and I use, the one that runs beside the field across the lane."

*Were you tempted to tackle her before she reached the river?*

"Not for a minute," I said. "Bree doesn't require a heroic intervention, Dimity. She once told me that she never seriously considered ending it all, despite everything that happened to her in New Zealand. Her modus operandi is to run away when times get tough, and she hasn't even done that. Besides, she swims like a fish." I kicked off my shoes and rested my stockinged feet on the ottoman. "I reckon she took the dirt track because she wants to avoid the village."

*She's not ready to face the villagers yet—too many sympathetic looks, too many people asking in hushed voices if she's all right, if she needs anything, if there's anything they can do to help. . . . It could become quite oppressive.*

"I wouldn't be surprised if Peggy Taxman asked her if she'd lost her mind," I said.

*I'm no longer surprised by anything Peggy Taxman says.*

"Peggy would only be saying what everyone else is thinking," I said. "Bree returned Tommy's love letter *unopened*, Dimity."

*At least she's found the courage to face him.*

"No such luck," I said. "She knew he'd come to her house to try to talk her around, so she taped the love letter to her front door for him to find."

*I would have used a push pin. Push pins are more reliable than tape, especially in an outdoor setting.*

"The reliability of the fastener may not have been foremost in Bree's mind when she was figuring out how to return Tommy's love letter," I said dryly. "She scrawled a pathetic little note across the back of the envelope, telling him to forget about her because she's not worthy of him. He showed it to me."

*You didn't tell me you'd seen him today.*

"It's been a busy day," I said. "I caught up with him when he came back from a job to fetch some tools for his uncle."

*I'm relieved to hear that they're still working together.*

"They may not be working together for much longer," I said. "Tommy isn't feeling too charitable toward Mr. Barlow. He ignored his uncle's text and he wasn't in a tearing hurry to get back to the job site. He even talked about moving out of Mr. Barlow's house."

*Would he leave Finch?*

"He might," I said, "if Bree doesn't change her mind. At the moment, she won't answer his calls or his texts and she refuses to see him. I think it's finally dawned on him that it won't be as easy to win Bree back as he expected it to be."

*I wonder how much Mr. Barlow knows about Bree's turbulent childhood.*

"He knows that she had a tough time as a kid," I said, "but I doubt that he knows just how tough it was. She hasn't even told Tommy the full story. When we were flying back from New Zealand, she made it clear to me that she intended to put that chapter of her life behind her. She didn't want to be treated as a charity case."

*Wouldn't you agree that both Tommy and Mr. Barlow would understand Bree better, and cherish her more, if they understood her past?*

"I would," I said, nodding, "but Bree isn't likely to spill her guts to them now, is she?"

*No, she isn't. But someone should tell them about Bree's father.*

I eyed Aunt Dimity's words uncomfortably. "Do you want *me* to tell them?"

*I think it would be advisable, under the circumstances. I realize that you would be betraying a confidence, but I believe that Bree will thank you for it in the end.*

"She'd never speak to me again," I protested.

*Do you want to heal the breach between her and Tommy or don't you?*

"I do," I said. "I want to heal the breach between her and Mr. Barlow, too, but Bree's secrets aren't mine to tell."

*A choice lies before you, Lori. Say nothing and a bad situation will become a far worse one—Bree will lose the love of her life, Tommy's heart will be broken beyond repair, and Mr. Barlow will be cut off from two young people who mean the world to him. Speak up and there's a very good chance that all will be well. It's entirely up to you.*

"I guess it is an emergency," I said reluctantly. "Tommy's a great guy. Everyone in Finch would be gutted if he left." I frowned into the middle distance, then lowered my gaze to the journal. "I suppose it could be argued that it's my civic duty to intervene."

*It could.*

"Then there's Tilly," I went on. "She was looking forward to the wedding. We all were, but Tilly had her heart set on being the step-aunt of the groom. She doesn't have any nieces or nephews of her own."

*You wouldn't want Tilly to be disappointed, would you?*

"No," I said.

*Well, then?*

"Bree left a note for me, too," I said, "telling me not to fret about her. If I do as you ask, it'll probably be the last note she ever leaves me."

*Of course it won't be. You're her best friend, Lori. Bree may be upset with you at first, but she'll forgive you.*

"Or she'll have my guts for garters," I said.

*All right. Keep silent. Avoiding conflict is clearly more important to you than Bree's happiness, or Tommy's, or Tilly's, or Mr. Barlow's, or Finch's, for that matter.*

"Okay, okay," I grumbled. "You can stop tugging on my heart-strings, Dimity. I'll do it."

*You won't regret it, my dear.*

"I probably will," I muttered.

The sound of singing crackled through the baby monitor. My sleeping beauty was awake.

"Naptime's over," I said, sliding my feet from the ottoman.

*You'll speak with Tommy as soon as possible, won't you, Lori? You'll explain why Mr. Barlow's good opinion means so much to Bree? And you'll continue to let me know what happens at Pussywillows?*

"You can rely on me," I told her.

*As can everyone who knows you.*

"Let's not get carried away," I said, "but barring the unforeseen, I'll be here tomorrow with a full report."

*Thank you, my dear. I look forward to it, as always!*

When the elegant copperplate had faded from the page, I slid the blue journal back onto its shelf, touched a finger to Reginald's snout, and went upstairs to the nursery, wondering if Bree would thank me or smack me for telling Tommy about her past.

# Thirteen

During the early years of our marriage, my husband had spent a massive amount of time away from home on business trips. After missing the boys' first steps, their second birthday, their introduction to the joys of horseback riding, and their first cricket match—which their team of five-year-olds won handily—Bill had seen the error of his ways, reduced his workload, and delegated most of the travel to childless subordinates in his firm's London office. He still left home from time to time to meet with special clients, but he'd never missed another cricket match and he'd witnessed nearly all of Bess's milestones.

I wasn't shocked, therefore, when he announced on Tuesday morning that he'd be happy to do the school runs and to look after Bess on his own for the rest of the day.

"I have no pressing business on my docket," he said, closing the dishwasher, "and I know how eager you are to reconvene Windle Watch. I could make dinner, too, if you like. How does roast chicken sound? Will and Rob like my roast chicken."

"I adore your roast chicken," I said, and after giving my husband a very thorough kiss, I said good-bye to the children, picked up my shoulder bag, and waltzed down the flagstone path to the Range Rover.

The leaves were filling out in the hedgerows and the birds seemed to flit from branch to branch with increasing urgency as they strove to feed their rapidly growing chicks. I couldn't scan the clear blue sky for goshawks while driving, but I had every intention of slowing down to scan Bree's door for further messages.

I'd already slowed to scanning speed when I spotted a familiar van parked in Bree's driveway. My heart rose at the thought of Mr. Barlow swallowing his pride and issuing an unreserved apology to his former apprentice, but it sank again when I saw Tommy leaning idly against the van, looking peevish. Though opportunity was pounding on the door, I wasn't ready to open it. I needed to work my way up to betraying Bree.

There was no point in pretending that I hadn't seen Tommy, but as I raised a hand to wave at him, he shook his head and made a thumbs-down gesture to indicate that Bree had not responded to his knocks. He then pointed to himself and hooked a thumb over his shoulder to indicate that he was taking off. His use of mime suggested that he wasn't in a chatty frame of mind.

I nodded to show I understood, then watched in my rearview mirror as he climbed into the van, backed out of the driveway, and drove toward Jim Teller's farm. I wondered how long he'd kept Mr. Barlow waiting this time.

"Reprieved," I murmured thankfully and continued on my merry way to the village.

I arrived in Finch much earlier than usual, but I wasn't the first to arrive at the tearoom. As I crested the top of the humpbacked bridge, I saw that Lilian and Amelia were already there, waiting for the tearoom to open. By the time I caught up with them, Sally Cook was unlocking the front door. Since her husband usually wielded the key, I asked her if he was okay.

"Henry's fine," Sally replied. "I left him in the kitchen to keep a batch of flapjacks from burning while I have a word with you."

I'd lived in England long enough to know that Sally's flapjacks weren't pancakes but sweet and chewy bar cookies reminiscent of granola bars in the States. Sally knew that I was fond of flapjacks, but instead of assuring me that she'd bring some out as soon as they were done, she hustled the three of us to our coveted table, then stood staring at the floor while she fidgeted with the hem of her spotless apron. Since Sally Cook was rarely, if ever, tongue-tied, I knew that something was amiss.

"I have a confession to make," she said.

"It might be better to make it to a vicar rather than to a vicar's wife," said Lilian. "Would you like me to ring Teddy?"

"It's not that sort of confession." Sally took a deep breath, then blurted, "Mr. Windle escaped."

"Escaped?" said Lilian, smiling. "You make it sound as though he's broken out of jail."

I didn't take the news as well as she did. I sat bolt upright in my chair and exclaimed, "Escaped? When? How? I thought you were watching him!"

"I can't watch him every second of the day," Sally retorted, her round face reddening. "I have work to do!"

"Sorry," I said, trying to calm down. "Just tell us what happened."

"I don't know when Mr. Windle left Pussywillows," Sally admitted, "but I saw him let himself in through the back door at half past six yesterday." She sighed heavily. "He must have slipped out while I was feathering the icing on the napoleons. Feathering requires concentration!" she added defensively.

"Never mind, Sally," said Lilian. "It was courageous of you to come forward, but I was already aware of Mr. Windle's escape."

"You couldn't have seen him leave Pussywillows," Sally objected. "You were doing Meals on Wheels."

"I didn't see him," said Lilian. "Teddy did."

"The vicar didn't come to the tearoom yesterday," Sally pointed out.

"Teddy didn't see Mr. Windle from the tearoom," Lilian explained patiently. "He was at his desk in the vicarage, revising his sermon, when he looked through our French windows and saw Mr. Windle walking beside the river."

"When?" I asked.

"Around half past two," said Lilian. "Teddy dropped everything, of course, and ran after Mr. Windle to volunteer his services as a local guide."

"Clever ruse," I said, impressed by the vicar's resourcefulness.

"It would have been, had it worked," said Lilian. "Unfortunately, Mr. Windle declined the offer. Teddy couldn't force his company on Mr. Windle, so he had no choice but to stay behind while Mr. Windle carried on alone."

"Did the vicar follow him?" I asked. "I would have."

"That's the interesting part." Lilian leaned forward and clasped her hands on the table. "Teddy didn't feel compelled to follow him. Mr. Windle didn't seem to be withdrawn or upset or dejected. If anything, his mood seemed lighter than it had been when Teddy and I spoke with him on Sunday, and he was much more communicative. He asked Teddy to thank me again for the lemon bars, commented favorably on the fine weather, and admired a pair of coots who'd built a nest close to the riverbank."

"Three sentences?" said Amelia, sounding amused. "My goodness. He's turned into a chatterbox."

"Nevertheless, Teddy was anxious about our new neighbor," Lilian went on. "He couldn't concentrate on his sermon until he saw Mr.

Windle again, returning along with riverbank with a small but noticeable bounce in his step."

"A bounce in his step?" I said doubtfully.

"The healing powers of nature are quite marvelous," said Amelia.

"It's not the healing powers of nature," Sally said wisely. "It's Pussywillows. The enchanted cottage is already working its magic on Mr. Windle. I told you it would." Absolved of guilt for missing the great escape, she smoothed her apron and got down to business. "Well, ladies? What can I get for you?"

We ordered a large pot of breakfast tea and a plateful of freshly baked flapjacks to share between us. Sally hurried back to the kitchen, and a short time later Henry took up his post behind the display case, looking relieved. His wife was very particular about her pastries.

A stream of early risers began to trickle into the tearoom to buy cinnamon rolls and loaves of unsliced raisin bread still warm from the oven. Each nodded pleasantly to us, then left, bound for hamlets even smaller and more remote than Finch.

"Sally's got a point," I said. "She's too busy to keep an eye on Pussywillows. Maybe one of us should sit in the kitchen, in case Mr. Windle exits by the back door again."

"There's no need," said Lilian. "Teddy's still working on his sermon. If he sees Mr. Windle near the river, he'll ring me."

"Mr. Windle was gone for four hours," I said. "He must have walked a long way. I wonder where he went."

"I doubt that he had a specific goal in mind," said Lilian. "How could he? He hasn't been here long enough to know where he was going."

"I quite enjoy an aimless stroll along the river," said Amelia. "I also enjoy sitting beside it. For all we know, Mr. Windle could have walked until he found a pleasant spot and sat listening to the water for two hours."

"One thing's certain," said Lilian. "He didn't throw himself into the river."

"Maybe Sally's right," I said. "Maybe the enchanted cottage is working its magic on him."

"Sally will be insufferable if he falls in love with a local," said Amelia.

"I'll be delighted," said Lilian, "though I think we can rule out Opal, Millicent, and Selena as contenders."

"Why?" I asked. "What have you heard?"

"And from whom?" Amelia added.

"Charles Bellingham popped into the vicarage yesterday evening to find out if I'd made another batch of lemon bars," Lilian replied. "I hadn't, but he stayed for a cup of tea. According to Charles, the ladies reacted rather badly to being rebuffed by Mr. Windle. It sounds as though they've written him off as ill-mannered and unfriendly."

"Ouch," I said.

Henry delivered the tea and the flapjacks, then asked where Bess was.

"It's a daddy-daughter day," I told him.

"I don't know who's luckier," he said, "Bess or her daddy."

"You might want to remind Bill of his good fortune the next time Bess has a hissy fit," I said.

Chuckling, Henry departed to serve another customer. While Lilian filled our teacups as well as hers, Amelia and I helped ourselves to the cookies. It seemed as good a time as any to dazzle my friends with Aunt Dimity's brilliant idea. I couldn't wait to see their reactions.

"I'm pretty sure I've figured out what's making the thumping noises in Pussywillows," I began.

"I think it must be a loom," said Amelia.

"So do I," said Lilian.

"Um," I mumbled, more than a bit deflated, "so do I."

"The beater could make a thumping noise," said Amelia.

"It could," said Lilian, "if the beater were heavy enough and if Mr. Windle pulled it toward himself hard enough when he's pushing the weft threads into place. It's just a guess, mind you, but it makes sense of the bundles of wood, the snips, and the thumping."

I ate my flapjack in silence, wondering if everyone in Finch knew more about looms than I did. Then I remembered that Aunt Dimity had referred to the beater as the "bar thingy" and felt a bit better about my lack of expertise.

"I can't imagine why he'd put the loom in his dining room," said Lilian. "He has a perfectly nice spare bedroom upstairs."

"The spare bedroom is too poky for a loom," said Amelia. "I stored my painting supplies in it when I lived in Pussywillows. The dining room is larger and airier. Plenty of elbow room, good natural light, too, when the curtains are drawn. And, of course, the dining room is on the same level as the kitchen. Mr. Windle might not want to be bothered with running up and down the stairs every time he wants a cup of tea."

"He might find it taxing," Lilian conceded.

I swallowed a bite of flapjack and pointed at the window.

"Heads up, Windle Watchers," I said. "Annabelle Craven is on her way to Pussywillows, armed with a lap quilt."

"I wish her luck," said Amelia.

"Unless the enchanted cottage has changed Mr. Windle beyond all recognition," said Lilian, "she'll need it."

# *Fourteen*

Pussywillows had not changed Mr. Windle beyond all recognition. He exchanged more words with old Mrs. Craven than he had with any of his previous callers, but after accepting the colorful lap quilt, he closed his door as firmly on her as he had on everyone else.

Mrs. Craven didn't appear to be offended or abashed by Mr. Windle's behavior. She seemed quite cheerful as she turned away from Pussywillows, and she nodded amiably to us when we motioned for her to join us. She refused, however, to take the fourth seat at our table.

"I won't sit with my back to the window," she declared as Henry escorted her to the table next to ours. "I'd rather not have to spin around to see what's going on."

She ordered a small pot of tea and two slices of lightly buttered toast. It would have struck me as a pathetically meager meal had I not known that Sally's toast was thickly sliced and packed with hearty grains.

"We noticed that Mr. Windle didn't invite you in for a cup of tea," said Lilian.

"I noticed you noticing," said Mrs. Craven, her eyes twinkling. "To tell you the truth, I'd have felt like a traitor if he had invited me in. As it is, I feel a wonderful sense of solidarity with my fellow rejects."

"I wouldn't let Opal, Millicent, or Selena hear you describe them as rejects," said Amelia.

"How, I wonder, would they describe themselves?" said Mrs. Craven. "Choosy? Selective? Discriminating?" She chuckled. "Yesterday they were in here claiming that they'd never wanted to set foot in Pussywillows in the first place."

Amelia smiled and shook her head. "The things we do to protect our fragile egos . . ."

"I didn't hear them firsthand," Mrs. Craven admitted. "Grant Tavistock filled me in on the delicious details when he came by for a chat last night. Elspeth," she added significantly, "didn't have a bad word to say about Mr. Windle."

"He didn't close his door on her," I said. "He didn't open it, either, but still . . ."

"I think there's more to it than that," said Lilian. "I believe she feels a profound sympathy for Mr. Windle."

"You could be right," I said. "Why else would she describe him as a little lost waif?"

"Why else indeed?" said Lilian. "The others may have been engaged in their usual manhunt on Saturday, but Elspeth saw something in Mr. Windle that touched her heart."

"Wouldn't it be lovely if the waif saw something in her?" I said.

"He will," said Amelia. "Pussywillows will make sure he does."

Henry returned with the pot of tea and the toast, which Sally had cut into manageable triangles. Mrs. Craven thanked him, then filled her cup without waiting for the tea to steep. She had a well-known preference for weak tea.

"I must say that Mr. Windle looks a little healthier than he did on Saturday," she went on. "More color in his cheeks. The enchanted cottage must be giving him a new lease on life."

"I rather think it's a touch of sunburn," said Lilian. "He went for a stroll beside the river yesterday."

"Better beside the river than in it," said Mrs. Craven. She took a dainty bite of toast and chewed it thoughtfully. "He was more talkative than I expected him to be."

"As you may have noticed," I said, "we noticed. What did he say to you?"

"He thanked me for the quilt," Mrs. Craven replied, "and he asked if I could direct him to any local landmarks." She chuckled again. "I told him that the only landmarks in Finch were the church, the bridge, and the war memorial, and that he could see two of them from his front door!"

"He must have felt a bit foolish for asking," said Amelia.

"Not foolish," countered Mrs. Craven. "He seemed . . . disappointed. I've no idea why. If he wished to live in a place teeming with landmarks, he should have moved to a more exalted village than Finch."

I turned to Lilian, who prided herself on her knowledge of the area. "Are there any other local landmarks?"

"It depends on what you mean by a local landmark," she said. "The hill behind your house could be considered a landmark, but if Mr. Windle was referring to man-made landmarks, I'd add Fairworth House and Hillfont Abbey to the list. As they lie outside the village, however, they may not be local enough for him."

"You can tell Mr. Windle about Fairworth and Hillfont when you call on him tomorrow morning, Lori," said Amelia. "Be sure to let him know that William and I would be happy to show him round Fairworth House."

"I will," I said. "Anything else to report, Annabelle?"

"My toast is scrumptious," she said, licking the tip of a buttery finger, "but other than that, nothing."

"Who's next on the rota?" Lilian asked. "Who's taking the afternoon shift today?"

"Tilly Barlow," Mrs. Craven replied. "She's going to bring him a book, remember? I hope she'll bring us news from the home front as well. I'm dying to know if Tommy and Bree have kissed and made up."

"They haven't," I said. "I've spoken with Tommy. Bree won't even answer his calls."

"What a pity," said Amelia. "I was convinced that he'd win her back with his beautiful, handwritten love letter."

"She taped his love letter to her front door, unopened," I said.

Three jaws dropped in astonishment. My friends were speechless with shock for a moment, but Lilian soon recovered her voice.

"Poor Bree," she said. "She must be in a terrible state."

"Tommy must be absolutely furious with Mr. Barlow," said Amelia. "I'd be furious with him, if I were Tommy."

"It's Tilly I pity," said Mrs. Craven. "She must feel as if she's living in a war zone."

"If only Mr. Barlow would apologize to Bree," said Amelia. "I don't know why he's being so stiff-necked about her unfortunate indiscretion."

"Nor do I," said Mrs. Craven. "When it comes to failed proposals, Mr. Barlow is in excellent company. King George VI had to propose to Elizabeth Bowes-Lyon three times before she accepted him, and look how well their marriage turned out."

"Perhaps Mr. Barlow could do with a history lesson," said Lilian.

I was certain that Mr. Barlow would apologize to Bree once I told him about her turbulent history, but I kept my thoughts to myself. I was too seasoned a gossip to make the rookie mistake she'd made by discussing a sensitive subject in the tearoom.

"What's this?" said Amelia, peering intently through the window. "Is Elspeth about to try her luck again at Pussywillows?"

I followed her gaze and saw Elspeth Binney crossing the green, with Homer trotting at her heels. Elspeth was neatly but not showily dressed in a pair of pale-blue trousers and a pretty floral-print blouse.

"She deserves a second chance," said Lilian. "Mr. Windle didn't even come to the door when she called on him yesterday."

"He was too busy weaving," said Amelia.

"Is Mr. Windle a weaver?" Mrs. Craven asked interestedly.

"We don't know for sure," I said.

"But we think he is," said Lilian. "Elspeth has changed tactics today. She's carrying a tin instead of the book of photographs."

"She must have taken heed of your warning about making Mr. Windle homesick for Derbyshire," I said.

"I wonder what's in the tin?" said Amelia. "It can't be her boeuf bourguignon. The tin would leak."

"I'll bet the rest of the Handmaidens are watching her through their net curtains," I said. "No matter what they might say to protect their fragile egos, they haven't lost interest in Mr. Windle. They're just upset with him for showing so little interest in them."

"I agree," said Mrs. Craven. "If Elspeth succeeds where they failed, they'll make her feel as if *she's* living in a war zone."

As it turned out, Elspeth had nothing to fear from the disgruntled Handmaidens. Mr. Windle treated her much as he'd treated them, though he did appear to say something more to her than "thank you" after she handed the tin to him. She responded by pointing first at the bridge, then at the war memorial, and finally in the general direction of the church.

"He asked her about landmarks," said Mrs. Craven.

"No doubt about it," I said.

When Elspeth finished pointing, she gave Mr. Windle a friendly smile and left before he had time to close the door.

"Interesting strategy," said Amelia. "Keep the visit short and sweet, and end it on your own terms. No one will be able to paste a reject label on Elspeth."

We didn't have to wave to catch Elspeth's attention. She led Homer into the tearoom of her own accord, though she avoided the dreaded fourth chair by taking a seat at Mrs. Craven's table. Homer disposed of a few flapjack crumbs that had dropped to the floor, then settled into his customary position beside Elspeth's chair. She looked as if she hadn't a care in the world.

"Mr. Windle heard me knock," she informed us unnecessarily. "I didn't have to compete with thumping noises today."

"We think he's a weaver," Amelia informed her.

"How silly of me for not thinking of it myself," said Elspeth. "It's obvious, now that you mention it. The beater would make a thumping noise if he pulled it toward himself with enough force when he's pushing the weft threads into place. He must have a fairly large loom, mind you."

"And a heavy beater," I put in, as if I knew what I was talking about.

"Naturally," Elspeth agreed.

Henry appeared at her elbow with a bowl of water for Homer. While the terrier refreshed himself, Elspeth looked from the toast to the flapjacks, then ordered a green salad and a glass of sparkling water. Lunchtime was drawing nigh.

"Did you make something nice for Mr. Windle?" Amelia probed.

"I made Bakewell tarts," Elspeth replied. "They're named for Bakewell, the Derbyshire market town where they were invented. I wanted to remind Mr. Windle that he doesn't have to live in Derbyshire to enjoy a taste of home."

I had to suppress a smile as another aspect of Elspeth's interesting strategy revealed itself.

"I'm sure he'll enjoy them," said Lilian.

"He asked me a question," Elspeth continued, looking as if she'd won the lottery. "He asked if I was aware of any local landmarks. I told him I didn't know of any, apart from the bridge, the war memorial, and St. George's. I did mention the church's medieval wall paintings to him," she assured Lilian, "but he didn't seem to be interested in them."

"I wonder what does interest him," said Lilian.

"Landmarks," Amelia, Mrs. Craven, and I said in unison.

"Mr. Windle asked me about landmarks, too," Mrs. Craven explained when Elspeth's eyebrows rose in surprise. "Did he seem disappointed by your reply?"

"I suppose he did," Elspeth said reflectively.

"Perhaps you should have told him about Fairworth House and Hillfont Abbey," said Lilian.

Elspeth looked chagrined. "You're right, I should have, but it simply didn't occur to me. They're private houses, after all, and neither one has open days for the public."

"For future reference," said Amelia, "William and I will open our doors to Mr. Windle whenever he wishes to visit."

"I'll let him know," said Elspeth, "the next time I speak with him."

"Well, then," said Lilian, eyeing Amelia and me. "Have we spoiled our appetites with the flapjacks, or shall we order lunch?"

We ordered lunch, of course, but even as we debated the relative merits of still and sparkling water, we watched for Tilly Barlow and her book.

# *Fifteen*

As a wedding present, Mr. Barlow had cleared out the catchall room at the back of his house and transformed it into a library for the fairly extensive collection of books his bride had brought with her from her home in Oxford. Some of the books were both old and valuable, but their monetary worth meant nothing to Tilly Barlow. Tilly collected books because she liked to read, not because she regarded them as a potential source of revenue, and she was always glad to lend them to her neighbors.

"What kind of book will Tilly select for Mr. Windle?" I asked my companions as Henry cleared our table after lunch. "Fiction or nonfiction?"

"Whatever she chooses, I hope it's a lighthearted read," said Amelia. "The last thing the poor man needs right now is a tragedy."

"Sally should lend him one of her romance novels," said Elspeth, who'd just returned from walking Homer. "They always have a happy ending."

"I can't quite envision Mr. Windle engrossed in a bodice ripper," said Mrs. Craven, "but you never know—he could surprise us!"

"Here comes the afternoon shift," said Lilian.

Since Tilly Barlow tended to dress like an old-fashioned librarian regardless of the circumstances, no one took the trouble to comment on the fact that she was wearing a plain white blouse, the brown skirt she'd worn to church on Sunday, and a sensible beige cardigan that would have blended into Mr. Windle's couch. The calf-bound book she cradled in the crook of her arm as she crossed the green appeared to be on the elderly end of the scale, but it seemed commonplace compared with Elspeth's outsized tome.

"Not a book of photographs, I'll wager," said Lilian.

"I doubt that Tilly owns a book of photographs," said Elspeth. "She prefers words to pictures."

At first it seemed as if Tilly were staging a reenactment of Elspeth's first visit to Pussywillows. When her knock received no answer, she pressed her ear to the door, then straightened, frowning. Instead of slinking slyly to the dining room window, however, Tilly marched over to it as if she didn't care who saw her and rapped her knuckles on the curtained pane.

"Bold move," said Amelia.

"Since when is Tilly bold?" I asked.

"Since Mr. Windle refused to answer his door," said Mrs. Craven.

Tilly's atypically bold move worked. When she resumed her stance on the doorstep, Mr. Windle was there, waiting for her. She presented the book to him, conversed with him for several minutes, pointed at her house, and seemed to part company with him on amicable terms. I was so curious to find out what had passed between them that I would have considered tackling her had she turned toward home. Happily for all concerned, especially my knees, she entered the tearoom.

Tilly certainly didn't seem to be herself. She sat at Elspeth's table without waiting to be invited, scratched Homer absently behind the ears, and forgot to say "please" when she asked Henry to bring her a pot of tea and a chocolate eclair.

"Heaven knows I've earned a treat," she said after he left.

"Did you have a hard time picking out a book for Mr. Windle?" I inquired, though I had a feeling that book selection was the least of her worries.

"Not at all," she answered. "As Mr. Windle is new to the area, I thought he might enjoy *A History of the Wool Trade in the Cotswolds.*"

"Bestseller, is it?" Amelia teased.

"I'll have you know," Tilly retorted more loudly than was strictly necessary, "that Mr. Windle expressed a *keen interest* in it."

I'd never heard her raise her voice before, and to judge by my friends' expressions, neither had they.

"Bad day, my dear?" Lilian asked gently.

"A succession of bad days," Tilly retorted, "with no end in sight."

Henry, who'd overheard her outburst, as had everyone else in the tearoom, approached her as he would approach a ticking time bomb, placed her order on the table, and asked cautiously if there was anything else she needed.

"A holiday," she snapped.

Henry backed away, and Elspeth reached down to reassure Homer, who'd awakened with a jerk. Rushing in where the rest of us mere mortals feared to tread, Lilian tried again. As a vicar's wife, she was adept at defusing human bombs.

"How are things at home?" she asked.

"Excruciating," said Tilly. "Tommy and Mr. Barlow have stopped speaking to each other, Tommy's been stomping about the house like a bull elephant, and Mr. Barlow's been sulking in his workshop. I'd knock their heads together if I could, but I can barely reach Tommy's."

I bit my lip to keep myself from laughing. I didn't want Tilly to turn her ire on me.

"I wish there was something I could do to help," Lilian said sympathetically. "Would you like me or Teddy to have a word with them?"

"Thank you," said Tilly, "but I doubt that the good Lord Himself could talk any sense into those two at the moment." After a sip of tea, she seemed to gather herself. "Forgive me, Lilian. I shouldn't have spoken disrespectfully about our Lord."

"He won't mind," Lilian assured her. "He can see that you're under a great deal of stress."

"I'm as fed up as I can possibly be," Tilly agreed. "I don't know what Mr. Barlow is doing in his workshop, but he's hammering away at something. The noise is driving me mad. I suppose it's why I behaved so impolitely at Pussywillows." She blushed. "I shouldn't have knocked on Mr. Windle's window, but I simply couldn't stop myself. The noises coming from his dining room set me off."

"He must have been weaving," said Mrs. Craven.

"Is Mr. Windle a weaver?" Tilly asked.

"We've convinced ourselves that he is," said Lilian. "The beater, you know."

"Oh, yes, the beater," said Tilly, exhibiting the same breezy familiarity with looms as the rest of our group, apart from me. "The noise I heard could have been made by strong pulls on a heavy beater. If Mr. Windle is a weaver, I imagine he'll find *A History of the Wool Trade in the Cotswolds* fascinating. It stands to reason that a weaver would have a natural affinity for wool."

"So it does," Amelia said earnestly, as if to make up for her earlier teasing.

"If you don't mind me asking," said Lilian, "how are Tommy and Mr. Barlow able to work together if they're not speaking to each other?"

"Grunts and gestures," said Tilly. "It's like living with a pair of cavemen." She pursed her lips. "I lay the vast majority of the blame on my husband. I realize that he was vexed with Bree for telling tales out of school, but he had no business speaking so harshly to her." She took another sip of tea before continuing, "To be honest, I think he was as stunned as Tommy and I were when Bree reacted as she did. She's such a plucky little thing. I'm sure Mr. Barlow believed that she was strong enough to take a scolding without going to pieces."

It suddenly occurred to me that I could fulfill my promise to Aunt Dimity by telling *Tilly* why Bree wasn't as plucky as she seemed. I could then leave it to her to convey the sad tale to her husband and to her step-nephew in a manner and at a time she deemed appropriate.

I decided on the spot to invite her to dinner. The twinge of guilt I felt for having an ulterior motive was offset by my certainty that she would welcome an evening away from her maddening menfolk.

"You need a break from the bickering," I said to Tilly. "Come to my place for dinner tonight. Let the cavemen fend for themselves."

"Do you know," she said, brightening, "I believe I shall. Thank you, Lori. It will be a blessed relief to get away from the banging." She sighed. "I wish I hadn't interrupted Mr. Windle. He shouldn't have to pay for Mr. Barlow's pigheadedness."

"The interruption didn't seem to bother Mr. Windle," said Amelia.

"He was extremely gracious," Tilly acknowledged, "and he was sincerely grateful for *A History of the Wool Trade in the Cotswolds*. I showed him where I live, in case he'd like to borrow other books on the subject."

"How many books on the subject do you own?" I asked.

"Eight," Tilly replied promptly. "I acquired them quite by accident. They were in a box of books I bought at an estate sale in Stroud."

"If you were going to find such books anywhere," said Lilian, "it would be Stroud. Stroud was once a famous mill town."

"Indeed, it was," said Tilly. "Stroud's woolen mills produced the scarlet fabric that became the hallmark of the British army. Hence the irreverent nickname 'redcoats.'"

"I had no idea," I said. "I may have to visit Stroud one of these days."

"Very few of the mills are still in operation," Tilly explained, "but some of the older ones have been preserved as museums."

"We don't have a proper museum in Finch," said Mrs. Craven. "If we had, I would have mentioned it to Mr. Windle." She turned to Tilly. "Did he ask you about local landmarks?"

"He asked me if I knew of any," Tilly replied. "I didn't wish to insult his intelligence by pointing to obvious landmarks like the church, the bridge, and the war memorial, so I told him about Fairworth House and Hillfont Abbey instead."

"How did he react?" I asked.

"A bit oddly, now that I think of it," said Tilly. "I'm not sure how to describe it, but it was as if I hadn't given him the answer he wanted." She shrugged. "Perhaps I should have pointed out the obvious."

"Elspeth and I pointed it out to him already," said Mrs. Craven. "He asked us about landmarks, too."

"I think it's commendable of him to take an interest in his new surroundings," said Elspeth. "I just wish I knew what he was looking for."

"I have what I'm looking for." Tilly gazed down at her eclair and smiled for the first time since she'd entered the tearoom. "I do love Sally's chocolate eclairs."

"So do we all," said Lilian. "But I'm afraid it's too late for me to order one. Meals on Wheels beckons."

"I should go as well," I said. "If I'm to call on Mr. Windle tomorrow morning, I must cook for him tonight."

"Will you make your leek, kale, and goat cheese casserole?" Amelia asked.

"Naturally," I said. "It freezes well, so it won't go moldy while he's working his way through the other casseroles. And since we're having a guest to dinner tonight," I added with a nod to Tilly, "I must clear a path through the toys. Is six o'clock too early for you? We dine early because of the children."

"Six o'clock will be perfect," she replied. She patted the table. "In the meantime, until the tearoom closes, I shall be at my post, watching Pussywillows."

"I'll keep you company, Tilly," said Amelia. "William received a new orchid by special delivery this morning. He won't notice that I'm gone."

"I'll take Homer for walkies, then come right back," said Elspeth.

"You'll ring us if the vicar sees Mr. Windle near the river again, won't you, Lilian?" said Amelia.

Lilian promised that she would, walked with me to the Rover, and went on her way to the vicarage. I climbed into the driver's seat and bumped slowly around the green, searching my mind for a landmark the ladies hadn't mentioned to Mr. Windle.

The only one I could come up with was the hill behind my house, and I couldn't imagine why he'd be interested in it. It was a nice enough hill, as hills went, and it held a great deal of personal meaning for me, but there had to be much more impressive hills in the Peak District.

"Why else would they call it the Peak District?" I asked myself.

I crossed the humpbacked bridge and headed for home, still pondering Mr. Windle's fixation on landmarks.

# *Sixteen*

Bree Pym's front door was devoid of messages when I drove past her house, but I spotted her as I turned in to my driveway. I wouldn't have looked toward the old dirt track if I hadn't seen her striding down it the previous afternoon, but there she was, walking toward the river again, half hidden by the rows of spring wheat.

After a moment's thought, I decided to go after her. I promised myself that I wouldn't attempt to catch up with her. I simply wanted to make sure that she was okay.

If she happened to see me, however, and if she happened to be in a receptive mood, I wouldn't hesitate to invite her to dinner. If I could get her to sit face-to-face with Tilly at my dining room table, I was certain that Tilly would do everything in her power to convince Bree to let bygones be bygones with Mr. Barlow and to renew her engagement to her increasingly dyspeptic fiancé. And if Bree allowed Tilly to coax her back into the fold, I'd be spared the onerous task of revealing secrets that weren't mine to reveal. I wasn't a big fan of emotional ambushes, but I was so reluctant to betray my friend that I was willing to try just about anything.

The absence of Bill's car in the driveway told me that he and Bess had already left for Upper Deeping to pick up Will and Rob. Since I didn't want my husband to think I'd vanished into thin air, I sent a text informing him of my plan to follow Bree, then switched off my phone to prevent it from ringing at an inopportune moment. I shoved the silenced phone into the back pocket of my jeans, left my cumbersome shoulder bag on the passenger seat, climbed out of the Rover, and dashed across the lane to the dirt track.

Bree was so far ahead of me by then that she'd already entered the copse that stood at the end of the track, between the Little Deeping and the field. I didn't care for the copse. Bill and I tended to walk around rather than through it because of the uneven ground and the dense undergrowth. Dank, dark, and overrun with shrubs and brambles, it wasn't an ideal place for a demoralized young woman to think sad thoughts, so I redoubled my pace until I reached a cluster of crack willows at the edge of the wood.

I paused to catch my breath, then crept forward, working my way along a thicket of blackthorn bushes to avoid being seen. I wasn't worried about being heard. The river narrowed and flowed more swiftly as it passed the copse, creating a rumbling roar that swallowed the sounds of my footsteps. Since it swallowed the noises around me as well, I was wholly unprepared for the sight that met my eyes when I saw Bree.

She wasn't sitting by herself in a murky corner of the copse's shadowy recesses, contemplating a bleak future without Tommy. She was standing at the water's edge, facing the wood and gesticulating while she spoke animatedly with Mr. Windle.

I was so surprised to see Mr. Windle with Bree that I lost my footing and slithered into a muddy depression in the moss-covered ground. Concerned that the sudden movement and my high-pitched yelp might have alerted the pair to my presence, I stayed put for a moment, despite the mud, then crawled to the rim of the shallow bowl to peer furtively at them through a stand of unfurling bracken. To my relief, they were so caught up in their conversation that they didn't even glance in my direction.

Mr. Windle was almost unrecognizable. It was as if the pale, frail ghost of a man had been replaced by someone more robust and radiant. He listened intently to Bree's lively comments and he responded to them with equal animation, drawing his arm through the air as he spoke and pointing from one misshapen mound of brambles to another. I was too far away to hear what he was saying, but whatever it was, it held Bree's attention. She followed his every movement and hung on his every word, nodding occasionally, as if to show that she understood.

I was about to creep closer to them when a fox padded through the bracken not five feet from my head. Startled, I slid into the mud again, and though I stifled a second yelp, I chose to retreat rather than risk a third tumble. Bree and Mr. Windle were getting along so well that I had no desire to intrude on them, on purpose or inadvertently, so I retraced my steps to the dirt track.

I returned to a cottage filled with familiar sounds as well as the savory scent of roast chicken. Bill and the children were enjoying an after-school snack in the kitchen, but when Bill heard me close the front door, he came down the hallway to greet me. When he saw how grubby I was, he somehow resisted the urge to hug me.

"Tricky footing in the copse," he observed.

"It's full of surprises," I understated. "Oh, and Tilly's coming to dinner. I meant to tell you in my text, but—"

"Tilly's not coming to dinner," Bill interrupted. "I just had a call from her, begging off. She tried to ring you, but she couldn't get through."

"My phone's off." I drew my cell phone from my back pocket delicately, using only a forefinger and a thumb, and passed it to Bill. "It's not too muddy, but it could do with a wipe. Why did Tilly beg off?"

"She had to drive Mr. Barlow to the hospital," said Bill.

"What happened?" I asked anxiously.

"Nothing fatal," Bill assured me. "Apparently, he smashed his thumb with a hammer while he was shaping a piece of sheet metal in the workshop. Why are you laughing? There's nothing funny about a handyman with a smashed thumb."

"I'll explain everything after I take a shower and change into clean clothes," I said. "I feel like a swamp monster. I must smell like one, too."

"I couldn't possibly comment," said Bill, but he stepped aside to avoid coming into contact with me as I sat on the hall bench to remove my shoes.

I explained everything to Bill after dinner, but I wasn't sure how much of it he took in. Daddy-daughter days always tuckered him out. He apologized for yawning so frequently and turned in at such an early hour that he very nearly beat the boys to bed. I stayed downstairs to make Mr. Windle's casserole, then went to the study to repeat the day's recap, confident that my narrative wouldn't be interrupted by yawns.

"Strange doings are afoot," I said to Reginald as I took the blue journal from its shelf. "Secret meetings in dark woods. There's no knowing where they might lead."

Reginald seemed suitably intrigued. I twiddled his pink flannel ears, then sat in one of the tall leather armchairs facing the hearth and admired my dry, clean jeans as I rested my stockinged feet on the ottoman.

"Dimity?" I said as I opened the journal. "It's been another big news day. Would you like me to start with the headline, or shall I get the smaller stories out of the way first?"

*Good evening, my dear. The smaller stories first, if you please. They'll make the headline shine even brighter by contrast.*

"It's blindingly shiny," I said, "but first things first. Bill looked after Bess today, so I arrived at the tearoom earlier and left later than usual. . . ." I told her about my wordless encounter with Tommy in front of Bree's house; Sally's alarming confession; the vicar's unsuccessful attempt to accompany Mr. Windle on his walk; and the odd bounce in Mr. Windle's step as he returned safely to Pussywillows.

*What, I wonder, could have put a bounce in Mr. Windle's step?*

"Sally credits Pussywillows," I said. "She claims that the enchanted cottage is working its magic on him."

*Mr. Windle's bouncing step does seem to verge on the miraculous. Do you know where he went?*

"I believe I do," I said, "but if I tell you, I'll be getting ahead of myself."

*In that case, carry on with the smaller stories. I prefer to let the anticipation build.*

"Opal, Millicent, and Selena have gone off Mr. Windle," I continued, "but Elspeth hasn't. She took advantage of the three-day-rule waiver and went back to Pussywillows this morning, shoehorning her visit between Mrs. Craven's and Tilly's."

*Did Mr. Windle open his door to her?*

"He did," I said, "but he didn't let her in. She gave him a tin filled with Bakewell tarts she made with her own fair hands."

*I hope Mr. Windle has a sweet tooth. Bakewell tarts are too sugary for some, but I retain a deep affection for them.*

"I'm not sure Elspeth took Mr. Windle's sweet tooth into account when she made the tarts," I said. "They were meant to demonstrate that he doesn't have to live in Derbyshire, where the Bakewell tart was invented, in order to enjoy a taste of home."

*A most thoughtful gift.*

"Lilian reckons that Elspeth has genuine feelings for Mr. Windle," I said.

*What do you reckon?*

"I reckon Lilian's right," I said.

*If she is, the Bakewell tarts could be regarded as sweets for the sweet. I do hope Elspeth's feelings will be reciprocated.*

"If they aren't," I said, "it won't be for lack of effort on her part. She hasn't knitted a pair of socks for Mr. Windle yet, but I won't be surprised if she does."

*I'll wager he didn't receive hand-knitted socks from Mrs. Craven or Tilly. Would I be correct in assuming that the former brought him a quilt and the latter, a book?*

"You would," I said. "As per usual, Mr. Windle received the gifts gratefully but did not invite the givers to enter Pussywillows."

*So far, so predictable.*

"I'll tell you something I didn't predict," I said. "Everyone in Finch knows more about looms than I do. Not a high bar, I admit, but still, it was discouraging to have my big announcement about the thumping noises preempted by Lilian and Amelia. Mrs. Craven, Elspeth, and Tilly talked about looms as if they'd been raised in a loom factory."

*If it's any comfort, I don't know much about looms, either.*

"It is comforting," I said, "in a misery-loves-company sort of way. But the fact of the matter is that we won't know whether or not Mr. Windle actually has a loom until one of us manages to look inside his dining room. We're certain, however, that he's interested in local landmarks, but not in the church, the war memorial, the bridge, Fairworth House, or Hillfont Abbey."

*There aren't any other local landmarks.*

"There aren't any other *man-made* landmarks," I pointed out, "but Pouter's Hill counts as a natural landmark. If he asks me about landmarks tomorrow, I'll tell him about Pouter's Hill."

*I don't know why Pouter's Hill would captivate him.*

"Nor do I," I said, "but Elspeth thinks it's commendable of him to take an interest in his new surroundings."

*So it is. Have we reached the end of the smaller stories?*

"Not quite," I said. "Tommy and Mr. Barlow are giving each other the silent treatment, although Mr. Barlow has been getting on Tilly's nerves by shutting himself in his workshop and making a racket. Tilly was so irritable when she joined us in the tearoom that she snapped at Henry."

*I didn't realize that she was capable of snapping at anyone, let alone at someone as inoffensive as Henry Cook.*

"She was way beyond peevish," I said. "I felt so sorry for her that I invited her to dinner. She couldn't make it, though, because she had to take Mr. Barlow to the hospital." Though I tried, I couldn't suppress a snort of laughter.

*I fail to see the humor in Mr. Barlow's misfortune.*

"You haven't heard the punch line yet," I said. "Mr. Barlow whacked his thumb with a hammer while he was sulking in his workshop. Just deserts for driving Tilly crazy, I'd say."

*Mr. Barlow is paying for his ill-judged fit of pique in more ways than one. He's lost his apprentice, he's alienated his nephew, he's annoyed the most mild-mannered woman in Finch, and now he's injured himself.*

"He won't be a very handy handyman with a damaged thumb," I agreed.

*Have you spoken to him or to Tommy about Bree's past?*

"With Tommy communicating through mime," I said, "and Mr.

Barlow shut away in his workshop, I haven't had a chance to speak to either one of them. I would have said something to Tilly after dinner if Mr. Barlow's accident hadn't altered her plans."

*You may not have to speak with any of them, my dear. Pain has a way of concentrating the mind. It's quite possible that Mr. Barlow's aching thumb will bring him to his senses. If it does, one word from him to Bree will start a chain reaction that will heal the many ruptures his intemperate behavior caused. I hope it will, at any rate.*

"Sounds good to me," I said, "not least because it would get me out of doing something I really don't want to do." I leaned back in my chair. "And so we come at last to the headline you've been anticipating."

*I'm on tenterhooks.*

I recounted the reasoning behind my decision to follow Bree, leaning heavily on my concern for her well-being and skipping lightly over my self-serving dinner-with-Tilly scheme, then set the scene, describing the crack willows, the blackthorn thicket, and the river's rumble before going in for the kill.

". . . and there she was, standing on the riverbank," I continued, "but she wasn't alone."

*Please tell me that she was with Tommy.*

"I wish she had been," I said, "but she wasn't with Tommy. She was with *Crispin Windle*."

*Good gracious! I confess to being blinded by your headline.*

"I hoped you would be," I said with a satisfied nod. "I've already had my thunder stolen several times today. I didn't want it to happen again."

*You had nothing to fear from me, my dear. You took me completely by surprise.*

"I was thunderstruck," I said. "Never in a million years did I expect to see Mr. Windle with Bree. Lilian was supposed to call the rest of us if he went walkabout again. I turned my phone off, though, so she may not have been able to reach me."

*Do you suppose that Bree and Mr. Windle stumbled across each other yesterday, after he rejected the vicar's offer of companionship?*

"I do," I said. "Mr. Windle's stroll beside the river and Bree's walk down the farm track would have put them in the copse at about the same time. Besides, when I saw them there today, they weren't acting as though they'd never met before. They were getting along like a house on fire. Mr. Windle was expressive, enthusiastic—nothing like the man I've seen in Finch."

*And Bree?*

"She held up her side of the conversation," I said, "but she seemed to be absolutely riveted by every word he said."

*What did he say?*

"I don't know," I said. "I couldn't hear him or Bree because of the river, but I'm pretty sure they were talking about the copse. They kept pointing at it." I shook my head. "It's so strange, Dimity. What could two such different people have in common?"

*Mr. Windle was a teacher and Bree has a hungry mind. Perhaps he's found a new pupil.*

"What's he teaching her?" I asked. "Advanced dankness? Introduction to brambles?" In a moment of exquisite irony, I interrupted my narrative with a gaping yawn. "Sorry, Dimity. I guess I'm more tired than I thought."

*Of course you are. Chatting with friends in the tearoom all day is hard work. Run along to bed, my dear. Your headline has given me much to contemplate. We'll speak again tomorrow.*

As the graceful handwriting faded from the page, I thought of something else Mr. Windle and Bree had in common.

"Loneliness," I said, looking up at Reginald. "Mr. Windle is a newcomer and Bree must feel like an outsider. It's an unlikely friendship, but if it helps them to feel less lonely, I'm all for it. Though why they'd choose to meet in a damp, dark patch of woods instead of a sunny spot on the riverbank is beyond my comprehension."

I returned the journal to its shelf, traced Reginald's hand-sewn whiskers with a fingertip, and went upstairs, wondering why anyone would be fascinated by the copse.

# *Seventeen*

I didn't see a note on Bree's door or a jilted fiancé in her driveway when Bess and I passed her house on our way to Finch on Wednesday morning. Since I refused to believe that Tommy had thrown in the towel, I reckoned that he'd come and gone while I was taking Will and Rob to school in Upper Deeping.

I was very much looking forward to renewing my acquaintance with Mr. Windle. As three days had passed since he'd moved into Pussywillows, no one could accuse me of knocking on his door prematurely. I could call on him with my head held high, undaunted by the sight of twitching curtains.

I intended to tell him about Pouter's Hill, on the off chance that it was the landmark he was seeking, but I couldn't ask him directly about his budding friendship with Bree Pym without admitting that I'd spied on them. To save face, I decided to drop her name casually into the conversation and hope that he would need no further prompting to describe their meeting in the copse.

Bess and I said hello to the ducks as we crossed the humpbacked bridge, and I waved to Amelia and Lilian as we passed the tearoom. They were seated at their customary table in the front window, sipping tea and keeping watch over Pussywillows. I parked the Range Rover in front of Bill's office and released Bess from her car seat.

To keep my fearless daughter from going walkabout, I held her hand with one of mine while balancing my casserole dish on the other.

With both hands fully occupied, I could do nothing but nod at Amelia and Lilian as we passed the tearoom a second time, and when we reached Pussywillows, I had no choice but to kick the front door. Mr. Windle answered my kick much more rapidly that he'd answered my knocks on Saturday. Perhaps, I thought, he was getting used to visitors.

"Good morning, Mr. Windle," I said brightly. "Remember me?"

"How could I forget your daughter's quacks," he asked good-humoredly, "or your rather unusual inquiry regarding suicide?"

"Sorry about that," I said, blushing.

"There's no need to apologize, Lori," he said. "It was a generous impulse."

"It was definitely impulsive," I agreed, blushing redder still.

"You were concerned about me," he said, "and I'm grateful. Do you come bearing a gift this time?"

"Leek, kale, and goat cheese casserole," I said. "My specialty. I hope you like it."

"I'm sure I will," he said. "Thank you."

The casserole dish teetered on my open palm as I held it out to him. To keep it from crashing onto the doorstep, I let go of Bess's hand for a nanosecond and she took off, charging straight past Mr. Windle and into his cottage.

"Bess!" I commanded. "Get back here!"

"I don't think she's listening," said Mr. Windle, taking the casserole from me. "You'd better go after her."

I didn't have the presence of mind to glance toward the tearoom before I scurried into Pussywillows, but I was later informed by reliable witnesses that Amelia and Lilian cheered.

Bess had already toddled into the front room by the time I caught up with her. She stood amid a maze of empty cardboard boxes that cluttered the polished plank floor, looking bemused. Mr. Windle followed us into the room, beaming beneficently at Bess.

He looked and sounded so much more vigorous than he had on Saturday that I began to think I'd overestimated his age. He suddenly seemed like a man in his early sixties rather than his midseventies. I could have sworn that his clothes hung less loosely on him, too, though it was probably wishful thinking. He hadn't been on the high-calorie casserole diet long enough to gain a perceptible amount of weight.

"I'm sorry, Mr. Windle," I said. "Bess hasn't quite grasped the concept of common courtesy."

"She's delightful," he said. "If you'll excuse me, I'll take the casserole to the kitchen. Shall I put the kettle on while I'm there?"

"Yes, please," I said. "I never say no to a cup of tea."

"Excellent." He gestured toward his beige sofa. "Please, make yourself at home. Bess can play with the boxes while we chat. Children her age like to play with empty boxes."

"Bess is no exception," I said. "On her second birthday, she spent more time playing with the boxes than she spent with the toys that came inside them."

"I'll be back directly," he said, and he went up the central corridor to the kitchen.

Mr. Windle seemed to know more about children than most single gentlemen of my acquaintance. I wondered if he had nieces and nephews, or friends with young families. Whatever the case, he was clearly enchanted by Bess.

A glance across the hallway confirmed that the dining room door was shut. I didn't wish to be caught in the act of snooping, so I stayed in the front room, turning some boxes upside down and others onto their sides, to make things more interesting for Bess. By pure coincidence, the task also allowed me to take a sightseeing tour of Mr. Windle's possessions.

He'd placed his sofa against the interior wall, facing the curtained windows across a decrepit coffee table that was covered with papers, some of which appeared to be maps. Draped across the back of the sofa, Mrs. Craven's quilt added a much-needed touch of coziness to the decor, such as it was.

The pair of bookcases flanking the fireplace at the far end of the room were crammed with well-thumbed books that didn't appear to be arranged in any discernible order. A sagging armchair and a wobbly pole lamp built in to a small, circular table sat before the fireplace. Tilly would have been pleased to see that her book about the wool trade lay on the circular table, with a scrap of paper serving as a bookmark. It looked as though Mr. Windle had read just over half of it.

During Amelia's tenure at Pussywillows, she'd placed a framed photograph of her late brother on the mantel shelf, and Tilly had used it to display a photo of her late parents. Mr. Windle hadn't put anything on the shelf, apart from Amelia's exquisite watercolor of the flag iris.

I was about to take a closer look at the maps when Mr. Windle returned. He cleared the coffee table by shoving the papers into a box, which he placed on top of one of the bookcases, well out of Bess's reach.

"Nearly there," he said. "Would Bess care for a glass of milk? I bought some fresh this morning from the extraordinary woman in the shop."

"Peggy Taxman," I said, nodding. "Peggy can be a bit much at first, but you'll soon get used to her, or as used to her as it's possible to get. She's the driving force behind all of our community events, with an emphasis on force." While I spoke, I rooted around in my shoulder bag, finally unearthing a slightly sticky and somewhat linty sippy cup. When I hesitated to hand it to Mr. Windle, he took it from me, assured me that he would rinse it thoroughly before he filled it with milk, and went back to the kitchen.

He returned a short time later carrying a wooden tea tray laden with a classic Brown Betty teapot, a pair of blue-and-white striped mugs, a cracked sugar bowl, a chipped creamer, two slightly tarnished teaspoons, and Bess's sippy cup, which was immaculate. He placed the tray on the coffee table and we sat side by side on the sofa, which sagged a bit under our combined weight.

Bess forgot her manners again, snatched the sippy cup from the tray before it was offered to her, and downed a few gulps of milk before handing the cup to me and resuming her exploration of the box maze. In the meantime, my host filled the striped mugs with tea.

"Thank you, Mr. Windle," I said, "on Bess's behalf as well as my own."

"You're very welcome," he said. "I must admit that I didn't expect to find an American living in a place as small and out of the way as Finch. You are American, aren't you, Lori?"

"My accent gives me away every time," I said, shaking my head with mock ruefulness. I sped through a short version of my family's move to England, then, seeing an opening, I zeroed in on it. "We're not Finch's most exotic imports, though. Bree Pym lives a stone's throw from here, but she's from New Zealand."

"She's a long way from home," he conceded without missing a beat, "but since New Zealand is still a member of the Commonwealth, its citizens have closer ties to the United Kingdom than you and your family do."

He hadn't taken the bait and I saw no point in pressing him. It was entirely possible that Bree had asked him to keep their meetings confidential, so I moved on.

"You're from Derbyshire, I believe," I said.

"Did my accent give me away?" he asked with a quizzical smile.

"No," I replied. "Village gossip did. It's something else you'll have to get used to if you intend to stay in Finch."

"I have every intention of staying," he said. "It's a lovely village. You mentioned community events earlier. How does one find out about them? Is there a newsletter?"

I laughed. "We don't need a newsletter. We have the village grapevine. If you want to find out what's happening in Finch, just keep your ears open."

"How do the villagers find out about events in other communities?" he asked.

"To tell you the truth, they don't pay much attention to other communities," I said. "There's enough going on in Finch to keep them occupied. Some of them subscribe to the *Upper Deeping Dispatch*, but only for the coupons and the sales notices." Influenced, perhaps, by the cottage's magic, I found myself putting in a good word for Elspeth. "Elspeth Binney's always on the lookout for cultural events as well. She enjoys broadening her horizons. I believe you've met Elspeth."

"I have," he said. "She was kind enough to make Bakewell tarts for me. I had one last night, after dinner. A perfect end to a sadly imperfect meal. I'm afraid I left the chicken-and-dumpling casserole in the oven too long." He looked momentarily disconcerted. "Forgive me. I should have offered you a tart."

"I'm glad you didn't," I said. "If I have one, Bess will want one." I nodded at my daughter, who was using an upturned box as a bongo drum. "Can you imagine her after a sugary treat?"

"Understood," he said. "Is the *Upper Deeping Dispatch* as venerable as it is useful?"

"It's been around for a long time," I confirmed. "I spent a happy afternoon in the archives last winter, poring over a bound volume of issues from 1837, but they go back much further than that."

"A valuable resource," he said. "I'm intrigued by Finch's history. When I finish unpacking, I intend to visit the church. I understand that it has medieval wall paintings."

"You could have seen the paintings quite easily, if you'd come to St. George's on Sunday," I said.

"I'm not a churchgoer," he said candidly. "I was once, but I'm afraid I lost my faith."

"You don't have to be a man of faith to come to St. George's," I assured him. "There are many mansions in the vicar's house. Our local witch plays the angel of the Lord every year in our Nativity play, and she's a pagan."

"Your vicar has a pleasingly ecumenical outlook," he said, "but no, it's not for me."

"Word has it that you're interested in local landmarks," I ventured.

"It's a hobby of mine," he acknowledged. "I've already heard about the church, the bridge, the war memorial, and a pair of stately homes. Are you aware of any other landmarks in Finch's general vicinity?"

He nodded politely as I described Pouter's Hill, but like Mrs. Craven, I sensed that he was dissatisfied with my answer.

"Are you looking for a specific type of landmark?" I asked.

"I seem to be looking for one that doesn't exist." He saw my puzzled expression and said gently, "Forgive me, Lori. I jest. My students always told me that I had a strange sense of humor."

"It's true, then," I said. "You were a teacher."

"Until my retirement, I was a professor at the University of Derby," he said.

"Shouldn't I be calling you Professor Windle?" I asked.

"I'm not a professor anymore." A wistful note entered his voice as he added, "A long time ago it seems now, like another life."

"You must miss it," I said.

"I miss my students," he said. "I miss the tutorials and the lecture hall. I miss the moment when a student's eyes lit up because a piece of knowledge had clicked into place." He smiled. "I don't miss departmental meetings, though. They tended to send me to sleep."

I nodded. "You preferred the classroom to the conference room."

"Well put," he said.

"What subject did you teach?" I asked.

"History," he replied. "Industrial history. Derbyshire's industrial history, to be precise."

So much for reading poetry aloud, I thought. Grant Tavistock would be disappointed.

"I have to confess that I know next to nothing about Derbyshire's industrial history," I said. "Less than nothing, to be honest. I thought Derbyshire was a natural wonderland, with the lion's share of the Peak District within its borders."

"It's a natural wonderland now," said Mr. Windle, "but Derby was one of the birthplaces of the Industrial Revolution. It never became a powerhouse like Manchester or Leeds, but it had its share of dark, satanic mills."

I recognized the snippet from William Blake's "Jerusalem" and thought that Mr. Windle might be a poetry lover after all.

"Blake took a dim view of the Industrial Revolution," I said.

"You see?" said Mr. Windle. "You do know something about it.

Blake's view was shared by many others, and with good reason. Mill owners tended to prioritize profit over their workers' health and safety."

"What did the mills produce?" I asked.

"They spun silk, cotton, and wool," he said, "and they wove, finished, and dyed textiles for the home market and abroad."

"Like Stroud," I said, recalling Tilly's comments on the wool trade in the Cotswolds. "Home of the redcoats."

"There is some similarity," he acknowledged, with the diplomacy of a scholar who could have gone on for hours delineating the difference between Stroud and Derby but who kindly chose not to bore me with it.

"It's a fascinating subject," I said. "Even nincompoops like me know that large-scale manufacturing changed everything, everywhere. Snowdrifts high in the Himalayas are tainted with microplastics, thanks to the Industrial Revolution."

"And millions of people who would have starved half naked in the street before it were adequately fed, housed, and clothed after it—because of it," he said. "As with most world-changing events, the Industrial Revolution was a double-edged sword."

"Sorry," I said, coloring to my roots. "I should know better than to lecture a professor."

"Not at all," he said. "I'm gratified by your zeal."

Having wrung all the enjoyment she could from the boxes, Bess marched out of the front room and into the corridor. I sprang to my feet and chased after her, but she managed to open the dining room door before I could stop her.

"You'll want to grab her," Mr. Windle cautioned, following close upon my heels. "The room's not childproofed."

It was, in my opinion, the understatement of the century. As I lifted Bess into my arms, I beheld an assemblage of objects guaranteed to intrigue—and quite possibly maim—a curious toddler. Bess was definitely intrigued by the pair of bookcases to my left, which were filled not with books but with a veritable rainbow of fine woolen yarns wound neatly around cone-shaped holders similar to those I'd seen in a craft shop in Upper Deeping.

The danger zone was to my right, where a long wooden table beneath the curtained window held compartmented trays filled with deadly-looking tapestry needles, a tempting selection of scissors, including the newly purchased snips, and an array of other tools about which I knew nothing except that I didn't want Bess to get anywhere near them.

At the center of the room stood a wooden loom. It wasn't quite as big as I'd expected it to be, but it was big enough, and it seemed every bit as complicated as the one Aunt Dimity's friend had attempted to explain to her. I hoped to high heaven that Mr. Windle wouldn't make the same mistake with me.

Having solved the twin mysteries of the thumping noises and the bundles of finished wood, I should have experienced a preening sense of triumph. Instead, I was overcome with a combination of awe and cringing inadequacy as I took in the many parts of a device I couldn't have operated if my life depended on it.

"Wow," I said. "A loom."

"Well spotted," Mr. Windle said dryly. "It is, in fact, a four-harness, six-treadle floor loom with suspended harnesses, a thirty-six-inch weaving width, a friction brake for tension control, and an adjustable beater to accommodate reeds of different heights and widths."

"So," I said, after his words had flown over my head, "you're a weaver."

"A mere amateur," he said. "I took it up after my—" He caught himself, then continued, "—after I retired. In a way, it's related to my field. Long before the first mill was built, weavers wove on floor looms in their cottages." He patted the unfinished length of black fabric in the loom, as if to test the tension. "Some people find weaving tedious. I find it meditative. Once the threads are set up, a loom is quite easy to use." He turned to me. "Would you like me to show you how this one works?"

"I would," I said, "and I'm sure Bess would, too."

"Bess too," Bess confirmed.

Mr. Windle seated himself on a low wooden bench before the loom, like an organist addressing a keyboard, but before he could do anything else, we were distracted by the sound of someone pounding thunderously on the front door.

"I believe I have another caller," said Mr. Windle, getting to his feet. "A rather insistent caller, I'd say."

Tilly again? I wondered.

With Bess still held safely in my arms, I trailed after Mr. Windle and peered past him as he opened the door. The insistent caller was none other than Tommy Prescott.

"Forgive me, Mr. Windle," Tommy said, "but I need to speak with Lori Shepherd."

*Need* to speak? I thought. Must be serious.

"Tommy!" Bess crowed happily.

Tommy followed the sound of Bess's voice, saw me, and reiterated in urgent tones, "I need to speak with you, Lori. *Outside. Now.*"

"Mr. Windle," I began, but he waved me to silence.

"Go," he said, and he stepped aside to let me pass.

"Bye-bye," said Bess.

"Good-bye, little one," said Mr. Windle, but he didn't close the door after we left. He stood on the doorstep watching as Tommy hustled me to the humpbacked bridge, presumably to thwart potential eavesdroppers.

"Lori," Tommy said, rounding on me, his scarred face pale with fear. "Bree is *gone*!"

# Eighteen

I felt a jolt of alarm, but I clamped down on it. Since Tommy was clearly out of his mind with worry, I had to at least pretend to be levelheaded.

"Gone?" I said. "What do you mean, Bree's gone?"

"I was at her house five minutes ago," he said. "Her car isn't in the garage."

"She could be in Upper Deeping," I suggested.

"Or she could be halfway to Heathrow," Tommy said frantically. "She could've booked a seat on the next flight to New Zealand. *She packed a bag, Lori!*"

I stared at him, nonplussed. "How do you know she packed a bag?"

"I have a key to her place," he replied. "She forgot to take it back when she returned her ring. When I saw that her car was missing, I let myself into the house and had a look around. She's not there and her blue carry-on is missing."

"Duck!" said Bess.

"Yes, sweetie, Mummy sees the duck," I said absently while I digested Tommy's unsettling discovery. "Did she leave a note?"

"I couldn't find one," he said desperately.

"Did she take her passport?" I asked.

"I don't know where she keeps her passport!" he exclaimed, flinging his arms wide in exasperation.

"I do," I said. "Bree showed me where she hid it. She thought her hiding place was a hoot." I passed Bess to Tommy, saying, "You can move faster with her than I can. Let's go."

Bess giggled as Tommy and I clambered hastily down the bridge. She was enjoying our speedy exit much more than we were.

Mr. Windle had withdrawn from his doorstep, but he watched us from his doorway as we dashed past Pussywillows, and he leaned forward to peer at us as we raced past the tearoom. I had a vague impression of startled faces in the tearoom's front window, but I was too preoccupied to acknowledge them. When Tommy began to veer across the green toward his uncle's van, I called him back.

"We'll take the Rover," I stated firmly. "You're in no condition to drive."

I strapped Bess into her car seat in record time, hopped behind the wheel, and left the village at a speed that wouldn't have shattered any records but would, I hoped, keep Tommy from pounding the dashboard in frustration. He exhibited laudable self-control, though I could almost hear him grind his teeth when I slowed down to negotiate the sharp bend in front of Bree's house.

I pulled into the driveway, climbed out of the Rover, and started toward the backseat but changed direction when I saw that Tommy was already there. Knowing that I wouldn't leave Bess in the car on her own for more than five minutes, he carried her to the front door, where I stood waiting for him.

"It's not locked," he said impatiently.

He reached across me to turn the doorknob and followed me across the threshold, through the hall, and into the front parlor. The room had changed very little since Bree had inherited the house from her great-grandaunts. To honor their memory, Bree had kept the front parlor almost exactly as they'd left it. If I hadn't known that Ruth and Louise Pym were dead and buried in St. George's churchyard, I would have expected to see them look up from their knitting to greet me.

The aspidistra still flourished on its little rosewood stand near the window; the finely crocheted antimacassars still graced the backs of the dainty matching armchairs before the hearth; and the rolltop desk Ruth and Louise had inherited from their father still sat against the back wall, looking as out of place among the more delicate furnishings as it always had.

I crossed to the mantel and fished around in a delftware posset pot, where Bree kept the key to the rolltop desk, just as her great-grandaunts had done. Key in hand, I unlocked the desk, raised the rolltop, pushed Bree's laptop to one side, and pressed a lever hidden at the back of a pigeonhole. A slender panel to the right of the pigeonhole popped open. I slid my hand into the narrow compartment and breathed a sigh of relief as my fingers touched Bree's passport.

"Well?" Tommy asked anxiously. "Is it there?"

"Yes." I took the passport from the compartment and showed it to him. "She hasn't bolted for New Zealand, Tommy. She's still in the UK."

Tommy swayed slightly, but he didn't drop Bess. If anything, he held her more tightly, as if his strong emotions couldn't overcome his protective instincts. He would, I thought, make a wonderful father.

"Where is she?" he asked helplessly.

"Her laptop might tell us," I said, "but let's take it to my place. Bess needs lunch and you need to be somewhere other than here." I picked up the laptop, slid the passport back into its hidey-hole, secured the desk, dropped the key in the posset pot, and left the parlor, calling over my shoulder, "Don't forget to lock the door on your way out."

After feeding Bess, reading her a story, and settling her in the nursery for her nap, I returned to the living room. I'd left Tommy sitting on the sofa with a roast chicken sandwich and a glass of water on the coffee table and Bree's laptop on his lap. When I saw Stanley sniffing the untouched sandwich, I shooed him away, picked up the plate, and waved it between Tommy's face and the laptop's screen.

"Eat," I said. "You can't think clearly on an empty stomach."

"Yes, I can," he said.

"Humor me," I insisted.

I stood over him, arms folded, while he polished off the sandwich in four gargantuan bites, which he washed down—prematurely, in my opinion—with the water. Satisfied, I sat in Bill's armchair. Despite my shooing, Stanley jumped onto my lap and curled into a purring ball of contentment. He wasn't a cat who held grudges.

"Was I right about the laptop?" I asked. "Did it tell us where Bree went?"

"I think so." Tommy closed the laptop and set it on the coffee table. He didn't appear to be as pleased by the results of his detective work as I'd thought he'd be. "I scrolled through her most recent searches. She was looking for the shortest route to a market town in Derbyshire, a place called Bakewell."

"Bakewell?" I said, my eyebrows rising. "Where the tarts were invented? Seems like a long way to go to appease a sugar craving."

"It's not the dark side of the moon," said Tommy. "Depending on traffic, Bree could have driven from her house to Bakewell in a little over two hours. And I don't think she went there to sample the baked goods."

"Why did she go there?" I asked.

"Bakewell's a popular tourist spot," he explained. "Since it's inside the national park, it's big on outdoor adventures—hiking, cycling, rock-climbing, caving, water sports, that sort of thing."

"Bet it can't beat Finch for kayaking," I said, knowing full well that it could.

Tommy smiled halfheartedly and went on. "Quite a few shops in Bakewell cater to the adventure trade. They sell outdoor clothing and gear, and rent equipment. Visitors can find pretty much anything they need to enjoy an active holiday."

"Is that what you think Bree's doing?" I asked doubtfully. "Enjoying an active holiday in the Peak District?"

"She concentrated on one shop in particular," Tommy continued. "Bike Well Cycles. It's an independent cycle shop owned by a couple—Fred and Alice Taylor. The Taylors rent, sell, and repair bicycles, but they also give guided tours of the Peak District."

"Busy couple," I commented.

"Their most popular tour includes a visit to Chatsworth House," said Tommy. "It's just up the road from Bakewell. Customers cycle there, take a walking tour of the house and gardens, then cycle back. Have you ever been to Chatsworth?"

"No," I said, "but it's high on my list of stately homes to visit. I hear it's magnificent."

"I went there once with my mum and dad," said Tommy. "I was about ten at the time, so I didn't have much say in the matter. I wasn't keen on the house—too many things for a gangly boy to bump into—but the gardens were spectacular, like a fun fair, only greener."

I laughed. "Sounds like the kind of gardens a ten-year-old boy would like."

"They're not tacky," Tommy stressed. "Far from it. Even I could see how beautiful they were, but they definitely weren't boring. There's a cascade, a maze, a rockery with boulders the size of cars, and a fountain that shoots a jet of water hundreds of feet into the air." He looked down at the laptop. "I told Bree about Chatsworth's marvelous gardens. We talked about going to see them together." He lifted his gaze to meet mine. "I think she decided to go on her own."

"She wouldn't," I protested.

"Why not?" said Tommy. "She could do with a change of scenery, she loves gardens, and she enjoys cycling. Bike Well's Chatsworth tour would tick all three boxes."

"I don't care if it ticks a trillion boxes," I retorted. "Bree wouldn't go to Chatsworth without you, not if you talked about going there together."

"You may not have noticed, Lori," he said with an air of resignation, "but Bree and I aren't together anymore."

"Maybe not officially," I argued, "maybe not right this minute, but you will be together again, I promise. She'll come back to you, Tommy. She just needs to figure things out."

"What is there to figure out?" he asked. "She knows how much I love her, she knows I'd do anything for her, but it doesn't seem to matter to her." He bowed his head. "I don't seem to matter to her."

He looked so young and so utterly defeated that I could hold my tongue no longer. I ceded the armchair to Stanley, moved to the sofa, and sat facing Tommy, with my leg folded under me.

"Has Bree ever talked to you about her childhood?" I asked.

"No," he replied. "She told me once that she envied me for having a normal childhood, but when I asked her what she meant, she said she'd rather look forward than back. I sensed that it was a no-go area, so I let it drop." He frowned. "Why? What does Bree's childhood have to do with her running away to Chatsworth?"

"Pretty much everything." I took a deep breath, apologized silently to Bree, and began the difficult task of telling Tommy about his beloved's abnormal childhood. "Bree wasn't much older than Bess when her parents' marriage crashed and burned. They weren't fit to raise a child, so she was raised by her paternal grandparents until her feckless father turned up, out of the blue, and took over the household.

"Bree's father was a bully, a thief, a liar, a cheat, a gambler, and a mean drunk. He drove Bree's grandmother into an early grave and he terrorized Bree's grandfather. Bree lived in fear of his drunken rages. She tried to shield her grandfather from them, but what could she do? She was just a kid."

Tommy's jaw tightened ominously, but he said nothing.

"Bree was eighteen when her grandfather died," I continued. "She made sure he had a decent burial, then took off to look for her mother. Bree didn't have much trouble locating her, but the reunion wasn't a happy one. She couldn't stay with her mother and she wouldn't go home to her father, so she ran and she kept on running, driven by anger, guilt, grief, and an unshakable conviction that she was not only unloved but unlovable."

"Unlovable," Tommy muttered, shaking his head in disbelief.

"I arrived in New Zealand shortly after Bree's father finally drank himself to death," I said. "I managed to track her down about ten days later. When I broke the news to her, she didn't shed a single tear."

"Why would she?" Tommy said bitterly.

"I found her in Queenstown, in a garden on the shores of Lake

Wakatipu." I paused as the memories came flooding back. "I told her that a pair of very old ladies in a very small English village had sent me to act as their emissary because they wanted very much to meet her before they met their maker. I brought her to Finch and introduced her to her great-grandaunts, who fell in love with her at first sight. They died the next day."

Tommy groaned softly.

"When your uncle took Bree under his wing," I went on, "he became a surrogate father to her—the father she wished she'd had. She hates herself for letting him down because she knows all too well how it feels to be let down. And how could someone who betrayed a man as upstanding as Mr. Barlow be worthy of marrying his nephew?"

"Unloved, unwanted, unworthy," Tommy murmured. "My poor Bree." He closed his eyes briefly, then turned to me. "Has she told my uncle about her childhood?"

"What do you think?" I asked.

Tommy sighed. "I think he's as much in the dark as I was. He'd never have come down so hard on her if he'd known about her father. We both thought Bree was as tough as nails."

"She is tough," I said, "and resilient and courageous and astoundingly self-assured—most of the time. But she's also vulnerable, especially when it comes to father figures. A harsh word from Mr. Barlow carries a lot more weight with her than it would if it came from you or me."

"I've never spoken a harsh word to Bree," said Tommy.

"Nor had Mr. Barlow, until she broadcast his private business in the tearoom," I reminded him. "I don't think he'd ever raised his voice to her before. Your uncle isn't an ogre, Tommy. He had a right to be upset with her."

"He also has a right to know why his lecture on privacy ended with his tough-as-nails apprentice bursting into tears," said Tommy. "I'll fill him in. He'll want to kick himself for losing his temper with Bree."

"He shouldn't," I said. "It's not his fault that she couldn't bring herself to tell him the truth, the whole truth, and nothing but the truth about her past."

"I suppose she didn't want him—or me—to feel sorry for her," said Tommy.

"She didn't want anyone to feel sorry for her," I said, "which is why she asked me to keep my mouth shut about her childhood. She enjoyed the pity party Grant and Charles threw for her after her rotten Aussie fiancé dumped her, but she'd hate it if everyone pitied her all the time."

Tommy raised his prosthetic leg. "No one understands better than I how demoralizing pity can be."

"Feel free to pity me after Bree finds out what I've done," I said glumly. "She'll probably clobber me for talking about her behind her back, but with you looking like a sad puppy, and Mr. Barlow smashing his thumb, and Tilly snapping at Henry—"

"Tilly snapped at Henry?" Tommy interrupted incredulously.

"You and your uncle have been driving her nuts!" I exclaimed. "You gave me no choice. I had to tell you about Bree's past for everyone's sake, including hers. I imagine the whole sorry story will come out eventually—secrets don't stay secret for very long in Finch—but until it does, I'd appreciate it if you wouldn't chat about it in the tearoom."

"I'll file it under 'Need to Know,'" Tommy promised, "and my uncle is the only one who needs to know." He smiled wryly. "It could be argued that Bree's as touchy about her privacy as my uncle is about his. No wonder they get along so well."

"Birds of a feather," I said, smiling back at him. "When you get home, apologize to your aunt, talk to your uncle, and above all, be patient with Bree. She's a clever girl. She'll figure things out."

"If a change of scenery helps her to figure things out," said Tommy, "then I don't mind her going to Chatsworth without me. She can show me her favorite spots when we go there together." He picked up the laptop and stood. "I'd better be on my way. I'll put the laptop back where we found it."

"What's your hurry?" I said, patting the sofa. "Stick around. Bess will be up in a few minutes. We can give you a lift home."

"Thanks, but I'll walk back to the village," he said. "I'm so bloody furious with Bree's dad I could put my fist through a wall. I need to work it off before I speak with Uncle Bill."

"A brisk walk sounds like a great idea," I said, jumping to my feet.

I accompanied him to the door and opened it. Before he stepped outside, he bent down to hug me. It was like being hugged by a mountain.

"Thank you, Lori," he said, straightening. "For the sandwich, for the truth, and for being a good friend."

"What's the watchword with Bree?" I asked.

"Patience," he replied, and he strode down the flagstone path to the lane.

I watched him go, feeling as if I'd had a narrow escape. I had a sneaking suspicion that Bree's trip to Derbyshire had something to do with Mr. Windle, but I had no intention of telling Tommy about the strange encounter I'd witnessed in the copse. He'd had enough revelations for one day, and I'd given away enough of Bree's secrets. I'd leave it to her to tell him about her friendship with our new neighbor.

I didn't want to be clobbered twice.

# *Nineteen*

In an effort to impress my sons during dinner, I told them about the fox I'd seen in the copse. I should have known better. Instead of reacting to my wildlife sighting with a gratifying degree of awe, they informed me nonchalantly that they'd seen the fox at least a dozen times while riding past the copse on their ponies.

"In fact," Will said, "we've seen a *pair* of foxes in the copse."

"We think one is a vixen," said Rob.

"Which one did you see?" Will asked.

"A red one," I said, avoiding Bill's amused gaze.

The boys took the opportunity to educate their ignorant mother, regaling me with fun fox facts until the meal was, mercifully, over and I had a reasonable excuse to send them to their room to do homework.

Even if Bill hadn't called me "foxy lady" for the rest of the evening, I would have stayed downstairs after he'd gone to bed. I had so much to tell Aunt Dimity that my head was spinning. I waited until the cottage had grown still and silent, then went to the study, lit the mantel lamps, and knelt to light a fire in the hearth. The room wasn't particularly chilly, but I found the sight, sound, and scent of a wood fire as soothing as the warmth.

"I stormed the castle," I told Reginald, sitting back on my heels. "To be accurate, Bess stormed it, but I was right behind her. When you have a toddler, you don't need a battering ram. Although, come to think of it, they're pretty much the same thing."

Reginald's black button eyes glittered in the firelight as I stood, took the blue journal from its shelf, and curled up in a tall leather armchair. I'd managed to impress him, at least.

"Dimity?" I said, opening the journal. "I had tea with Mr. Windle in Pussywillows this morning."

Aunt Dimity's fine copperplate appeared almost instantly on the blank page.

*Well done, Lori! How did you succeed so spectacularly where so many before you had failed?*

"Bess," I said. "My little barbarian barreled into the cottage without waiting for an invitation. I followed her, Mr. Windle followed us, and the next thing I knew, he and I were having tea in the front room while Bess played with his empty cardboard boxes. I couldn't have planned it better if I'd tried."

*Barbarians have their uses, especially when they're as adorable as Bess.*

"Mr. Windle would agree with you about Bess's high degree of adorableness," I said. "He couldn't stop beaming at her. He seems to know a fair amount about children, more than I would expect from a bachelor."

*He might be an uncle or an honorary uncle. I never had children of my own, but I knew how to look after a toddler. Tell me about your visit. Did you observe anything unusual in Pussywillows?*

"Mr. Windle is still getting himself organized," I said.

*Hence the cardboard boxes.*

"I think they must have been filled with books," I said, "because the bookcases in his front room are stuffed with them. He seems to like maps, too. I saw several on his coffee table before he made room for the tea tray. He's reading the book Tilly gave him, and he keeps Annabelle Craven's lap quilt on his sofa, but the only thing he has on his mantel shelf is Amelia's painting."

*No photographs?*

"None," I said. "You'd think an uncle or an honorary uncle would have photos of his nearest and dearest on display, if only to bring back happy memories."

*Perhaps he hasn't unpacked them yet. Were you able to ascertain why he moved away from his nearest and dearest?*

"No," I said, "but I can confirm everything Marigold Edwards told us about him. In addition to being single, he is indeed a retired professor from Derbyshire. He taught industrial history at the University of Derby. I think he wishes he was back in the classroom. He loved teaching."

*Retirement can be a difficult transition, but he'll come through it better if he makes an effort to find new friends.*

"He won't look for them at St. George's," I said. "He's not a churchgoer."

*Once he learns that the church is Finch's beating heart—as well as the best place to hear the latest gossip—he may change his mind.*

"He asked me if Finch had a newsletter," I said, chuckling. "I told him that word of mouth is our preferred form of communication. I let him know about the *Upper Deeping Dispatch*, though, in case he wants to take in a concert or wander through an art gallery. I'm sure Elspeth would be willing to show him the sights."

*Did he mention Elspeth?*

"He mentioned her Bakewell tarts," I said. "He described them as a perfect end to an imperfect meal. I guess he's not much of a cook. Elspeth, on the other hand, is a dab hand in the kitchen."

*You're matchmaking, Lori.*

"It's not me," I protested with feigned innocence. "It's Pussywillows!"

*Ah, yes, the cottage that casts a romantic spell over anyone who lives there. Well, it certainly seems to be having a salutary effect on Mr. Windle. He's gone from a haggard shell to a charming host in four short days. What else did you talk about?*

"I dropped Bree's name into the conversation," I said, "but he acted as though he'd never heard of her. I think she may have asked him to keep their meetings to himself, though I don't know why she would."

*If Mr. Windle admits to befriending Bree, the villagers might subject him to the kind of interrogation Bree herself is working assiduously to avoid. Bree's a kindhearted young woman. She wouldn't want him to be caught up in her personal drama. Did you drop Pouter's Hill into the conversation as well?*

"I did," I said, "and it went over like a lead balloon. Not a flicker of interest from Mr. Windle. When I asked him what kind of landmark he was looking for, he made a joke about looking for one that doesn't exist, so maybe he's stopped looking."

*I may have another suggestion for him, but we'll come to it in a moment. Did you ask him if he owns a loom?*

"I didn't have to ask," I said. "After my little barbarian broke into his dining room, I saw the loom with my own eyes."

*I hope you kept her away from it.*

"She viewed it from the safety of my arms," I said. "Heaven knows what she would have done if I'd turned her loose on his yarn supplies."

*To paraphrase Sir Walter Scott: Oh, what a tangled web she would have woven!*

"I'd still be untangling it," I agreed, shuddering. "Mr. Windle's collection of colored yarns would make a painter's palette look dull, but he loaded the loom with black yarn. Can you believe it?" I frowned slightly. "I hope he's not making a shroud."

*Shrouds are usually made of unbleached linen.*

"Good to know," I said. "I'd hate to think that he contemplated death every time he sat down to weave."

*Why didn't you ask him what he was weaving?*

"I might have," I said, "but I didn't get the chance. We were interrupted by Tommy Prescott pounding on the front door like a maniac and demanding to speak with me in private."

*Oh, dear. What was the matter with Tommy?*

"He thought Bree had taken off for New Zealand," I said. I told Aunt Dimity about the missing car, the missing carry-on bag, the missing note, and the immense relief Tommy and I had felt when I'd discovered that her passport wasn't missing. "She'd left her laptop behind, too, and she would never have gone to New Zealand without her laptop."

*Do you know where she went?*

"I put Tommy to work, searching her laptop for clues," I said. "He's ninety-nine percent certain that she went to Bakewell."

*The market town in Derbyshire?*

"Yes," I said. "It seems to be a mecca for outdoorsy types as well as tart aficionados. Tommy thinks Bree went there to take a cycling tour run by a local couple who own a shop called Bike Well Cycles."

*What a clever play on words!*

"Tommy was too miserable to get a kick out of it," I said. "The cycling tour includes a tour of Chatsworth House. He and Bree had planned to go there together, to see the gardens. He was crushed by the thought of Bree going there without him. He saw it as the final nail in the coffin of their relationship."

*Good grief. They've only been apart for a few days. Bree hasn't had time to design a proper coffin, let alone to drive the final nail into it. Apart from that, Tommy can't be certain that she went to Chatsworth. Bree could have been using her laptop merely to daydream about the trip they'd planned.* There was a pause, and when the handwriting began again, the royal-blue ink took on a darker hue, as if Aunt Dimity were emphasizing her words. *Tommy isn't thinking clearly, Lori, because he doesn't have all the facts.*

"He's thinking clearly now," I said, "because I gave him all the facts before he left."

*You told him about Bree's childhood?*

"I did," I said. "And he'll tell Mr. Barlow. If all goes according to your plan, there'll be a hug fest at Bree's house as soon as she gets back from Derbyshire."

*If she went to Derbyshire, which I doubt. I'm sorry, Lori, but I find it very difficult to believe that Bree and her broken heart are gadding about on a cycling holiday in the Peak District.*

"I don't think she's gadding about," I said. "I'm merely suggesting that she might go to Derbyshire if she thought she could help Mr. Windle."

*How on earth would a cycling tour help Mr. Windle?*

"No idea," I said, "but I do know that Bree wasn't behaving like someone with a broken heart when I saw them together in the copse. They were enjoying each other's company, maybe lifting each other's spirits, possibly confiding in each other." I uncurled my legs and bent over the blue journal. "Think about it, Dimity. Bree befriends a troubled man from Derbyshire one day and drives to Derbyshire the next. There has to be a connection."

*I suppose Bree could have discovered why Mr. Windle appeared to be so full of woe when you and Tommy saw him from the bridge. If she did, she wouldn't hesitate to put her own problems to one side in order to solve his. As I observed earlier, she's a kindhearted young woman.*

"Exactly," I said, leaning back in the chair. "The cycling tour has me flummoxed, but you can't expect me to work out every tiny detail all at once, can you?"

*I would never dream of doing so, my dear. You've had a day filled with stellar achievements. You should rest on your laurels this evening. Before you get too cozy, however, I'd like to return to the topic of landmarks.*

"The ones that exist or the ones that don't exist?" I asked.

*The one I have in mind is a bit of both. I'd almost forgotten about it, but your visit to the copse brought a hazy memory into sharper focus.*

The fire crackled and the ivy fluttered in a vagrant breeze while Aunt Dimity marshaled her thoughts. When the handwriting recommenced, it flowed slowly across the page, as if she were looking back a long way. Which, as it turned out, she was.

*I was in my second year at the village school when a schoolmate whispered to me that the copse was haunted. Her grandfather had told her that, in his youth, he'd seen ghostly figures drifting through the underbrush, and that she should avoid the copse, lest the ghostly figures follow her home.*

A log shifted in the fire, sending up a shower of sparks, and I nearly jumped out of my skin.

"Sorry," I said, readjusting my grip on the journal.

*Don't apologize, my dear. I, too, was spooked by the tale, but when I ran home after school, round-eyed with fear and gibbering about ghosts, my mother sat me down and talked some sense into me. She told me that a grist mill had once stood at the end of the dirt track across the lane from our cottage. The builder chose the location because the river's flow was strong enough to turn the mill's waterwheel at a steady rate.*

I remembered the river's rumble and nodded.

*My mother went on to tell me that at some point, long before she was born, a businessman from Upper Deeping converted the grist mill into a textile mill.*

*With so many sheep about, he had a ready supply of wool, and the river was an endless source of power. As it turned out, the mill was too small to be profitable, but the owner kept cutting corners and piling pressure on his workers until the inevitable happened. A poorly repaired machine malfunctioned, resulting in the deaths of four mill workers.*

"The ghostly figures," I murmured.

*I will repeat what my mother said to me when I spoke those same words to her: Stuff and nonsense! My friend's grandfather invented the ghostly figures in order to discourage his granddaughter from playing near a dangerous stretch of the river. Since I was an intelligent girl, she said, I didn't have to be tricked into avoiding danger. I was flattered, of course, and eager to live up to my mother's opinion of me, so I never played near the narrows.*

"Your mother was a wise woman," I said.

*She was a thousand times wiser than the businessman from Upper Deeping. The ensuing court cases bankrupted him. The mill was closed, the machines and the waterwheel were auctioned off, and the building was left to decay.*

"No wonder the ground in the copse is so treacherous," I said. "The bushes and brambles must have grown over whatever parts of the building are left. Trip hazards everywhere you step."

*My mother told me that the villagers wanted to erase the mill from their memories. They were appalled by the tragedy and deeply humiliated by the fact that Finch was cited in many court documents as the village closest to the mill. They felt as if they'd been tarnished by the same brush as the mill owner. Which brings me to Mr. Windle.*

"The mill can't be his landmark," I objected, putting two and two together. "There's hardly anything left of it."

*On the off chance that it is his landmark, I would, if I were you, urge him to proceed with caution. His new neighbors take a vast amount of pride in their community. They might not appreciate a reminder of a painful chapter in Finch's past.*

"I can't ask him to suppress his findings," I said.

*You can, however, counsel him to present his findings in a sensitive manner.*

"Okay," I said. "I'll have a word with him, but—" I broke off as my cell phone pinged, alerting me to an incoming text. I glanced at the ormolu clock on the mantel and saw that it was approaching midnight. "Forgive me, Dimity. I don't know who would be texting me at this hour."

*You'd better find out. There could be some sort of emergency at Fairworth House or in the village.*

Since Willis, Sr., had a history of heart problems, Aunt Dimity's words hit home. I pulled the phone from my pocket, looked at the screen, and did a double take.

"I don't believe it," I said. "It's *Bree*. She wants to know if I'm still awake. She has something important to tell me." I looked down at the journal. "She must be back from Bakewell."

*Tell her to come over at once! You and I can speak again tomorrow.*

I wasn't a speedy texter, but even my sons would have been impressed by how quickly I replied to Bree.

# *Twenty*

I was waiting on the doorstep when Bree pulled into the driveway. She got out of her car and scurried up the flagstone path, her heart-shaped face alive with suppressed excitement.

"I'm glad you're up, Lori," she said, making an effort to keep her voice low. "I have a lot to tell you!"

"Come through to the kitchen," I told her. "I've put the kettle on."

Bree was wearing black jeans, black leather boots, and a formfitting, finely woven woolen pullover I hadn't seen before. I couldn't have carried off the sweater's red, orange, and dark-purple diagonal stripes, but the bright colors and the bold pattern were just right for Bree. When we reached the kitchen, she held her arm out to me.

"Feel it," she said. "Extra-fine merino wool from New Zealand. There's nothing else like it in the world."

"It's gorgeous," I said, stroking the downy sleeve. "You didn't buy it in New Zealand, did you?"

She blushed and let her arm fall. "I know I've been out of touch for the past few days, Lori, but I wouldn't go to New Zealand without telling you."

I was tempted to ask if Mr. Windle had woven the merino wool for her, but it was too early in our reunion to admit that I'd followed her to the copse. I closed the kitchen door and nodded at the plate of oatmeal cookies I'd placed on the scrubbed pine table.

"Help yourself to a cookie," I said. "I'll see to the tea."

"A midnight feast," Bree said, reaching for a cookie as she lowered herself onto a chair. "Yum!"

Once I'd set the table with everything we'd need to enjoy our midnight feast, I sat across from her and filled our cups with tea. After a strenuous internal debate, I'd concluded that, as Tommy was bound to tell her about our unsanctioned visit to her house, I might as well tell her myself. Before I could commence the tale of the purloined laptop, however, she was off and running with her own tale.

"So much has happened since the moving-van vigil that I don't even know where to start," she said. "It's not just you I didn't want to talk to after I left Mr. Barlow's house. I didn't want to talk to anyone."

"You needed some time on your own," I said, as if I weren't the sort of person who would get down on her hands and knees to make sure that a car was still in a garage. "I understand."

"You probably know what I did with Tommy's letter," she said, toying with her teaspoon.

"He may have mentioned it," I acknowledged breezily.

"On Sunday it seemed only fair to make a clean break with him," she said earnestly, "but by Monday, I was having second thoughts. I was too wound up to stay at home, but I didn't want to bump into anyone while I was out, so I walked away from the village and down the dirt track to the copse. No one ever goes there. It's too creepy."

"It's a spooky spot," I agreed, recalling Aunt Dimity's ghost story.

"I was sitting on the riverbank, trying to think things through," she said, "when I got the surprise of my life." Her eyes twinkled with anticipation as she approached the big reveal. "You'll never guess who walked up to me."

"I might," I said, more or less truthfully, "but I'd rather hear it from you."

"It was Mr. Windle!" Bree exclaimed.

"Good heavens," I said with as much astonishment as I could muster.

"If I'd seen him coming, I'd have ducked into the copse," she admitted, "but you know how loud the river is in the narrows. I didn't have a clue that he was there until he said, 'Good afternoon.'" She folded her arms and rested them on the table. "I'm glad I didn't run away. Mr. Windle may have retired, but he's still a professor, a brilliant professor. I learned all sorts of things from him."

"Such as?" I said.

"Did you know that there used to be a textile mill in the copse?" Bree asked. "I didn't, but Mr. Windle did. He came across a reference to it in some obscure academic journal while he was still living in Derbyshire. When he moved here, he assumed that the mill would be a local landmark. He couldn't understand why it wasn't."

"I think I may have heard something about some sort of mill somewhere near Finch," I said vaguely. Bree did not need to know that my knowledge of the mill had come from an extraordinarily obscure journal. "I couldn't have told him where the mill was, though. How did he figure it out?"

"Deduction," said Bree. "It didn't show up on any of his maps, but Finch wasn't on some of them, either, so he made a few educated guesses. He studied the river's twists and turns and reckoned that the narrows would be a good location for a water-powered mill."

"He must have been disheartened when he saw the copse," I said.

"You'd think so, wouldn't you?" Bree marveled. "But the copse didn't bother him at all. He read the ground as if he were reading a diagram, and he described the mill so clearly I could almost see it." For a moment her gaze turned inward, as if she were back on the riverbank, following Mr. Windle's sweeping gestures and hanging on his every word. "The channel that brought water from the river to the mill pond; the flume from the mill pond that fed the waterwheel; the tail race, where the water drained back into the river . . . All that from a few indentations in the ground." She came out of her reverie and laughed at herself. "It was uncanny, Lori. He could tell where the mill building had stood by clearing the brambles from a handful of flagstones and some stumpy bits of wall."

"Amazing," I said.

"He told me his research into the mill's history was ongoing," she said, "and he offered to give me an update on Tuesday, if he hadn't bored me to tears already."

"It doesn't sound as though you were bored," I said.

"Mr. Windle is the best kind of teacher," said Bree, "the kind who makes you *want* to listen. So I agreed to meet him at the copse on Tuesday." She looked down and toyed with the teaspoon again. "I also asked him to keep quiet about meeting me. He didn't demand an explanation. He just said, 'Okay.' Then he walked back to the village and I went home."

I wondered if the sight of the forlorn young woman sitting by herself beside a cheerless stand of trees had struck a chord with Mr. Windle. Having gently but firmly rebuffed a steady stream of well-meaning visitors, he might have empathized with Bree's desire to avoid the village spotlight, whether he understood the reason for it or not. A good teacher had ample reserves of empathy, and by Bree's estimation, Mr. Windle was one of the best.

"What happened on Tuesday?" I asked.

"We saw a fox," Bree said, grinning. "It came out of a patch of bracken and dove under a blackberry bush. I think it was diving into its den."

I made a mental note to thank the fox for his exquisite timing. If he hadn't distracted Bree and Mr. Windle, they might have noticed me sliding back into the mud.

"We talked about the mill again on Tuesday," Bree went on, "but he didn't have much to add to what he'd said about it on Monday. He told me there must have been other buildings in the copse, but he'd need a machete to prove it." She smiled. "He said he was glad he didn't own one because it was too fine a day to work up a sweat. So we sat on the bank and just talked."

"About what?" I asked.

"Ourselves, mostly." Her smile faded as she said solemnly, "He's a widower, Lori. His wife's name was Olivia."

"A widower?" I said, frowning. "Marigold Edwards told Sally Cook that he was a single gentleman. She never said anything about him being a widower."

"Marigold never spoke with him directly," Bree reminded me. "When he decided to leave Derbyshire, he hired a broker to find a cottage for him. I imagine he was too grief-stricken to discuss Olivia's death in an office. The broker must have noticed that he wasn't wearing a wedding ring and assumed that he'd never worn one."

"Bill's father wore his wedding ring for years after his first wife's death," I said. "I wonder what Mr. Windle has done with his."

"It's with Olivia," said Bree, "in her grave. She asked him to bury it with her. She wanted him to marry again and she was afraid that a wedding ring would make it harder for him to find a new wife."

"She must have been a remarkable woman," I said. "How long ago did she die?"

"Six months," Bree replied, "but she was ill for several years before she passed away. She had motor neuron disease. Mr. Windle retired early to look after her full time, but since there's no cure, there wasn't much he could do except to keep her as comfortable as possible while she wasted away."

I recalled the cloud of anguish that had enveloped Mr. Windle when Tommy and I had seen him from the bridge. I could think of nothing worse than to stand by helplessly while someone I loved suffered without the least hope of recovery. It would, I told myself, be enough to test anyone's faith.

"He found little ways to make Olivia happy," Bree was saying. "She was an accomplished weaver. Before she lost the use of her hands, she taught him how to weave. When she became bedridden and unable to speak, he set up the loom in their bedroom, so she could watch the shuttle fly back and forth and listen to the clatter." She shook her head sadly. "He'd have swapped places with her in a minute, Lori. He loved Olivia with his whole heart."

"And now he's alone," I said softly.

"But he's not alone," Bree said, leaning forward abruptly. "He has a daughter. Her name is Alice. She and her husband live up north, in Derbyshire. I couldn't believe it when he mentioned her."

I stared at her. "If he has a daughter in Derbyshire, why did he move to the Cotswolds?"

"It didn't make any sense to me, either," said Bree. "I didn't get the impression that his daughter hated him or vice versa. His face lit up like a Christmas tree when he talked about her. Then he went all quiet and wistful, as though he missed her so much it hurt."

"I wonder if she knows how much he misses her," I said.

"So did I," said Bree, "so I drove to Bakewell to tell her."

"Bakewell?" I said alertly. "Does Mr. Windle's daughter live in Bakewell?"

"I didn't know where she lived," said Bree, "but Mr. Windle told me that she owned a shop in Bakewell. He didn't mention the shop's name, but anyone with a laptop and half a brain could have figured it out."

"And you have considerably more than half a brain," I said.

"I don't know about that," Bree said modestly, "but I did figure it out. There's only one shop in Bakewell owned by a woman named Alice. It's called Bike Well Cycles and it's situated on the edge of town."

I felt like crowing. I could hardly wait to tell Aunt Dimity that I'd been right all along. Bree hadn't gone to Bakewell to enjoy a cycling holiday. She'd gone there to speak up for her new friend, just as I'd predicted.

"I wasn't sure how long it would take me to fight my way through traffic," Bree went on, "so I packed a bag in case I had to stay overnight. I got to the shop around ten o'clock this morning."

"Was Alice there?" I asked.

"She was restocking shelves," said Bree. "I recognized her as soon as I saw her. She has her father's eyes."

I nodded. "How old is she?"

"Midthirties, maybe. She's tall, like he is, and she has short blond hair, even shorter than mine." Bree ran her fingers through her spiky crop, which had reverted to its natural dark-brown color. "She's in great shape."

"All that cycling," I said.

"No doubt," said Bree. "She dropped an armload of jumpers when I told her where I was from. She thought something awful had happened to her father. I calmed her down and helped her to pick up the jumpers, but I felt so guilty for scaring her that I bought one." She plucked at her sleeve. "The wool's from New Zealand, but it was woven in Derby."

Birthplace of the Industrial Revolution, I thought, but I kindly chose not to bore Bree with my erudition.

"Alice's husband was out with a tour group," Bree continued, "so she asked an assistant to mind the shop and took me next door to a café filled with cyclists. It was quite a sight." Bree grimaced. "Some men should not wear Lycra, Lori."

"No, they should not," I agreed with heartfelt sincerity, remembering the many unfortunate exemplars I'd seen pedaling through Finch.

"Alice had good reason to be concerned about her father," Bree said, returning to the main subject. "He'd worn himself to a thread looking after Olivia. When she died, he became very ill. It took Alice a couple of months to get him back on his feet, but even then, she had to keep an eye on him, to make sure he was eating and drinking and getting enough sleep. For a long time he didn't have the strength to pick up his grandchildren."

"He has grandchildren?" I said, nearly choking on a sip of tea.

"He has *three* grandchildren," Bree replied. "Alice and her husband have two sons and a daughter."

"Like Bill and me," I said.

"Their sons aren't twins," Bree explained, "and they're younger than Will and Rob, but their daughter is about Bess's age."

"Good Lord," I said as comprehension dawned. "That's why Mr. Windle has taken such a shine to Bess. She must remind him of his granddaughter." I clapped a hand to my forehead as another penny dropped. "No wonder he knows so much about toddlers. He was used to having them around before he moved to Finch." I lowered my hand and looked imploringly at Bree. "How could he bear to leave them?"

"I asked Alice the same question," she said. "She was stunned when he told her what he planned to do. She and her husband begged him to stay, invited him to move in with them, but he wouldn't hear of it. He told them that with three children to raise and a business to run, they had more than enough on their plate without adding him to it as well."

"He left Derbyshire because he didn't want to be a burden on his family," I said slowly. "He had to remove himself from their orbit to keep Alice from dropping in on him to make sure he was eating and drinking and sleeping."

"Exactly," said Bree. "He'd worn himself out looking after his wife. He must have been afraid that his daughter would wear herself out looking after him. He insisted on giving them his good furniture. He pulled a few old pieces out of his attic to keep for himself."

"Which explains why he has so little," I said, "and why everything he owns is so rundown."

Bree nodded. "He gave them his car, too, and kept the one Olivia bought secondhand a few months before she became ill." She smiled wanly. "So you were right, Lori. He does drive the old Renault for sentimental reasons."

"The saddest of sentimental reasons," I murmured, wishing I'd been wrong.

"Can't imagine a sadder one," Bree agreed.

We drank our tea in silence. I wasn't sure what was going on in Bree's mind, but I was struggling to comprehend the magnitude of Mr. Windle's noble but needless act of self-sacrifice. When I tried to imagine what my world would be like without Willis, Sr., in it, I wanted to weep.

"They'll visit him, won't they?" I asked.

"They'll try," said Bree, "but the boys are in school, their shop is always busy, and you know how tricky it can be to travel with a toddler. It won't be easy for them to get away."

"Are you going to tell him about your trip to Bakewell?" I asked.

"Alice has probably told him about it already," Bree replied. "She calls him every day."

"She's doing her best to stay in touch," I said. "How do you think he'll react to your mission of mercy?"

"He knows I like to learn," said Bree. "He can't be too upset with me for wanting to learn more about him. If he raises any objections, I'll blame Finch for turning me into a world-class snoop."

"Speaking of snoops . . ." I cleared my throat. "There are one or two or possibly three things I should tell you, now that you're back."

"Have you been snooping, too?" Bree asked.

"It's pretty much all I've done since you pulled up the drawbridge," I said.

To ease my way into a potentially hazardous series of confessions, I started with Windle Watch. After I described the haunting scene Tommy and I had witnessed from the bridge, Bree had no trouble understanding why so many of us had volunteered to act as Mr. Windle's guardian angels. She understood why I'd followed her to the copse, too. When I told her about the laptop episode, however, she was outraged, not because Tommy and I had burgled her house, but because Tommy had jumped to a transparently erroneous conclusion.

"I'd never go to Chatsworth without him!" she protested. "How could he think I would?"

"Oh, I don't know," I said with a nonchalant shrug. "The broken engagement might have had something to do with it."

"Right," said Bree, simmering down.

"Right," I repeated more forcefully. "You left a trail of destruction behind you when you ran out of Mr. Barlow's house in tears. Tommy didn't know what was going on because he didn't know what had gone on before you came to Finch. So . . ." I looked her squarely in the eye. "I told him. Everything. If you want to knock my block off, go ahead, but—"

"You promised me you wouldn't ever tell anyone anything," Bree interrupted. She regarded me reproachfully, then looked down at her teacup. "But I guess I gave you a pretty good excuse to tell Tommy, so you can relax— I won't knock your block off." She smiled sheepishly at me. "The thing is, I was going to tell him myself. Mr. Windle said I should."

"What?" I said stupidly.

"After I told Mr. Windle about my dad—" she began, but I cut her off.

"You told Mr. Windle about your dad?" I said with unfeigned astonishment.

"I told him about my dad and Mr. Barlow and Tommy and all sorts of things." She ducked her head self-consciously. "It was kind of like when you came up to me in Queenstown. I didn't know who you were or why you were there, but I poured my heart out to you anyway. Sometimes it's easier to talk to a stranger than to a friend."

"Yes," I conceded. "Sometimes it is."

"Mr. Windle told me that I should talk to Tommy and to Mr. Barlow about my dad," she said. "He said keeping secrets is a waste of time, and time is too precious to waste, especially the time we spend with the people we love."

I felt a lump rise in my throat as I thought of the precious time Mr. Windle had spent with his late wife, but I refused to allow our midnight feast to end on a mournful note.

"Since his advice coincides precisely with mine," I said gruffly, "I can only praise him for his wisdom."

Bree grinned, grabbed a handful of cookies, and got to her feet.

"I'll be off," she said. "Sorry to keep you up so late. I just had to tell you about, well, everything."

"I'm glad you did," I said, standing. As we walked to the front door, I asked, "Do you know if Mr. Windle is planning to publish an article or to give a lecture about the old mill?"

"I imagine he'll do both," said Bree. "He might even invite the villagers to the copse for a show-and-tell."

"If I were him, I'd wait awhile before I gave guided tours of the copse," I said. "The villagers might resent a newcomer lecturing them about their own history."

"Don't be silly, Lori," said Bree. "The villagers think Finch is the best place in the world. They'll love having another landmark to brag about." She gave me a hug and whispered, "I missed you."

"I missed you, too," I said, hugging her back. "Go home and get some sleep. You have a reengagement party to plan."

She laughed and scampered down the flagstone path to her car. As she drove away into the darkness, I felt as if my brain would collapse under the weight of so many revelations. I wanted to share them with Aunt Dimity, but when I realized that a tricky toddler would be waking me in a few hours, I decided to take my own advice and get some sleep.

Though my brain was overloaded, one thought stood out with absolute clarity as I went upstairs. I wouldn't drive straight to the tearoom after I took the boys to school. I'd go to Fairworth House first, so my baby girl could spend time with her grandfather.

# Twenty-One

Willis, Sr., was so delighted by our impromptu visit on Thursday morning that he requested permission to keep Bess with him for the rest of the day. I gave it readily, knowing that his housekeeper would be on hand to supervise the playdate. Since Deirdre's son wasn't much older than Bess, I suspected that she'd put all three of her charges down for naps after lunch.

The first thing I noticed when I crossed the humpbacked bridge was that Bree's car was parked in front of Mr. Barlow's house, behind his paneled van. It looked as though Bree had wasted no time in convening a meeting with her nearest and dearest in order to dispose of a few secrets. I doubted that any voices would be raised while she described her father's reign of terror, though Mr. Barlow would almost certainly be so angered by her mistreatment that he might have put his fist through a wall if he hadn't already smashed his thumb.

The second thing I noticed from the apex of the bridge was that Windle Watch was already in full swing. Amelia and Lilian were seated at the best table in the tearoom, while Charles Bellingham and Annabelle Craven had colonized the table next to theirs. All four of them greeted me warmly when I entered the tearoom and took the seat Amelia and Lilian had saved for me.

I was given a cooler reception by Opal Taylor, Millicent Scroggins, and Selena Buxton. Though they were sipping cups of tea at a table some distance away from the front window, I could feel their gimlet gazes as soon as I stepped through the door. I assumed they'd either witnessed or heard about my gaining access to Pussywillows and were none too pleased with me for avoiding the ignominious fate that had befallen them.

"Where's our little princess?" Henry Cook asked, arriving at our table to take my order. "Is it daddy-daughter day again?"

"No," I said. "It's granddad-granddaughter day."

"Bess is at Fairworth?" said Amelia, smiling. "William will be pleased. He was saying just last night that he wished he could spend more time with his darling girl."

"His wish is my command," I said. "I'm not allowed to pick her up until dinnertime." I ordered a buttered crumpet and a pot of breakfast tea, then turned to Charles. "Where's Grant? Has he resigned from Windle Watch?"

"Certainly not," said Charles. "He's in the midst of restoring an eighteenth-century landscape painting he should have finished a week ago, but he'll keep an eye on Pussywillows from his workroom." He exchanged a meaningful look with Lilian. "Not that he'll see much."

"Why not?" I asked. "Has Mr. Windle gone for another riverside stroll?"

"Mr. Windle went for a drive this time," said Lilian. "I was on my way to the tearoom when he drove past me. I don't know where he was going, of course, but he was driving toward Upper Deeping."

Henry had just finished placing my tea and my buttery crumpet on the table when Elspeth Binney and Homer arrived at the tearoom. Elspeth surveyed the three Handmaidens haughtily, then accepted Charles's invitation to sit with him and Mrs. Craven. Homer licked Mrs. Craven's proffered hand, then assumed his customary position at Elspeth's feet.

"They're always going on about how unfriendly Mr. Windle is," Elspeth said in such a confidential murmur that I could hardly hear her. "I'm tired of their grumbling."

"I would be, too," Charles said supportively. He nodded at the plateful of fruit scones he was sharing with Mrs. Craven. "Have a scone, my dear."

"Thank you, Charles." Elspeth helped herself to a scone, asked Henry to bring her a pot of Earl Grey, and informed us that she'd risen early to make another special treat for our new neighbor. "It's called a fidgety pie. I don't know why it has such a silly name, but it originated in Derbyshire, so I thought Mr. Windle would enjoy it."

"What's in a fidgety pie?" Charles asked. "Jumping beans?"

"Very droll," Elspeth said dryly. "The principal ingredients of a fidgety pie are potatoes, onions, apples, sultanas, and ham. It should reheat beautifully, but there was no point in bringing it to Pussywillows this morning, not after I saw Mr. Windle drive away. Do we know where he's gone?" Her gaze flitted from face to face until it came to rest on mine. "Did he, perhaps, inform *you* of his itinerary, Lori?"

Every head in the tearoom, including Henry's, turned in my direction. I had a feeling that Sally had given her husband strict instructions to gather intelligence on my successful sortie, not that he would have needed her instructions. Henry did not share Mr. Barlow's disdain for gossip.

"No, Elspeth," I stated firmly, "Mr. Windle didn't say a word to me about his plans."

"What a pity," said Elspeth. "Still, it was very nice of him to ask you in."

"He didn't ask me in," I said. "My marauding daughter stormed the castle before I could stop her."

"Have you considered renting a fidgety toddler?" Charles asked Elspeth.

She gave him a withering look and he subsided.

"I think we can all agree that Bess is irresistible," said Lilian, "in every sense of the word."

Henry returned with Elspeth's tea and a bowl of water for Homer, then stood behind the counter and pretended to be busy while he eavesdropped on my report.

"Mr. Windle couldn't have been kinder to us," I said, and I told them about the empty boxes, the sippy cup, and the tea. "He's reading the book Tilly gave him, he's propped your painting on his mantel, Amelia, and he's thrown your quilt across the back of his couch, Annabelle. As for you, Elspeth," I said, hoping to make her day, "he described your Bakewell tarts as the perfect end to an imperfect meal." I lowered my voice as I explained, "He managed to burn Opal's casserole."

To her credit, Elspeth glanced sympathetically at Opal while making a valiant effort to conceal her delight. Homer gave a soft woof and wagged his stubby tail, as if he were applauding her.

"I should have warned him that the oven runs hot," said Amelia. "I burned two loaves of brown bread before I got the hang of it."

"Did he quiz you about landmarks?" Lilian asked.

"He did," I said, "but I didn't win a prize for Pouter's Hill. I can, however, confirm that he's a retired professor, though I'm afraid his specialist subject is industrial history rather than poetry."

"Not what Grant had in mind," Charles said. "Ah, well. Can't win 'em all."

"I'm afraid he's not a churchgoer," I said to Lilian.

"I hope you made it clear to him that our church is open to people of all faiths and none," she said.

"I told him about Miranda's role in the Nativity play," I said. "How much clearer could I be?"

"It sounds as though you had a pleasant chat with Mr. Windle," Mrs. Craven said impatiently, "and I'm very pleased for you, but I was rather hoping that you'd asked him the question we've been asking one another since Monday. Does he or does he not own a loom?"

"He does," I proclaimed triumphantly.

"I knew it!" said Amelia.

"Bravo, Lori," said Lilian.

"Well done," said Mrs. Craven.

Homer raised his head and barked.

"The pup's proud of you, too, Lori," Henry called from behind the till.

"High praise," I said, laughing.

"Did you sneak into Mr. Windle's dining room while he was in the kitchen making tea?" Charles asked.

"I didn't have to," I said. "I chased after Bess when she invaded his dining room, and there it was, in all its glory. He rattled off a list of the loom's features, but the only thing I can remember is that it has an adjustable beater."

"A most useful feature," Mrs. Craven said approvingly.

"Most useful," Amelia agreed. "With an adjustable beater, he can use reeds of varying heights and widths."

"He has lots of yarns, too," I said, clinging doggedly to a language I understood, "in lots of different colors."

"Did Mr. Windle demonstrate the loom for you?" Elspeth asked.

"He was going to," I said, "but we were interrupted."

"By Tommy," said Amelia, nodding. "We saw him banging on Mr. Windle's door."

"He seemed to be terribly upset," said Lilian.

"Rumor has it," said Charles, "that Bree Pym vanished without a trace yesterday morning."

"Is that why you left Finch in such a hurry?" Amelia asked. "Were you and Tommy worried about Bree?"

"We were," I admitted, "but we didn't have to be. It was a colossal misunderstanding. Bree explained it all to me last night, after she got back."

"Back?" said Charles. "Back from where? Speak, Lori! Everyone in Finch is dying to know where Bree went."

I'd given careful thought to how much I would reveal about Bree's trip to Derbyshire, and I'd decided that I would reveal nothing. Bree could tell the world about Mr. Windle if she chose, or Mr. Windle could tell the world about himself, but in this particular instance, I was squarely in Mr. Barlow's camp. Some subjects were too personal—and some, too heartbreaking—to be turned into gossip fodder.

"You can ask Bree," I said. "My lips are sealed."

"There's a first time for everything, I suppose," said Charles. "But surely you could open them long enough to give us a tiny hint. We'd be grateful for the merest scrap."

"Stop wheedling, Charles," Mrs. Craven scolded. "It's unbecoming."

"I do not wheedle," Charles protested indignantly.

The tearoom erupted in laughter.

"I rest my case," said Mrs. Craven.

"I can tell you one thing about Bree's trip, Charles," said Lilian, peering through the window. "It seems to have cheered her up."

I followed her gaze and saw Bree, Tommy, Mr. Barlow, and Tilly walking across the green toward the tearoom. Tommy had his arm around Bree, and Mr. Barlow was holding Tilly's hand with his undamaged one.

"Her trip seems to have cheered all of them up," Amelia observed. "Tilly and Mr. Barlow can't stop smiling at each other."

"Tommy doesn't appear to be upset anymore," said Lilian.

"Quite the opposite," said Elspeth. "He looks like a man who's found his heart's desire."

"Beautifully put," said Charles. "Accurate, as well."

Bree's solo trip to Derbyshire hadn't healed the breaches her secrets had caused in the family she loved best, I thought. She'd had to take her loved ones with her on a journey to New Zealand to make them understand how much they meant to her, and she'd done so without ever leaving Mr. Barlow's house.

As if sensing that a significant event was about to take place on the premises, Henry darted into the kitchen to fetch Sally. Their return coincided with the quartet's arrival. When Bree came through the door, the entire tearoom fell silent, and it remained in a state of suspended animation until, with Tommy, Mr. Barlow, and Tilly gathered around her, Bree said, "Boo!"

I jumped, Homer barked, and a few teaspoons clattered to the floor.

"Now that I have your attention," said Bree with a mischievous grin, "I'd like to announce that Tommy and I are engaged again." She held out her left hand and waggled her fingers to show that the ring Tommy had given her—twice—was back where it belonged.

"We'd like to announce our wedding date as well," said Tommy, "but we'll have to speak with the vicar about it first."

"Pick a date, any date," Lilian said instantly. "I promise you that Teddy will give it his blessing."

"I'll need time to make the cake," Sally cautioned.

"How about one month from tomorrow?" Tommy asked.

"Short notice," said Sally, rubbing her chin. "I usually need a minimum of three months to make a proper wedding cake—they have to age, you know—but I'll manage."

"You always do," Henry said, gazing admiringly at his wife.

"A June wedding," Elspeth said, sighing blissfully. "It's like something out of one of your novels, Sally!"

"It's better," said Sally, linking arms with Henry.

"I'll supply the flowers," said Amelia.

"I'll provide the flower girl," I said, "if you don't mind her running amok on the way to the altar."

"We don't mind what happens during the ceremony"—Bree tilted her head back to gaze into Tommy's eyes—"as long as we're husband and wife by the end of it."

I expected him to bend her backward with a kiss that would be talked about for years, but the gentle kiss he gave her, and the tender way he held her afterward, would live in my memory forever.

# *Twenty-Two*

"Then Mr. Barlow asked if there was any chance of getting a cup of tea," I said, "and the spell was broken."

*Finding out that you didn't know someone you thought you knew quite well is thirsty work.*

The study was still and silent, undisturbed by the crackle of a fire because I'd been too tired to build one. Bill and the children were in bed and asleep, but I'd dragged myself into the study to give Aunt Dimity a somewhat condensed account of everything that had happened since I'd received Bree's text. Though I was bursting to tell her every last detail, I couldn't stay up past midnight twice in a row without suffering serious consequences.

"Everyone rushed over to Bree and Tommy to congratulate them," I said, "and Sally sent Henry to the pub to grab a few bottles of champagne to go with her chocolate-covered strawberries. The news spread like wildfire, though, and people kept turning up, so she brought out trays of tea cakes. When the pub ran out of champagne, Dick Peacock made an emergency run to Upper Deeping to fetch more. It was the best reengagement party Finch has ever seen."

*Unless I'm misremembering, it's the only reengagement party Finch has ever seen.*

"Mr. Windle missed it," I said. "I don't know when he got back from wherever he was, but he didn't get back in time to behold the results of his handiwork."

*He'll be pleased to know that his wise advice led to such a satisfactory outcome, no matter when he hears about it. I wonder if he'll be equally pleased when he learns of Bree's fact-finding mission. And, yes, Lori, for the umpteenth time, I freely admit that you were right and I was wrong. I should have had more faith in Bree's good intentions.*

"I can only hope that Mr. Windle realizes how good Bree's intentions were," I said. "I'm sure his daughter will speak up for her. I think Alice was relieved to know that someone in Finch cared enough about her father to seek her out."

*I'm glad that Alice is staying in touch with Mr. Windle. He may need her support if he goes ahead with the mill project.*

"I'll support him," I said. "So will Bree."

*Will she? Bree's charmed by the mill's marvelous mechanisms, but I'm not convinced that she'll feel the same way about it if she learns of its human costs.*

"Maybe Mr. Windle won't dig deep enough to discover its human costs," I said, yawning. "Or maybe he'll publish his findings in an obscure academic journal." I nestled my head against the back of the tall armchair. "They don't usually carry advertisements for sales in Upper Deeping, so I doubt that they'll be widely circulated in Finch."

*It's time you were in bed, Lori. If you fall asleep in the chair, you'll have a stiff neck in the morning.*

"I believe I will head upstairs," I said, "but I couldn't have gone to sleep without telling you about Bree's adventures—in Derbyshire *and* at home."

*It's been a remarkable day, with an exceptionally happy ending. I'm rather hoping for your sake that tomorrow will be a bit boring.*

I smiled drowsily. "So am I, Dimity, but I'm not counting on it. Finch may be a backwater, but it's seldom boring."

*A truer word was never spoken, my dear. Sleep well.*

When Aunt Dimity's handwriting had faded from the page, I pried myself out of the chair, returned the blue journal to its shelf, touched a finger to Reginald's snout, and turned out the lights. I managed to crawl into bed before the ormolu clock chimed midnight, and though I had a strange dream about a pair of ghostly figures getting married in the copse, I did not have a stiff neck in the morning.

I was pleasantly surprised when Friday began on a boring note.

I was in the kitchen eating breakfast with my family when Lilian called to inform me that she'd suspended Windle Watch because its subject had driven past the vicarage shortly after she and the vicar had finished their own breakfast.

"I'll let you know if Mr. Windle returns to Pussywillows before the tearoom closes," she said. "Enjoy your day off!"

I needed no encouragement to enjoy my day off. I still believed that it would do more good than harm to keep an eye on Mr. Windle, but I found it comforting to return to a familiar routine. While Will and Rob were at school, Bess and I did laundry, baked chocolate chip cookies, played a rudimentary form of cricket in the meadow behind the cottage, watched a ladybug cross a vast expanse of Queen Anne's lace, drew highly abstract duck portraits, and took simultaneous naps.

My blessedly boring day became more interesting after dinner, when Lilian called again.

"I've been chatting with Mr. Windle," she informed me.

"You didn't interrupt his dinner, did you?" I asked.

"I didn't go to Pussywillows," she said. "Mr. Windle came to the vicarage."

"Good heavens!" I exclaimed. "What an honor. You may have to mount a plaque on the vicarage, singling it out as the first private home in Finch to be visited by Crispin Windle. It's not quite as eye-catching as 'The Queen Slept Here,' but it's not bad."

"I was as shocked as you are," Lilian admitted, "but I tried not to show it."

"My jaw would have dropped to the ground," I said. "What brought him to your doorstep?"

"He wanted to know if he could give a talk in the old schoolhouse tomorrow," she explained. "Apparently, Bree told him that the schoolhouse had become our village hall and that I oversaw the events schedule."

A sense of foreboding crept over me.

"There must be something scheduled for tomorrow," I said, staring bleakly at the blank square on my wall calendar.

"There's nothing," she replied. "Miranda Morrow's broom-making class isn't until next weekend."

"What will Mr. Windle talk about?" I asked, as though I didn't know the answer.

"The name of his talk is 'Finch's Hidden History,'" Lilian said. "It's a wonderful title, isn't it? I tried to coax a few details out of him, but he said he'd prefer to keep them to himself. It's perfectly understandable. No speaker worth his salt wants to spoil a presentation by giving away too much of it beforehand. He's chosen a popular topic, though. It should be a real crowd-pleaser."

"It should be," I said, wondering if it would be. "When will his presentation begin?"

"One o'clock," she said. "Can I count on you to arrive early? With a lame thumb, Mr. Barlow may need help setting up the chairs, and I won't be able to help him because I'll be setting out the refreshments."

"You can count on me, Lilian," I assured her.

"Thank you," she said. "It's all very last-minute, but I think I can guarantee that most of the seats will be filled. I intend to ring every member of the parish."

"Good luck," I said. "I'll see you tomorrow."

After Lilian rang off, the worries I'd pushed to the back of my mind ran forward, waving their hands. While it was heartening to know that Mr. Windle felt strong enough to visit her and to make a very public appearance before the rest of his new neighbors, it was distressing to think that he might be setting himself up for a setback. If he unveiled a shameful chapter in the village's hidden past, he stood a good chance of becoming the least popular man in Finch.

By Saturday morning I was in such a state that I would have driven to Pussywillows and pleaded with Mr. Windle to reconsider his presentation if Lilian hadn't called me after breakfast to inform me that he'd taken off again for parts unknown. With no way to contact him, I could do nothing but feel uneasy about the storm clouds that might be gathering on his horizon.

I had no doubt that the talk would draw a sizable audience, not least because Mr. Windle's failure to attend the Sunday-morning service at St. George's had deprived many of my neighbors of the chance to see him up close. To be on the safe side, therefore, my family and I arrived at the schoolhouse a full hour before the presentation was due to begin.

After heaving the lectern onto the dais at the front of the schoolroom, Bill took Bess to the humpbacked bridge to visit the pretty ducks, promising that they'd return in plenty of time to hear the vicar's opening remarks and that they'd leave promptly if Bess threatened to punctuate those remarks with quacks.

My ghoulish sons questioned Mr. Barlow minutely about his injured thumb, but when they asked him to unwrap it so they could get a good look at the damage, he told them he hadn't smashed it for their entertainment and put them to work setting up chairs.

Lilian, Tilly, and I took charge of the tea table. While Lilian dealt with the tea urn, Tilly and I laid out neat rows of cups and saucers, teaspoons, creamers, sugar bowls, and napkins on the white tablecloth Lilian had draped across the table. Tilly informed us that Bree and Tommy were so busy making up for lost time that they might or might not show up for the talk. Neither Lilian nor I inquired as to how they were making up for lost time, but her smile told me that she, too, was remembering what it was like to be young and in love.

We'd just finished adding a selection of Sally Cook's cookies to the tea table when Charles Bellingham and Grant Tavistock arrived, Grant in his white linen suit and Charles in a double-breasted blue blazer that made him look as if he'd sailed to Finch on his yacht. Each was carrying an easel that was at least six feet tall.

"Mr. Windle dropped by our cottage last night," Grant informed us, resting his easel on the floor.

"I nearly fainted when I answered the door," said Charles. "It was like answering the door to a yeti." He frowned. "I don't mean to imply that Mr. Windle resembles a yeti. I was alluding to the rarity of—"

"We understand," Lilian interrupted. "You were surprised when Mr. Windle came to your door."

"Evidently, Bree described our business to him," said Grant. "He assumed that a pair of art appraisal and restoration experts would have a few easels lying about, and he asked if he might borrow two of the larger ones."

"He must be using visual aids," said Charles.

"Thank you, Charles," Lilian said dryly. "I think we'd worked that one out for ourselves." As the two men arranged the easels on either side of the lectern, she continued, "I'm relieved that Mr. Windle's visual aids don't require an electrical hookup. I still have nightmares about the slide show Elspeth's niece presented last year."

"She didn't lose many slides in the fire," I said consolingly, "and she had copies of them at home."

Charles stepped down from the dais and laid claim to two front-row seats on the center aisle. Since he was as tall as the easels and quite a bit broader, it wasn't the most considerate choice he could have made and Grant vetoed it, directing Charles to sit at the far end of the row, where he'd pose less of a hindrance to those seated behind him.

If Mr. Windle had charged a fee, he would have spoken to a sellout crowd. Mrs. Craven, Miranda Morrow, Sally Cook, Jasper Taxman, Christine Peacock, George Wetherhead, and the Hobsons streamed into the schoolhouse early, as did the Handmaidens— all four of them, plus Homer.

Opal, Millicent, and Selena had evidently agreed to keep their complaints about Mr. Windle to themselves because Elspeth seemed quite content to sit with them. Homer trotted up and down the center aisle, greeting his many fans, then curled up for a nap beneath Elspeth's chair.

Bill and I elected to sit in the back row with our brood, in part because it would allow him to make a speedy exit if Bess began to quack, but also because it would allow me to watch my neighbors.

Having occupied the back row in church and in committee meetings for many years, I'd become adept at reading head movements that indicated attentiveness or drowsiness—a not-uncommon sight during the vicar's sermons—or shocked disapproval. I hoped for attentiveness and would settle for drowsiness, but I feared that I might detect shocked disapproval.

Amelia and Willis, Sr., were among the last to arrive. As soon as they'd seated themselves in the places we'd saved for them, Bess wriggled out of her father's lap and toddled over to chat with her grandfather.

As if sensing that his neighbors had not come to the schoolroom to hear a conversation between him and his granddaughter, Willis, Sr., announced that he and Bess were going to the churchyard to visit Dennis the marble shepherd. Amelia put her purse on his chair to reserve it in case he and Bess came back before the talk was over.

By half past noon, every seat except Willis, Sr.'s was filled. At ten minutes to one, our speaker arrived.

# *Twenty-Three*

Mr. Windle was wearing a charcoal-gray suit, a white shirt, a black tie, and a pair of black wingtip shoes. Though the suit fit him as poorly as everything else in his wardrobe, I interpreted his semiformal attire as a sign of respect for his audience.

He entered the schoolroom awkwardly, clasping a sheaf of papers in one hand while the other steadied the stack of large poster boards clamped beneath his arm.

"The visual aids," I murmured to Bill.

"No plugs," he murmured back. "We're safe."

The friendly chatter that had filled the schoolroom before Mr. Windle's arrival subsided gradually as he walked up the center aisle to confer with the vicar, who stood waiting for him on the dais. They spoke, then the vicar stepped aside while Mr. Windle deposited the sheaf of papers on the lectern and propped what appeared to be an equal number of poster boards on each easel. The outermost boards were disappointingly blank. Our speaker was clearly reluctant to spoil his presentation by giving anything away beforehand.

Mr. Windle and the vicar swapped places and the vicar began his opening remarks. His request that we turn off our cell phones triggered the usual flurry of activity, and he waited for the commotion to die down before he proceeded.

"It is my very great pleasure to introduce today's speaker, Mr. Crispin Windle," he said. "Before his retirement, Mr. Windle was a highly respected professor of modern history at the University of

Derby. Mr. Windle has implored me to forgo the privilege of citing his many academic honors and achievements, and I shall, of course, abide by his wishes. I will say only that we are indeed fortunate to have such a distinguished scholar address us on a topic of immense interest to us all. Ladies and gentlemen, I give you Mr. Crispin Windle on Finch's hidden history."

The vicar led the applause as Mr. Windle took his place behind the lectern. While the vicar seated himself next to Lilian in the front row, Mr. Windle peered out over the audience.

"I wonder if I might enlist a pair of volunteers?" he asked. Before Elspeth could raise her hand, he pointed at Will and Rob. "Perhaps the two young men in the back row would be good enough to assist me?"

Since Will and Rob were accustomed to performing before much larger crowds at gymkhanas, they didn't suffer from stage fright. They jumped to their feet and strode to the dais without a moment's hesitation. After a quiet word from Mr. Windle, the boys took up their positions beside their respective easels and awaited his cues. Though I felt a mother's pride in my sons, I couldn't help but think that Mr. Windle had chosen them simply because they reminded him of his grandsons.

Mr. Windle took a nervous breath and gripped the lectern tightly, but when he began to speak, he seemed to relax, as if he were in his element. Though he was not reciting poetry, his clear and resonant voice would, I thought, please Grant.

"Thank you, Mr. Bunting. I hope you haven't raised expectations too high with your generous introduction." He swept an arm through the air to indicate the schoolhouse. "It's been some time since I last spoke in an academic setting. I might be a bit rusty."

Indulgent chuckles rippled through the room.

"However faulty my delivery," he continued, "I hope you'll accept my presentation as a small repayment of the debt of gratitude I owe you for the many kindnesses you've shown me since I came to Finch one short week ago." His gaze traveled around the room, coming to rest in turn on Lilian, the vicar, Amelia, Tilly, Mrs. Craven, Charles, Grant, Opal, Millicent, Selena, Elspeth, and me. "As a newcomer, I expected to be held at arm's length, but you've embraced me as you would a long-lost friend. The warmth of your welcome has meant a great deal to me, and I thank you most sincerely for it."

Three of the Handmaidens shifted uncomfortably in their seats while the rest of us smiled modestly.

"I would not presume to lecture you on a subject I'd studied for no more than a week," he said, a change of tone indicating that he'd commenced his presentation. "Finch first captured my attention several months ago, when I came across a mystery that intrigued me: A landmark near the village that should have been preserved had instead all but disappeared.

"How could a sturdy structure that had stood for more than a century suddenly vanish, leaving scarcely a trace behind? Why had a building that should have been familiar to every householder in the village been forgotten? To answer those questions, we must uncover a hidden chapter of Finch's history.

"Before we delve into that history," he added as an aside, "please note that the illustrations I created to accompany my talk are approximations based on years of research and observation, as no contemporary illustrations of the buildings to which I will allude exist."

He nodded at Will, who removed the blank board on his easel to reveal a beautifully rendered pen-and-ink drawing of a tidy three-story stone building sitting at the edge of a wheat field, its waterwheel half submerged in a rustic wooden plume beside a river.

"In 1708, Elijah Bennett built a water-powered grist mill on the west bank of Little Deeping River," said Mr. Windle. "For over a hundred years, the Bennett family ground local grains into flour used by villagers and townspeople alike to make their daily bread. In 1821, however, the Bennett mill underwent a transformation."

He nodded at Rob, who revealed a drawing of the same building, expanded by at least a third, with an elaborate system of sluice gates and drainage channels leading to it from a large millpond that had intruded on the wheat field. The contrast between the original building and its successor was striking.

"In 1821," Mr. Windle continued, "Elijah Bennett's descendants sold the grist mill to Linus Johnson, a businessman from Upper Deeping. He converted it into a textile mill for the carding, spinning, and weaving of wool. Linus Johnson had big dreams, but he was both incompetent and greedy. Having overspent his budget on a slipshod conversion, he equipped the mill with outdated machinery and skimped on maintenance."

He nodded at Will, who revealed a cutaway drawing showing the interior of a small, water-powered textile mill. It was like looking into the workings of a very complicated clock. I could scarcely imagine the noise, the dust, and the heat that had been generated by the bewildering array of belts and shafts, cogs and rods, and tightly packed rows of machines.

"A mill was a dangerous place to work even when it was well run," said Mr. Windle. "When it was badly run, it could be, and often was, deadly. In 1823, an appalling incident took place in Johnson's mill. A shaft in a power loom snapped and four workers were killed."

At a nod from Mr. Windle, Rob slid the drawing of the mill's exterior from his easel to reveal a portrait, of sorts. It depicted a dark-haired boy standing before an industrialized metal version of Mr. Windle's wooden loom. The sleeves on the boy's oversized white shirt had been rolled up to free his hands, and his ragged trousers were held up by suspenders. He was barefoot and so tiny he had to perch on a metal plate at the bottom of the loom in order to pursue his assigned task.

My heart clenched as I studied the drawing. The boy was younger and much smaller than my sons. I wondered fleetingly if Mr. Windle had chosen them to act as his assistants because he'd known that others would make the same comparison. If so, I thought, Will and Rob were his most effective visual aids. While they radiated robust health and the confidence of youth, the boy's dull eyes were fixed on the machine, as if he could imagine no other life.

Mr. Windle waited for his listeners to absorb the drawing's details, then said, "The workers who lost their lives on that tragic day were children. Linus Johnson had purchased them from an orphanage in Upper Deeping."

"Purchased them?" Mr. Barlow exclaimed from the third row. "How could he buy children?"

Unfazed by the outburst, Mr. Windle explained, "He paid a small fee to the orphanage's governor and took the children on as apprentices."

"If they were apprentices, Mr. Johnson would have had to feed, clothe, and house them, wouldn't he?" asked Lilian.

"He fed them bread and milk," Mr. Windle answered, "he provided them with cast-off clothing once a year, and he allowed them to sleep on pallets in a corner of the mill. In exchange, he trained them in a trade."

"Trained them in a trade," Mr. Barlow muttered disgustedly. "It's child abuse, is what it is."

"Linus Johnson wasn't exceptional," Mr. Windle pointed out. "Well into the nineteenth century, children formed a significant part of Great Britain's labor force. They were, in many ways, ideal employees. They were cheap, easy to control, and small enough to squeeze into tight spaces to tend to machinery. It wasn't unusual for children as young as five to work twelve-hour days, six days a week, for the paltry sum of four shillings per week. Orphans were particularly useful, as they had no one to speak up on their behalf, or to protect them from a cruel master."

"It's like something out of Dickens," said the vicar, sounding queasy.

"Poverty forced Charles Dickens to work in a factory when he was twelve years old," said Mr. Windle. "The experience fueled his fiction and filled him with a crusader's zeal to bring about the end of child labor in Great Britain."

"I'm aware of Mr. Dickens's difficult childhood," said the vicar, "but I had no idea that such Dickensian horrors had played out so close to home."

"We tend to associate such horrors with large cities," said Mr. Windle, "but they occurred in rural mills as well."

"What about the law?" Mr. Barlow demanded. "Why wasn't this Johnson bloke arrested after the children died?"

"There were no health and safety laws in those days," said Mr. Windle, "and there were no workers' rights. If a mill worker lost her hand while on the job, she lost her job. In fact, police were often called upon by mill owners to round up runaway apprentices and return them to their masters."

"Johnson's so-called apprentices didn't run away," Mr. Barlow persisted. "They *died*."

"Industrial accidents were regarded as the cost of doing business," said Mr. Windle. "Linus Johnson was taken to court after the children died, but not because his negligence had caused their deaths. An investor sued him for financial malfeasance and won a large settlement. To avoid bankruptcy, Johnson had to close the mill and sell its accoutrements, including the waterwheel."

"I reckon he got away with murder," Mr. Barlow said bitterly.

"I believe your predecessors came to the same conclusion," said Mr. Windle. "I believe that they felt tainted by the tragedy, or ashamed of themselves for not paying closer attention to conditions at the mill." He paused, then asked again, "How could a sturdy building that had stood for more than a century suddenly vanish, leaving scarcely a trace behind? I suspect that the answer to my question can be found here and there in the village and, quite possibly, on some local farms."

Opal Taylor looked around the schoolroom, as if she expected to see a waterwheel she hadn't previously noticed.

"I have not yet had time to verify my theory, but I will let you judge its soundness for yourselves." Mr. Windle folded his hands on the podium. "The mill had survived floods, storms, and a jury-rigged expansion, but it could not survive the villagers' guilt and anger. To rid themselves of a place they detested, they pulled it down. They may have thrown some of the material into the river, but I believe they salvaged and reused most of it. It would not surprise me to discover that a low wall on a hillside or a shed in a back garden contained dressed stone taken from the mill."

Grant and Charles looked off into the distance, as if they were trying to envision their garden shed.

"I can state unequivocally," said Mr. Windle, "that the farmer who owned the field adjacent to Linus Johnson's property bought the mill site. He lodged no complaints about the mill's disappearance. He never cultivated the land, nor did he sell it to another entrepreneur. He allowed it to be reclaimed by nature."

He nodded at Will, who pulled aside the drawing of the mill's interior to reveal a haunting landscape of gnarled trees, creeping vines, and dark, dank shrubs.

"With the passage of time," said Mr. Windle, "the site of Linus Johnson's mill became the somewhat sinister stand of trees known as the copse."

It was a lot for my neighbors to take in. They'd hoped to hear a story that would give them bragging rights in neighboring villages—evidence of a recently discovered Roman villa, perhaps, or proof that Charles II had escaped his enemies by hiding in the room above the pub. Instead, they'd heard a wretched tale of child abuse, neglect, and exploitation that had taken place in their own backyard. Their discomfort was palpable.

Some bowed their heads, others stared at the drawing of the boy, and still others turned their faces away, as if they couldn't bear to look at it. The cheerful anticipation with which they'd greeted Mr. Windle had been replaced by somber reflection tinged with revulsion and a slight hint of resentment. Aunt Dimity had been right to worry about their reaction to Mr. Windle's talk, I told myself. He'd presented them with a chapter of their history they did not wish to read.

"History is hidden for many reasons," said Mr. Windle. "I believe that the story I've uncovered faded from local memory because the villagers took no pride in it. You may believe that such things are best forgotten, but are they? By forgetting Linus Johnson's mill are we not doing a disservice to the children who died there? Why should he have a name while they have none?"

"He shouldn't," said Mr. Barlow, "but that's how it is. Big-shot businessmen get their names in the papers. Kids no one cares about, don't."

"Sometimes they do," said Mr. Windle. "I've spent the past couple of days searching the archives of the *Upper Deeping Dispatch*, but it wasn't until this morning that I discovered a brief article—no more than a filler—about the accident at the mill. In it, the victims were named." He consulted his notes, then raised his head and spoke in ringing tones. "Timothy Welland, aged nine; Sarah Smith, aged seven; Agnes Mayhew, aged eleven; and Richard Shard, aged ten. They were buried—"

"I know where they were buried," Lilian interrupted. She turned in her chair to look at Mr. Barlow.

"Dear Lord," he said faintly. "The lambs."

# *Twenty-Four*

"The lambs?" said Mr. Windle.

"It's what Mrs. Bunting and I call the four children buried at the back of the churchyard," Mr. Barlow explained. As our church sexton, it was his responsibility to keep the churchyard tidy and, when necessary, to dig graves. He was intimately familiar with every headstone, memorial, and tomb.

"The headstones are quite small," said Lilian, whose knowledge of the churchyard was second only to Mr. Barlow's. "Each is surmounted by a stone carving of a lamb. In a churchyard, lambs tend to signify children."

Mr. Windle leaned forward on the lectern, but he didn't interrupt the dialogue. He listened to it intently, as did everyone else in the schoolroom.

"The headstones are so weathered we had to do rubbings to read them," said Mr. Barlow. "But the rubbings didn't tell us much. No birth dates and just the one death date, 13 July 1823, repeated four times."

"And four names," said Lilian. "Timothy Welland, Sarah Smith, Agnes Mayhew, and Richard Shard."

The villagers seemed to exhale simultaneously in an extended "Oh!" of comprehension.

"The mill children were right there under our noses all this time," marveled Mr. Barlow, "and we never knew it."

"By law," Mr. Windle said quietly, "they would have been buried in the churchyard closest to their place of death."

"Yes, I know," said Lilian, "but we didn't know where they'd died, or how they'd died, or why they'd been buried beside one another. The burial record was no more forthcoming than the headstones. Since no one in the village shared their surnames, I assumed that they were the children of itinerant farm laborers."

"We thought maybe they'd been carried off by measles or influenza or some such thing," said Mr. Barlow. "Outbreaks happened in Finch in the bad old days, same as everywhere else, and they usually hit the little ones and the old folk worst."

"If they'd died of a contagious disease," said Lilian, "they would have been buried quickly, to prevent the disease from spreading. Their families would have attended the burial service, but at some point they would have moved on to another agricultural job in another region."

"I've always felt a bit sorry for the lambs," said Mr. Barlow, "lying there all on their own, with no grandmas or granddads or uncles or aunties around them." He sighed. "It's worse somehow, knowing they were orphans. They'd've been buried by strangers, with no one to grieve for them."

"But someone did grieve for them," said Mr. Windle. "They weren't laid to rest in paupers' graves. They were given decent burials with embellished headstones. The villagers may not have been able to ensure that young workers were treated humanely at the mill, but they could see to it that Sarah, Agnes, Timothy, and Richard were buried with the same care and compassion they would have shown their own children."

"A small mercy," Lilian acknowledged, "but a mercy nonetheless. I, for one, am grateful to know the truth. The lambs were imaginary figures based on guesswork and supposition. I feel even more sympathy for them, now that I know who they really were. I shall amend the burial record to reflect the information you've shared with us today, Mr. Windle."

"I've not yet consulted the coroner's report or examined the orphanage's records," he said. "If you look into them, you may be able to learn even more about the children."

"I shall look into them," Lilian said firmly. "I'll see to it that the mill children are not forgotten again in Finch."

Though Mr. Windle spoke in response to Lilian's comment, he addressed the room at large.

"It may surprise you to learn that, in the wider world, the mill children were never quite forgotten," he said. "I found their names listed, along with many others, in a report compiled by a parliamentary commission. The report led to major reforms in child labor laws and eventually to the abolition of child labor in Great Britain."

He nodded at Rob, who revealed the final pen-and-ink drawing. In it, four young children—two boys and two girls—stood on either side of a telescope, gazing wide-eyed at the stars.

"I'd like to think," said Mr. Windle, "that the four orphans who were laid to rest in the churchyard with such tender loving care would be proud to know that their tragic deaths led to better lives for generations of children to come."

There was a moment of silence as Mr. Windle gathered his papers, shook hands with Will and Rob, and collected his poster boards. The clapping began a bit patchily, led at first by the Windle Watchers and Mr. Barlow, but it quickly built to a crescendo as the entire audience gave Mr. Windle a standing ovation before descending on the tea table.

Lilian commandeered Mr. Windle's poster boards and his papers, placed them atop the upright piano, and drew him toward the tea table, where his hand was shaken many, many times. I doubted that the villagers would brag about the textile mill while chatting with friends in neighboring villages, but they would, perhaps, visit four graves in the churchyard to pay their respects and to reflect on a poignant chapter in Finch's hitherto hidden history.

When Amelia turned her cell phone on, she found a message from Willis, Sr., informing her that he and Bess had repaired to Fairworth House. When Bill turned his phone on, he found a similar message, to which Willis, Sr., had appended a request to drive Amelia home when she was ready to leave the schoolhouse.

"If it's all the same to you, I'd rather walk," she said. "But not until we finish clearing up."

After the tea table had been politely pillaged, the crowd thinned rapidly. Having left their respective spouses to run their respective businesses single-handedly, Sally Cook, Christine Peacock, and Jasper Taxman were the first to depart. Grant and Charles reclaimed their easels and took Mrs. Craven home with them for a proper tea. Opal, Millicent, and Selena left for the shops in Upper Deeping, and Elspeth took Homer for a walk along the river. Elspeth didn't say outright that they would walk all the way to the copse, but I had my suspicions. She was as keenly interested in history as she was in a certain historian.

Since Miranda Morrow wouldn't need the lectern for her broom-making class, Bill moved it from the dais to the back room. Under Mr. Barlow's supervision, he, Will, and Rob began folding chairs and putting them away. Lilian, Amelia, Tilly, and I cleared the tea table and, with the vicar's help, did the washing up. When Tilly complained that she couldn't imagine where Bree and Tommy had gotten to, Lilian said innocently, "Can't you?" and I gave an unseemly snort of laughter.

Mr. Windle offered to help everyone with everything, but Lilian refused to allow it. She led him to a chair, provided him with a plate of lemon bars she'd stashed in the back room, poured him a fresh cup of tea, and told him that, as the guest of honor, it was incumbent upon him to relax.

When order had been restored to the schoolroom, Amelia asked Will and Rob to escort her to Fairworth House on foot; Tilly took Mr. Barlow home to change the dressing on his thumb; the vicar returned to the vicarage to revise his sermon; and Mr. Windle made a request Lilian couldn't refuse.

"I wonder if you would introduce me to the lambs?" he inquired. "I haven't explored the churchyard, so I don't know where the graves are located."

"I'll show you," she said. "I'll take you to them right now, if you feel up to it."

"I feel better than I have in quite some time," he said. Then he turned to Bill and me. "Would you care to join us?"

"Very much," I said.

"We can pay our respects to the children together," said Bill.

Lilian turned off the lights and led the way out of the schoolhouse. She didn't bother to lock the door behind us because the schoolhouse, unlike Bree's house, was under twenty-four-hour curtain-twitching surveillance.

We didn't bombard Mr. Windle with questions or act as his tour guides as we made our way to the church. I think we were tired of talking, but apart from that, it was a solemn occasion, and we all seemed content to allow it to unfold in silence. We passed through the lytch-gate and walked to the back of the churchyard on the neatly raked graveled path that encircled the church. When Lilian stepped off the path, we followed her across a stretch of clipped grass to four graves near the churchyard's rear wall.

The stone lambs on the headstones sat with their legs folded beneath them, as if they, too, were at rest. The honey-gold headstones had gone gray with age, but a colorful clump of pansies grew at the foot of each grave.

"Mr. Barlow planted the pansies," Lilian said. "He's always had a soft spot for the lambs, and he thought the bright colors were the sort of thing a child might like."

"They're perfect," said Mr. Windle. He looked out over the low stone wall and across the water meadows to the river. "I can't conceive of a more beautiful or a more peaceful resting place. It, too, was chosen with care. Thank you for showing it to me, Mrs. Bunting."

"Not at all," she said. "You're welcome to visit the children whenever you like, Mr. Windle. I may come back tonight"—she turned her face skyward—"and look up at the stars."

He nodded to show he'd caught the reference, then said he was ready to go. As we retraced our steps around the church, he fell back to walk beside Bill and me.

"This may not be the most appropriate time or place for gift giving," he said, "but when I was in Upper Deeping yesterday, I found a little something for Bess."

"My daughter would tell you that it's always the right time for gift giving," said Bill.

"I would have given it to her earlier," said Mr. Windle, "but I was afraid it would annoy some of my listeners."

He reached into his suit coat's inner pocket and produced a small stuffed animal. It was a duck, but it wasn't just any duck. To judge by its green head, its yellow beak, and the white ring around its neck, it was a mallard. It wasn't quite as abstract as Bess's drawings, but there was nothing fancy about it, no choking hazards or wings she could tear off. It was a simple, and simply adorable, little mallard.

"To commemorate our first meeting," he said, handing the duck to me. "When I heard Bess quacking on the bridge with you and Tommy, I was reminded of another little girl." He lowered his eyes, as if overcome by thoughts of the granddaughter he'd left behind in Derbyshire.

Barbarians have their uses, I thought. If Bess hadn't made such a ruckus after the moving-van vigil, Mr. Windle wouldn't have emerged from his house, Tommy and I wouldn't have seen his anguished tears, and Windle Watch wouldn't have come into existence. The gratitude he'd expressed at the beginning of his presentation suggested that we'd managed, in some small way, to ease the sorrow he felt at leaving his nearest and dearest behind in Derbyshire. And we owed it all to my duck-loving daughter.

"It's so sweet," I said, caressing the mallard's green head. "How could such a cute little ducky annoy anyone?"

"Ah, yes," said Mr. Windle, regaining his composure. "I forgot to mention that it has a hidden charm." He reached over and squeezed the duck, which emitted a series of remarkably authentic quacks.

"Bess will go out of her mind when she hears it quack," I said, laughing delightedly.

"She'll love it," said Bill with a chuckle. "Thank you very much, Mr. Windle."

"You're very welcome," he said, smiling.

A comfortable silence settled over us once more as we left the churchyard, but it didn't last long. We'd just said good-bye to Lilian at the vicarage when Bree came tearing up the lane, shouting excitedly. Tommy followed her at a more sedate pace, with a broad grin on his face.

"Mr. Windle," Bree said breathlessly, skidding to a halt before us.

"Bree!" I exclaimed. "Where have you been? You missed Mr. Windle's talk."

Bree waved a hand dismissively. "He read it to Tommy and me this morning, after he got back from Upper Deeping."

"You've been at Pussywillows?" I said incredulously.

"Yes, yes, we're learning how to weave, but never mind that," she said impatiently. She peered beseechingly at Mr. Windle. "I've been looking for you everywhere! Come with me! Hurry! You won't believe it! You simply won't believe it!"

Bree seized his hand and would have dragged him after her if Tommy hadn't intervened.

"Take it easy, love," he said gently. "You'll break his wrist if you're not careful."

"Sorry," she said.

Bree dropped Mr. Windle's hand and began to prance backward in front of him, beckoning to him as if he were an infant on the verge of his first step. Tommy strode beside her with his arm out, ready to catch her if she stumbled, while the rest of us watched her, both amused and confused by her antics. We were almost to the tearoom when Mr. Windle looked past her and froze. The color drained from his face and he swayed so alarmingly that Bill put a hand under his arm to steady him.

Bree stopped prancing and got out of his way so she wouldn't obstruct his view of Pussywillows. A man, a woman, and three children stood before the cottage, between the front door and a parked SUV. The two boys were younger than Will and Rob, but the girl was about Bess's age. The woman was tall and fit, and her blond hair was shorter than Bree's.

"Dad!" cried the woman, grinning from ear to ear.

"Granddad!" bellowed the boys.

The toddler didn't say anything. She ran straight into Mr. Windle's widespread arms, and he scooped her up as if she weighed nothing. He buried his face in her dark hair and hugged her so tightly she squirmed.

"Down!" she commanded imperiously.

Laughing and crying at the same time, he obeyed, but the boys were there by then, and he hugged them instead. The man chased after the toddler, who was making a break for the green, and the woman flung her arms around the boys and Mr. Windle in a group hug that was so infectious it prompted Bill and me to wrap our arms around each other.

"It's Alice!" Bree told me, in case I hadn't guessed. "She and Fred left Stefan in charge of the shop and drove all the way down from Bakewell to spend the weekend with her father."

I had no idea who Stefan was, I only vaguely remembered that Fred was Alice's husband, and I didn't know any of the children's names, but I didn't need a scorecard to follow the game. I recognized a family reunion when I saw one, and this reunion was one of the most joyous I'd ever seen.

It may have been a trick of the late-afternoon sunlight, or wishful thinking on my part, but Pussywillows seemed to emit a golden glow that enveloped Mr. Windle and his family. Love came in many forms, I thought, and each one was touched by magic.

After the initial euphoria had eased, Mr. Windle introduced everyone to everyone else. Fred was indeed married to Alice, the boys were Crispin and Freddy, and the girl's name was Olivia, though she was called Ollie.

Tommy, Bree, Bill, and I helped them to unload the car, which took some time, as it was stuffed to the roof with sleeping bags, pillows, toys, and toddler paraphernalia as well as boxes of household items Alice assumed her father would need. When Mr. Windle invited us to join him and his loved ones in Pussywillows, however, we declined. Even Bree understood why we should leave them in peace, after Tommy explained it to her. She was still a tad overexcited.

"I love happy endings," she said as Mr. Windle closed his door.

"So do I, but this isn't an ending," I said, gazing fondly at the enchanted cottage. "It's a new beginning."

# *Epilogue*

Bree Pym and Tommy Prescott were married in St. George's Church on a cloudless summer day in late June. Bree wore a slinky, floor-length, matte white dress that displayed every tattoo of which I was aware. She would have nothing to do with a veil, but she colored the spiky tips of her lustrous brown hair with gold glitter, which produced a twinkling halo effect a veil would have spoiled.

Tommy gazed at her as if she were his angel as she walked up the aisle on Mr. Barlow's arm. To the disappointment of some, military regulations prevented Tommy from wearing his uniform, but most of us thought he looked even more dashing in the immaculate three-piece black suit Willis, Sr.'s tailor had fashioned for him.

Amelia filled the church with fragrant blooms from her garden, and Sally's three-tiered cake was a masterpiece, despite its truncated preparation time. Elspeth Binney's niece took the wedding photographs, while Elspeth played a selection of familiar and less familiar pieces on the organ. Bree had chosen the less familiar pieces, all of which were quite loud and quite percussive.

I kept Bess on the straight and narrow by positioning Homer beside the vicar, at the far end of the center aisle. The pup's bright eyes and wagging tail held her attention far better than any picture book could. Since Bess and her mallard—whom she'd dubbed Greg for reasons beyond my understanding—had become inseparable, she carried him in her basket of rose petals. The sound of quacking in the rear pew during regular church services never fails to annoy Peggy Taxman, but whenever I invite her to confiscate Greg, she backs down in a hurry. Not even the mighty Peggy Taxman is a match for a two-year-old.

Bree and Tommy went to Derbyshire for their honeymoon. According to Tilly, they elected to stay in a remote cottage on the Chatsworth estate "so they wouldn't disturb people with their loud music." When they weren't enjoying their music, Bree and Tommy took advantage of every outdoor adventure the Peak District had to offer. They hiked, they parasailed, they climbed cliffs, they wriggled through caves, they took several cycling tours with Bike Well Cycles, and they explored Chatsworth's marvelous gardens together.

Tommy moved into Bree's house when they returned from Derbyshire, but they still spend lots of time at Mr. Barlow's. Bree is as willing as ever to learn new skills from her mentor, and Tommy's proud to work beside his uncle. Thanks to Tilly's expert nursing, Mr. Barlow's thumb healed in record time, and though the story of his multiple proposals made the rounds via the grapevine, it was greeted with respect rather than ridicule. Persistence is a valued trait in Finch.

Tommy and Bree spend time with Mr. Windle, too. As it turned out, the black fabric I'd seen in Mr. Windle's loom hadn't been woven by him but by Bree. It took her about two weeks to finish her first project, a black scarf with a white fern that symbolized New Zealand. It was as if ridding herself of the secrets she'd carried with her for so long had freed her to acknowledge the country of her birth without flinching.

Bree never revealed what she'd learned about Mr. Windle's past to anyone other than Tommy and me, but the story came out gradually as the villagers got to know him. Since many of them were in his age bracket, they had no trouble understanding his reluctance to be a burden on his family.

His family still doesn't regard him as a burden, but they've stopped trying to persuade him to move back to Bakewell. Alice and Fred bring the grandchildren to see him once a month, even during the height of tourist season, and take comfort in the knowledge that he's found friends who care about him almost as much as they do.

Mr. Windle and Lilian Bunting worked in tandem to fill in some of the blank spaces in the history he'd presented at the schoolroom. Mr. Windle discovered that Linus Johnson had defrauded quite a few investors. Though by Mr. Barlow's reckoning Linus Johnson had gotten away with murder, he paid for his financial crimes with a sentence of seven years' penal servitude in a prison infamous for the harsh treatment of its inmates. He emerged a shattered man, immigrated to Australia, and was never seen again in Upper Deeping.

To her dismay, Lilian learned that the orphanage's records had been destroyed in a fire that had gutted the building in which they had been stored. The coroner's report was still on file in a dusty municipal archive, and though it made lamentable reading, it contained the children's birth dates, which she added to the burial record.

She was more than dismayed by the report's determination that their deaths had been caused by simple misadventure rather than gross negligence. It also noted that the children had, like so many others, been abandoned as infants by parents who'd been too impoverished to raise them.

Mr. Windle and Lilian presented their findings to another gathering in the schoolhouse on a stormy afternoon in early August. I presented them to Aunt Dimity in the evening.

The storm hadn't abated. If anything, it had gotten worse. Gusts of rain crashed against the diamond-paned windows above the old oak desk, and the guttering fire in the hearth filled the study with wavering shadows. Reginald looked quite relieved to be high and dry in his special niche in the bookshelves.

"The villagers took a grim satisfaction in learning of Linus Johnson's fate," I said, "especially when Mr. Windle specified the details of his incarceration: a minimal diet, a thin mattress in a locked cell, and long hours of hard labor."

*It's hard to imagine a more fitting punishment.*

"They did unto him what he'd done unto his apprentices," I agreed. I summarized Lilian's talk, then described a few proposals she'd made at the end of it. "Everyone was in favor of dedicating a memorial tablet in the church to the mill children."

*They should be memorialized. They and children like them are the unsung heroes of the Industrial Revolution. They played a more important role in our history than many of the lords and ladies whose names are displayed prominently in our places of worship.*

"There was some debate about whether the original headstones should be updated or replaced with new ones," I went on, "but Lilian suggested a third course. She proposed leaving the original headstones as they are but mounting a plaque on the churchyard wall behind the graves, listing additional details about the children."

*Did the villagers support her suggestion?*

"They supported it unanimously," I said. "She, Mr. Barlow, and Mr. Windle are working on a design. Once the plaque is in place, the vicar will conduct a graveside service combined with an unveiling ceremony."

*I'm certain the event will be very well attended. If Mr. Windle has taught the villagers anything, it's to look the past—every part of the past—squarely in the face. By ignoring the difficult chapters, we fail to recognize those whose sacrifices should be honored.*

"Why didn't your mother tell you that the workers who died in the mill were children?" I asked.

*She may not have known. The story had been filtered through a sieve of willful forgetfulness by the time it reached her.*

"Will and Rob have been asking Bill and me all sorts of questions about child labor," I said. "They've been asking their teachers about it, too. They were stunned to learn that children their age and younger still go to work instead of school in many countries."

*Do you regret exposing them to such knowledge?*

"No," I said. "I think I may be raising a pair of activists Charles Dickens would salute."

*Has any decision been made regarding the copse?*

"Yes," I said. "We've decided to leave it as it is. The mill's too far gone for restoration, but even if we could afford to put it back together again, we wouldn't. Its destruction is an important part of the story we'll hand down through the generations." I leaned back in my chair. "We've recovered a lost chapter in the river's story, too."

*The Little Deeping's power was harnessed to drive the machinery in a textile mill owned by an unscrupulous and contemptible man.*

"I prefer Romans and Vikings and medieval pack trains," I said, "but I won't forget the role the river played in the dark side of the Industrial Revolution. None of us will."

*Perhaps Lilian could devise an explanatory plaque and place it in the copse.*

"I'll suggest it," I said. "If it were up to me, though, I'd put a plaque there commemorating the day Bree Pym met Crispin Windle. She was incredibly lucky to run into him when she did."

*He was lucky, too. Mr. Windle was a professor in need of a pupil, and he found one in Bree. Their interactions gave him a new purpose in life—or revived an old one. She helped him every bit as much as he helped her.*

"He's certainly come a long way from the man Tommy and I saw from the bridge," I said.

*He was alone and lonely when you and Tommy saw him from the bridge, but you and Bree and everyone who watched over him helped him to realize that he didn't have to be either.*

"The stranger at our table has become our friend," I said, "and Finch is his classroom now. If Lilian has a gap in her schedule, she can count on him to fill it with a guided tour of the copse, or a lecture in the schoolhouse, or a lesson in pen-and-ink drawing, or a weaving demonstration. Fortunately for Elspeth, he still can't cook."

*She knows the way to a man's heart.*

"She has the enchanted cottage on her side as well," I said. "It may work its magic on Mr. Windle yet."

*It was his wife's fondest wish that he remarry. She didn't want him to spend the rest of his life grieving for her.*

"A truly remarkable woman," I said. "I'm sure she'd approve of Elspeth."

*She does.*

"Let's hope she gives Mr. Windle a nudge in the right direction." I stretched my legs out on the ottoman and gave a satisfied sigh. "I'd love to see Grant win the bet he made with Charles after Sally's prediction. Grant believes that fairy tales can come true"—I smiled down at the journal—"and I have a very good reason to believe it, too."

# *Elspeth Binney's Bakewell Tarts*

MAKES 12 TARTS

## Ingredients

Crust:

*12 3-inch unbaked tart shells*

*¼ cup raspberry jam*

Filling:

*¼ cup butter, softened*

*¼ cup granulated sugar*

*1 large egg*

*¼ cup all-purpose flour*

*5 tablespoons ground almonds*

*1 teaspoon baking powder*

*1 teaspoon almond extract*

Icing:

*5 tablespoons confectioners' sugar*

*1 tablespoon boiling water*

## Directions

1. Preheat the oven to 450°F. Arrange the tart shells on a baking sheet.

2. Bake the tart shells at 450°F for 6 minutes. Remove the shells from the oven and cool them.

3. Reduce the oven temperature to 375°F.

4. Spoon 1 teaspoon of raspberry jam into the bottom of each tart shell.

5. Beat the butter and granulated sugar together in a bowl with an electric mixer until smooth and creamy. Add the egg, flour, ground almonds, baking powder, and almond extract and mix well.

6. Spoon 1 tablespoon of the butter mixture on top of the raspberry jam layer at the bottom of each tart shell.

7. Bake the tarts at 375°F until the filling is bubbling, 25–30 minutes.

8. Stir the confectioners' sugar and boiling water together in a bowl until the icing is smooth. Drizzle it over the warm tarts. Allow the tarts to cool and enjoy a sugary treat!